PRAISE FOR LEON ROOKE

"Rooke's language is a riotous, tumultuous force of nature . . . completely riveting." – *Publishers Weekly*

". . . echoing Barth and Borges, Dostoevsky, Kafka and Poe."
– *Canadian Literature*

"He never wastes his considerable comic sense simply to get laughs. His humour is like a searchlight freezing a criminal against a prison wall—in a single flash it can illuminate life's sinister shadows . . . Rooke tosses off superb imagery with the largesse of a king dispensing gold coins . . . Rooke is an exceptional storyteller." – *Maclean's*

"Rooke has lured us into the *terra incognita* of the soul, and it's our loss, proof of our mediocrity, if we don't follow, with gladness in our hearts."
– *The Georgia Straight*

"Rooke's vision is Manichaean, melodramatic, exaggerated, and sometimes intentionally cartoonish. At its root, it is pure antithesis—angels against devils. This formal opposition, though, is the engine of his furious style. Leon Rooke doesn't write like any of those precious minimalists or Kmart realists cluttering the literary marketplace these days. He is the high priest of maximalist panache, the standard-bearer for a hyper-rhetoric that is at once strange, eccentric, and beautiful."
– *Globe and Mail*

PRAISE FOR *The Fall of Gravity*

"Intoxicating." – *Quill & Quire*

"Touched by genius." – *The Georgia Straight*

"*The Fall of Gravity* is a comic improvisation on middle America at the end of the millennium. Like any good trip, it's a series of Zen moments . . . [I]t's vintage Rooke, fast and funny, sweet but not sentimental, an intimate glimpse of a world where suspension of disbelief has collapsed . . ." – *The Globe and Mail*

"*The Fall of Gravity* . . . demands and deserves indulgence and delivers deep rewards by the time the last page is turned." – *The National Post*

"In this tale of a runaway wife, Leon Rooke is a magician 'with long sleeves' at the wheel in a road movie—populated with fallen priests, suicidal dogs, the Minnesota Chicken War, 27 rains, and a reoccurring ghost story from Guelph province—all linked by a dark and tender tale of permanent courtship and escape." – Michael Ondaatje

PRAISE FOR *A Good Baby*

"A haunted and haunting novel . . . deliciously inventive."
– *Washington Post Book World*

"Story-telling at its most compelling, a narrative to rivet a reader's attention, told in a bardic idiom that gives the novel the authentic lilt of a hillbilly yarn . . . irresistible." – *Chicago Tribune*

"Extraordinary language and imagination . . . Twain and Faulkner come to mind. It is a sign of Rooke's tremendous range and his deftness that he can shape this wild story into a cliffhanger." – *New York Newsday*

"A fine and rambunctious novel . . . a veritable find." – *The New York Times*

PRAISE FOR *Shakespeare's Dog*

"It is lickerish, witty, and full of panache." – *Publishers Weekly*

"Leon Rooke's capacity for unusual kinds of empathy was already amply demonstrated in his last novel, *Fat Woman*. In *Shakespeare's Dog* he's put his talent to the test and passed triumphantly. Rooke's brisk and earthy tale has something to say about Shakespeare and a great deal to say about dogs . . . a robust delight . . ." – *Harper's*

"A sculpted novel with a largeness of imagination and wit, a book for literate dogs like ourselves." – *The New York Times Book Review*

Books of Merit

Painting the Dog

Painting the dog

paintin

the Dog

The Best Stories *of*

Leon Rooke

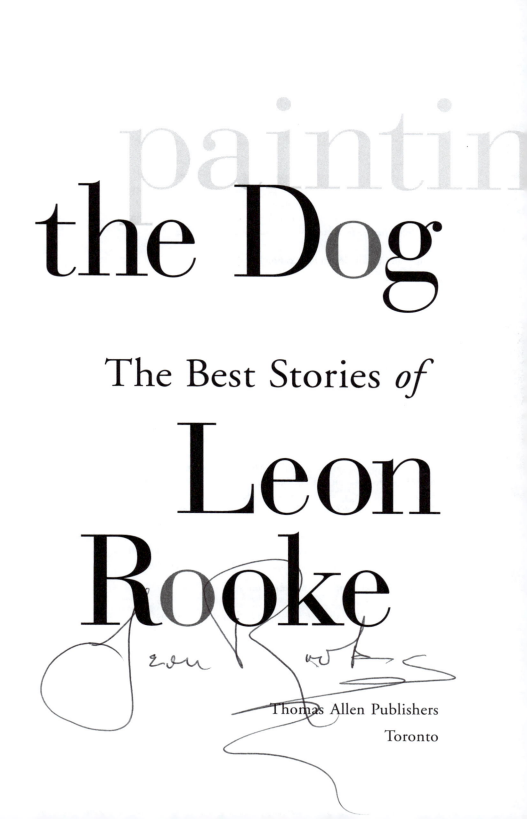

Thomas Allen Publishers
Toronto

Canadian Cataloguing in Publication Data

Rooke, Leon
    Painting the dog: the best stories of Leon Rooke

ISBN 0-919028-44-6

I. Title.

PS8585.O64P34 2001   C813'.54   COO-933236-7
PR9199.3.R66P34   2001

These stories, in slightly different forms, have been previously published.
"Art," "The Blue Baby," "Pretty Pictures," and "Want to Play House?" in *Who Do You
Love?* (McClelland & Stewart, 1992); "A Bolt of White Cloth," "The Only Daughter,"
"The Woman's Guide to Home Companionship," and "Saks Fifth Avenue" in *A Bolt
of White Cloth* (Stoddart Publishing, 1985); "Early Obscenities in the Life of the World's
Foremost Authority on Heidegger" in *Muffins* (Porcupine's Quill, 1995); "The Heart
Must From Its Breaking" in *The Happiness of Others* (Porcupine's Quill, 1991); "The
Birth Control King of the Upper Volta" and "Sing Me No Love Songs I'll Say You No
Prayers" in *The Birth Control King of the Upper Volta* (ECW Press, 1982); "Painting
the Dog" in *Toronto Life* magazine (August 2000); "Lady Godiva's Horse" in *Death Suite*
(ECW Press, 1981); "The Woman Who Talked to Horses" in *Sing Me No Love Songs I'll Say
You No Prayers* (Ecco Press, 1984); "Dust" in *Saving the Province* (Oolichan, 1989); and
"Wintering in Victoria" in *Broad Back of the Angel* (Fiction Collective, 1977).

Cover and text design: Gordon Robertson
Editor: Patrick Crean
Cover photograph: From *What Dogs Do* by Sharon Beals © 1995.
    Reprinted by permission of Chronicle Books, San Francisco.
Author photograph: Donald Denton

Published by Thomas Allen Publishers,
a division of Thomas Allen & Son Limited,
145 Front Street East, Suite 107,
Toronto, Ontario M5A 1E3 Canada

Printed and bound in Canada

For Mike and Carol
For Branko and Francesca
For Barry Callaghan
For P. K. and Michael and Linda
For Austin Clarke

For Connie,
Constance,
Constanza,
& Constancia
  – always

Many people made suggestions for stories to be included in this volume. I want especially to thank John Metcalf, Mike Matthews, Terence Young, Patricia Young, Douglas Glover, Branko Gorjup, Connie Rooke, and Patrick Crean.

ALSO BY LEON ROOKE

NOVELS

The Fall of Gravity
Fat Woman
Shakespeare's Dog
A Good Baby
Who Goes There
The Magician in Love

SHORT STORY COLLECTIONS

Last One Home Sleeps in the Yellow Bed
Vault
The Love Parlour
The Broad Back of the Angel
Cry Evil
Death Suite
The Birth Control King of the Upper Volta
Sing Me No Love Songs and I'll Say You No Prayers
A Bolt of White Cloth
How I Saved the Province
The Happiness of Others
Who Do You Love?
Muffins
Arte
Oh! Twenty-seven Stories

PLAYS

Sword/Play
Krokodile
Ms. America
A Good Baby
Shakespeare's Dog

Contents

Want to Play House?

H ERE. COME HERE. Yes. Now this is what you
do. You see where I have marked with my stick
that line in the dirt?

That is the back door. You come in the door and I am
standing here in the kitchen. That's right, this is the kitchen, see
my pots and pans? See my table?

All right, don't sulk. Look, I will draw the table in the dirt with
this stick. See? That is the table. It is polished nice and clean, and
it has our plates on it, and our silverware, and this nice stew I have
made.

No, no, you don't sit down yet. Let me explain. You go back
to the door—not yet!—and you come in with your muddy boots
and you see me here at the sink where I am washing the dishes
and looking out the window, and I don't see you yet. For heaven's
sake? My back is turned. Do you think I have eyes in the back of
my head? Use your imagination.

Very well, I will draw the sink and the windows. There. See
them? Take your hands out of your pockets and pay attention.

Let me see: what am I wearing? I am wearing my dressing

gown. Yes, this old quilted pattern gown like my . . . like mothers wear. It's seen better days. But I have on my stockings, and my make-up. Kind of pretty, you know. I am very pretty, and gay, but just worn out. With worry over you and the kids. I have lost my spunk. Bills, bills, bills, and I never get any help. You know, like when grandmama died. How grandpapa was, after that. You remember, don't you? Well, you were too young.

No, you don't whistle, you don't say anything. You have your lunch pail with you, and you just stand at the door, holding your pail in your hand, and you know I have just scrubbed the linoleum because of the sparkle. So you are there in your muddy boots, not speaking to me until I turn around and see you there. You like watching me secretly like that, because of how pretty I am and how much you love me. Why? Because I said so. That is how we play.

Now listen to me: you've got to try to look smart, and not smile, because my husband is very smart, and he almost never smiles, and his hair is combed back like this. Here, let me wet it. Yes, like that. But don't smile. Pretend you've been hard at work all day and this was just another one where you know you've not got one lick ahead, and you are in a foul mood because you know it is all my fault. I spend so much, on these pots and pans and the new linoleum—you are standing on the new linoleum, silly— and sometimes you wish I was dead. Forget I said you love me, this is better.

This is much better and totally realistic. Don't you see? Because if I am dead you can start over and get yourself a new wife who will look so pretty you can't keep your hands off her. Yes, you are the daddy. I told you, you are the daddy. You are the daddy and my husband. Yes, both, you can be both. Just do what I say, that's all you have to do, is what I say. Can't you see how it is done?

Okay, I will take you through it step by step, though that's precious little fun for me. I tell you, it is precious little fun for me, and I don't know why I go through it. All right, you are here at this line, which is the door, and you come in and I am sitting at the table crying my eyes out because I am full of woe.

That's right, I have changed my mind, I am not standing at the sink when you come in. Let's play this way instead. I have been full of woe all day and I have got nothing done, nothing is ever done because I am unable to rouse myself from the loathsome woe, and now I have lost all track of the time and don't know which way to turn.

Oh, which way to turn, my darling?

Forget the sink. I tell you I am at the table. Yes, weeping. I can weep really convincingly. Truly I can, so your heart would break. Now you are there, and you see me weeping. What do you do?

You don't know? Didn't I tell you? I thought you said you wanted to play. No, you can't back out now.

All right, so you hate me. That's good. You come in and what next? That's right. You put the pail on the floor, and then what?

Fine, you don't care about the polished floor. Of course you don't. I can clean it until I'm blue in the face and you never notice. Yes, do that if you want to. Sneak right up behind me and start strangling me if you want to. You won't hurt me. I'm bigger than you and I can whip your ass any day of the week. Don't think I can't. You're a worthless little limp ass and you don't scare me one little bit. Try it.

Try and hit me with that stick and you will regret it until your dying day. You are too stupid to live, do you know that? Go ahead, hit me. I dare you. I dee-double dare you. Use your rock. You think I am scared of your little rock? I'm going to whip the daylights out of you. You are being so bad I can't bear to look at you. Ugh. My skin crawls. Do it. Try that one more time and you are good as dead. You are mincemeat.

Yes. I say all that. And you are screaming, too. You are telling me exactly what you think. It is all my fault? Understand? You would like to beat me until you can't stand up. Have you been drinking? I bet you have been drinking. I bet you have been spending all our money down at your tavern, your beer hole, and now I and the children will have to starve.

Go on, start beating. You can't hurt me. A little nothing like you couldn't hurt anyone. Such rubbish. I never saw such rubbish in my life. You are Quitsville, do you know that? You are some little rodent thing in the road I would run over. Smush you flat, you lift a hand to me. Try it. See where it gets you. You can't even earn a decent wage.

Yes.

And then I run, you see, and you chase me. You are in a rage, shouting you will kill me. Shouting how for years you have been wishing me dead.

No. No, there is no kissing. You don't have to worry one bit about kissing.

What do you mean you can't do it without real furniture?

Out here in the yard. No one can see us, you know. No one cares. No one is looking. They don't even know we are here. We can do anything we want.

Got it? Ready?

Oh, wait. I have another idea. You see here where I've drawn in the sink, the counter? And up there, the windows? Now here on the counter is this knife. Mama's butcher knife. Mine, I mean, I'm the mama. It's under those leaves down in the dirt, where the pretend-counter is. And while you're chasing me you pick up the knife and when you catch me you stab me a thousand times. You go completely crazy and you're shouting all that stuff and stabbing me and I'm fighting back, just full of the awfullest woe, both of us, and then I will finally fall and lie still and not move a muscle because I will be dead.

Yes, pretend-dead, you'll like that part. No, in this one you are not dead, I am the dead one. Dead and gone to hell.

So you see what you have done and you roll me over in your arms and hold me. Your grief pours out. You tell me how much you love me. How sorry you are. You blubber all over the place. No, you don't have to kiss me. You rock and sob. You're sorry, so sorry you've hurt me. And you say things like this: you say how you wish we could start over. All over, fresh, and what a good time, what a wonderful life we would have. You didn't mean to hurt me. You never meant to. What went wrong? That's what you ask. You ask that a thousand times, as you rock and moan, and wish you had never been born.

What went wrong, my darling?

Okay? That's how we do it.

Yes, let's start.

Go to the door.

You come in.

You see me weeping.

You see the knife. Already you have spotted the knife. Good. It will be so much fun.

Come on, then. Ready, set, go!

The Woman's Guide to Home Companionship

W HAT FOLLOWS is not in my own hand. What follows is being delivered through the good graces of my friend and neighbour Mrs. Vee Beaverdeck of 101 Menzies, who is doing so without cost or complaint. She will aver, if asked, that this is the truth and the whole truth as I know it and that this story or tale is told first-hand and in a calm manner while we are here in my kitchen drinking our two coffees with now and then an ounce of something fortifying on the side.

It is 2:00 a.m. after what I'd call without exaggeration the roughest night of our lives.

We have been sitting around for hours since it happened, trying to figure out how we hooked up with such undesirables in the first place.

Vee says yes, that is the Lord's truth.

I shall now describe Mrs. Vee Beaverdeck to the degree I am able, so that there shall be no mistaking her for another person or persons and in order to assist the authorities. Vee is forty-six years old, two full years and three full months older than I am, though I think I can guarantee she has never acted funny about it. She is close to my own height and with a disposition similar to mine and on the issue of slenderness we both come in with identical high marks, though this was not always the case.

Why, you ask.

Since June I have shed eighteen pounds, all in the strategic places and without experiencing any undue psychological turmoil. Indeed, it was not because of psychological turmoil or unwholesome self-image in the first place that I embarked upon my physical-improvement program. It was a question of being Fulfilled or not being Fulfilled, as the expert told us. I have always been something of a compulsive snacker and the pounds seem to go right on me, right where they shouldn't, so from time to time my span-image of myself is such that without undue duress I engage in a crash program to eliminate all excess flabbiness, though that is hardly the word.

Mrs. Beaverdeck on the other hand has always been of the slim variety, though not so slim you could thread her through a needle, which has been her great good fortune down through the ages and which I think she will admit (she is nodding) she at times feels a little vain about.

I should intrude here to say Mrs. Beaverdeck keeps trying to interrupt me and change what I am saying, but I am not allowing this because it was the agreement we struck before we started out on this dictation. "You will get your turn," I keep telling her, "after I am done." I should explain too the employment of quotations in the previous sentence was because it was a direct quote or ultimatum delivered to Mrs. Vee Beaverdeck one second ago. I hope I will not have to use this technique hereafter, because it is most distracting to find yourself constantly interrupted and corrected and your every word questioned.

Back to the description.

Suffice it to say I took the aerobic course at Fitness Works Incorporated, 427 Fort Street with free parking, and dropped eighteen pounds, the first being always the hardest, as you know. Mrs. Beaverdeck only lost four, whereupon the expert let her know she need not lose any additional poundage. Be that as it may, I got my muscles toned and my stomach flat and now look smarter than I ever have, whereas Mrs. Vee Beaverdeck has since time immemorial been able to wear whatever she has wanted to wear without thinking twice about it. Now we wear the same size dress, with my feet maybe a half-size larger depending on the make, and double A whereas she's single A.

She paints her toes and I do not.

I am this minute wearing a house robe which belonged to her but which she gave to me because it looked so much better on me thanks to the colour of my eyes, which it picks up and highlights, together with my hair.

My bones are bigger so I think I still look larger and more cumbersome, though she claims this is my own personal delusion and little hang-up.

It is time we paused now to refreshen our drinks and sort out in a private and unpublicized manner the issue raised above, since as Vee says this is not a subject totally pertinent to this document and anyhow we have both got to stop crying.

We have got to face up, Vee says, to the consequences of what we have done.

Hi, we are now back, and Vee has sworn that she will take my dictation properly and not in any way undermine my account of our activities this awful evening.

To pick up where we left off:

I definitely have more bosom and we have agreed that this is why I feel larger than Mrs. Beaverdeck, when the truth is that for all practical purposes our bodies are identical. Mrs. Beaverdeck's breasts are sweet and certainly ample, if a little catty-cornered. On this score I feel the nod goes to her whatever the case, the reason being she is more in the Movement than I am and hence does not wear brassieres, which gives her a pronounced if unfair edge on the stares-and-whistles front, that being proved each time the two of us step out shopping. Let me insert also the news that while Mrs. Beaverdeck and I have numerous areas of conflict, on such matters for instance as the wearing of brassieres, we are in shining agreement on the abortion issue, women in the priest-hood, on how ninety percent of the world's husbands stack up, etcetera or for instance the politics of certain warmongering nations which shall remain nameless.

Vee is this minute dressed in a black chiffon gown bought from Coordinates Yes!, a stylish store in the heart of town which we both frequent and not too expensive though occasionally their manners could be improved. She has a striped black-and-white silk scarf around her throat, and sheer knee-high hose of mid-night blue, with a pair of old Capezio shoes on her feet because of how she came running out of her house so fast tonight she was practically hysterical. She has long black hair which is now pinned up to her head, along the sides anyway. I have more grey in mine, sorry to say, though it hardly ever shows because of a certain high-quality if expensive rinse which I swear by. Funnily enough, my skin is darker than Vee's with her black hair, despite my being in the blond spectrum thanks to my devoted parents who were both good Christians and will never again be able to hold up their heads once the newspapers get hold of this dictated confession. Vee's skin is definitely on the pale or albinic side, since she has not had more than an instant's sunshine strike her lovely figure since she was a child at Ocean View, which I understand is a beach-front-and-carnival type place outside Norfolk, Virginia. It is pretty bold and striking, if you've ever seen Vee—that contrast between black which is her favourite colour and her black hair with her dazzling white skin which does not have a blemish on it that I've ever seen.

Pardon. Mrs. Vee announces she has a cute birthmark the size of a dime on her left inner thigh next to what she calls her "chief asset."

As for yours truly I do not have any marks or disfigurations over the whole of my flesh save those administered in recent times by my objectionable husband.

Mrs. Vee Beaverdeck interrupts to say that I should say up there where she spoke of her most cherished parts she was speaking "in the ironical."

The subject's eyes are her best features. They are very large and entrancing, with naturally long lashes, plus she has a lively animated face, as I do myself, and more especially tonight as we sit here pouring ourselves coffee and spirits, which we are in part doing in order to keep up our spirits and to get done and accomplished the job we have set for ourselves before we close up shop and let come what must come: the terrible shame and our names and likenesses splashed in banner headlines across the nation.

Vee says thanks to God we do not have children, inasmuch as unbearable would be their agony and their lives ruined, because what we have done would be a bitter tonic.

Amen.

It may well be that we are having more to drink than is good for us under the circumstances, but let it be known we are of sound mind and strictly responsible for our actions and will not plead self-defence or temporary insanity or any of that stuff that you read about. Nor do we yet anyhow regret anything we have done or see how, given the circumstances and our emotional states and how over these past few months we have been driven to it, how it could have been avoided.

Nor do we intend to shrivel and cry and fall down in a faint when they come for us. Suffice it to say we mean to stand on our own two feet, giving as good as we get. We will go with our two v fingers high, like in the Movement.

Time out.

Time in.

We are back now, Mrs. Vee Beaverdeck with a pillow to soften her behind and a new writing tablet to take down this dictation as I hereby give it, each word the truth as I have always found the truth to be relevant.

Blemish and all, as Vee says.

Vee says that I should remind everyone that since June of the current year, together with our loyal attendance at Fitness Works Incorporated, a going and respectable concern, we have both been running on the shoulders of our noted highway one half-hour each morning and another half-hour around sunset and that we are now up to four and five miles without hassle or undue sudation. In fact, what we have noticed is that gentlemen of the male persuasion are frequently pitched into unseemly fits of passion by no more than the thin sheen of sweat over our jogging bodies, with the result that they often swerve off the road or beep their horns or sometimes even execute daredevil U turns and return to embark upon the most boring and impossible advances two women at our stage of enlightenment could conceivably imagine.

Whereas we could take or leave this behaviour, our abominable husbands have, from the beginning, pitched a gasket. We have taken immeasurable abuse, alternating with a certain stonewalling, over our fitness endeavours. Vee remembers that when we first went out on runs her husband would sit drinking his beer in front of the TV and laughing at her for (quote) "thinking you are some kind of female athelete."

What my own husband said, his chapter-one remark, was (quote), "What I wonder is what kind of effect all this exercising is going to have on your little red fire engine." Little red fire engine is my husband's he thinks quaint euphemism for my sexual parts. If the reader finds this sinister and distasteful and bespeaking of deep dark problems with his sexual attitudes then I am with that reader to the nth degree.

It is with a heavy heart that I utilize material of this x-rated type but accuracy dictates it and leaves me no choice.

Mind you, this was way back in June when there was still some semblance of sanity at 101 and 137 Menzies.

Vee says that I should take off the kid gloves and give a few more sterling examples of their truly rotten behaviour.

But I believe I can trust the reader to already understand what kind of "gentlemen" we have here.

Also, it is not my hope to give a full and documented account of their crimes against us and nature, for that would take a book and lots more time than I am willing to give to those two throwbacks.

Let it be known, in any event, that we have spotless reputations in this town and no one to our knowledge, among those with whom we carry on a daily business, has ever had occasion to say word one against us, nor have we been involved in any previous criminal wrongdoing.

Hold on a minute. Vee has gone and got my Polaroid and I have taken and labelled three pictures depicting her cut and bruised face, as well as two of the back porch and door which show what a rage my own husband was in earlier in the evening when he left this place.

Vee or Mrs. Beaverdeck has likewise taken a picture of me in knickers and bra, which shows I am anything but the "slick pig" he has since June been calling me.

Vee has said she can think of a number of men who would be willing to pay a hundred dollars for a copy of the above-named photo. I have said I can think of two or three I'd let have it for free.

We have had us another drink and are presently making a fresh pot of coffee.

We have also looked back over this document and read it aloud, because my friend and neighbour Mrs. Vee Beaverdeck claims I go off on too many tangents, for instance what she looks like.

Vee Beaverdeck is beautiful. She is beautiful and she is my dearest friend and I have threatened to go directly to the authorities and confess our cruel deed if she doesn't put on the page exactly what I dictate to her.

You should understand, however, that many of the comments and asides we make to each other are not being entered into this document, since we feel much of it is not your business to know and for once in our lives we are doing exactly what we want to do.

We shall now have another drink, and as Vee says, "screw the coffee."

Mrs. Vee Beaverdeck, I have discovered only this evening, has had business training, and I am proud of her. For six years before her unfortunate marriage she worked for Stan Bask Associates, a well-known investment firm in this city. She advanced in this period from clerk-typist to the position of receptionist-supervisor and customarily took dictation from Stan Bask himself, who twice tried to seduce her and once got her pinned down on the carpet floor in front of his desk.

Suffice it to say that Mrs. Beaverdeck now looks back upon that experience with a very different eye.

She is now back from the phone where she has got Mr. Stan Bask up from a sound sleep and told him exactly what we think of him.

He professes that he "does not remember," and reminds her that "we were both young then."

I have now been subjected to a long speech from Mrs. Vee Beaverdeck on the importance of the Woman's Movement and such questions as, "How can you, Violet Witherspoon, sit quietly by?" I have not heard many of these questions because I have gone to the bathroom. From my seat on the toilet, however, I have reminded Vee Beaverdeck of what we both have tonight done to our husbands.

"You can hardly say, after my actions this evening, that I have sat (quote) quietly by (unquote)."

That is a direct quote.

Vee Beaverdeck, who has admitted she said so out of tipsiness, has apologized for delivering inflammatory accusations against one Violet Witherspoon, domiciled at 137 Menzies.

By common vote we shall now pause, for we are overcome with giggles. Take five.

Back now. The old clock on the wall cries out the time, 3:12 a.m. In this interval have we skulked by devious route and cunning to 101 Menzies, there to "view the remains," to replenish our bar stock, and to secure an overnight bag for Mrs. Vee Beaverdeck, including toothbrush, stockings, underwear, make-up, hair dryer, the outfit she means to wear tomorrow for whatever official inquiries might involve us, together with the book I lent her years ago, inherited from my mother and containing numerous pressed flowers, entitled *The Woman's Guide to Home Companionship*.

We have had a great laugh over this volume, as you can imagine, though it put me in tears to think of my mother eternally slaving away and all for what?

The "remains" remain intact and unchanged. We did not long study the situation, however, for the macabre, as Vee stated, has limited appeal.

I shall now pick up some of the loose ends.

Vee Beaverdeck believes I should not have described her breasts as "catty-cornered." She has bared herself and I have taken a Polaroid and we are now researching the result. I say to Vee, "Your left nipple points to nine o'clock, your right to three o'clock, and I call that catty-cornered."

Vee Beaverdeck spends one half-hour in my bathroom behind locked door studying this matter. Then she calls for her drink, which I pass through. A minute or so later she calls me in. She is seated on the bath edge, crying out her beautiful eyes.

"Vee," I say, "I was only kidding."

"I know," she says.

"I mean it," I say. "It was only a joke."

"I know," she says.

Then Vee Beaverdeck looks at me and with a broken heart says, "I could get a plastic surgeon to make small cuts on the inside of each breast and get them pointed straight."

We then bawl, for it comes to us in the same split second that our men have totally undermined our self-image, and it is almost as if we can hear them laughing.

It is some time before we are able again to stand upright. This has nothing to do with strong drink, though our glasses stand empty.

Vee says, "I said I was going to get drunk, and I meant it."

So forthwith we pour ourselves another round.

We are both wide awake at 4:00 a.m. and wondering when grief or guilt, or fear or total despair, will set in, but to this hour, along those lines, we feel nothing.

"What will they do to us?"

"I will claim total amnesia."

These statements and others like them have been made and repeated since the perpetration of the very deed itself, though I have decided and Vee has agreed that such disclosures are not to be admitted into this chronicle. Even so.

"Should we get in the car and run?" says Vee.

"Vee," I say, "we have between us exactly twenty-seven dollars and eleven cents."

"Two beautiful women, alone in the dark night, cannot leave a cold trail. It is impossible. At the first gas station or truck stop we come to some man will make a pass at us, we will be compelled to resist his advances, and before we know it five thousand peace officers will be hot on our trail."

I mope. I tell Vee to put it down that I am moping because she has entered the above statement directly onto these pages. "Vee," I say, "I am supposed to be dictating my statement."

"So dictate," she says.

We have a little cry because we have fought with each other.

Vee asks if I meant it back there at the start of this piece when I spoke of her beauty. That interests her, she says, though she can not quite see its point in terms of this document.

"Take this down, Vee," I say. "The point of it was to stress that while our husbands found us objectionable and undesirable, men and in fact anyone with an objective eye would find us quite the opposite." I remind her that I did not kill myself those weeks at Fitness Works Incorporated for nothing, and that we have not run upwards of five thousand miles over the past six months so that our husbands could abuse us and poke fun.

"Also, we were pretty sharp cookies to begin with," I say.

Something in this remark drives Vee to reflect that seventeen men in the past year have propositioned her. Three of them, directly. That is, they put their arms around her and began kissing her and whispering about motels.

I am stunned. Only two have approached me.

"One was your husband," she says.

"Vee, put this in," I say. "I am not surprised."

"He was the one most adamant."

I am not surprised.

"Vee," I say, "are you sure? Seventeen?"

"I could be mistaken about a couple of them," Vee says. "But it was how they looked at me. I also didn't tell quite the truth about Mr. Stan Bask. The truth is I never knew to what extent I was willing. Alas, he was a handsome devil. So debonair."

We agree it is the debonair gent who most carries the day.

Vee Beaverdeck makes it clear she was never a fallen woman. She wonders whether this was a mistake. She laments that all she wants is a little happiness in her life. "Like," says she, "when jogging."

She says she is getting tired of taking dictay, and is feeling dopey and sentimental and would like to shoot herself.

She goes over to the kitchen faucet and lets cold water stream over her head.

I have gone into my bedroom and poked around in my cedar chest until I've found my husband's old love letters. I look at them a while. I don't know why and certainly I don't care. It strikes me with a jolt that his old letters are wholly illiterate. All he talks about is his job and drinking and the weather and what he'd do if he had me near him, and how dumb everybody is. He writes in a very large hand so he can fill nine or ten pages. He includes little drawings of what sheep do to each other. It is a funny thing to me how I would clutch this trash to my chest in those days and feel absolutely divine and glorious.

It is clear from his letters that he never had a brain in his head and that all was subterfuge from the start.

"He mentions you," I tell Vee. "He says his buddy Carl has taken up with 'a very weird woman who is very odd.'"

Vee says, "Let me see that."

She has now stopped receiving dictation to look it over.

I say, "All right, Vee." It is too late to save her from it. She's going to come to that part in the letter where my husband-to-be says that Carl tells him he's pretty sure he's going to get from her what he wants and that he's already had more than a taste of it. "She's hot-to-trot in the old backseat," Carl says. "Guess they just can't resist old Carl's charm."

"I don't want to take any more dictay," Mrs. Vee Beaverdeck has said. So I've dropped down here to do it myself. What I wonder about is why they've treated us the way they have. I don't think they originally set out to become demented. I know they don't think of themselves as mean. We've never mattered to them so they've gone about their lives exactly as they've wanted, never thinking about us except to say what trouble we've caused them. Floppy appendages, I guess we are, like an extra arm that nobody wants. It was not the big things anyway that led us to our mission. It was the little things they did, like how they would look at each other with sick smiles anytime we spoke, and how they pitched their beer cans out of the car window, and scoffed at flowers we brought into the house; it was how they left wet coffee spoons in the sugar bowl and abused our friends and swore up and down Richard Nix was such a great foreign-policy president, not to mention the whole cut-throat heathen gang our other halves aligned themselves with. Etcetera. Etcetera. It was how they looked, too: with their hair combed down over their brows, their ears sticking out, the stupid baseball caps on the back of their heads, and the seats of their pants flopping down to their knees. Mostly it was how you could never get out of them one word of moral support, not one word about their emotional feelings on the private home-front question as it relates to those closest and dearest to them, and if you expected support from those two on your personal dilemmas ranging from A to Z you'd be better off putting in a call to the Ayatollah what's-his-name.

The truth is we did it to them because they never seemed to feel anything. Not even when we did it.

My friend and beloved neighbour Mrs. Vee Beaverdeck is this moment overcome with uncontrollable fatigue and hereby demands that I cease with these memoirs. She declares with a shiver that she has this second had the most terrible thought; to wit, that we have not in point of fact succeeded in dispensing with our husbands, but that throughout the torment of this evening and the subsequent drenching of ourselves with alcohol we have merely been displaying wishful thinking. She urges that we abandon this post immediately and scurry post-haste to view the miserable bodies.

Agreed. A foul thought indeed. Take twenty.

Hi! I'm back.

Nope, we've done it, all right. They are definitely gone from this world. They shall never again take advantage of frail womanhood or sneer at a pile of dirty dishes or behave generally like inhuman scoundrels.

They shall know better next time.

"Let's put pennies over their eyes," Vee Beaverdeck said. "Let's pull the sheets up under their chins. Let's get rid of these beer cans and cigarette butts they've left here and take a Polaroid of them in their glory, in case we again have doubts."

The photo turned out ever so nicely. It seemed to catch mine flinching when the flash went off. It seemed to me I heard both of them groan, but that was only my nerves working overtime.

"Mine, too," said Vee. "I've had it."

She said hers looked nicer than he ever had. "You'd almost think him human," she said. She pointed out a dimple in his left cheek. "Or is that where I got him with the heel of my shoe?"

We sat out on the back deck measuring the dark houses all around and looking up out of tired relief at the man in the moon.

"It's no man," Vee said. "That's my grandmother."

"She's nice," I said. "She looks like she knows a woman's true place."

Vee Beaverdeck stretched out flat on her back. She sighed about a thousand times.

"This is a one-shot deal," she said. "I'm not cut out for murder and mayhem."

Ditto here. It's too gruesome, if that's any news.

A Bolt of White Cloth

A MAN CAME BY OUR ROAD carrying an enormous bolt of white cloth on his back. Said he was from the East. Said whoever partook of this cloth would come to know true happiness. Innocence without heartbreak, he said, if that person proved worthy. My wife fingered his cloth, having in mind something for new curtains. It was good quality, she said. Beautifully woven, of a fine, light texture, and you certainly couldn't argue with the colour.

"How much is it?" she asked.

"Before I tell you that," the man said, "you must tell me truthfully if you've ever suffered."

"Oh, I've suffered," she said. "I've known suffering of some description every day of my natural life."

I was standing over by the tool shed, with a big smile. My wife is a real joker, who likes nothing better than pulling a person's leg. She's known hardships, this and that upheaval, but nothing I would call down-and-out suffering. Mind you, I don't speak for her. I wouldn't pretend to speak for another person.

This man with the bolt of cloth, however, he clearly had no

sense of my wife's brand of humour. She didn't get an itch of a smile out of him. He kept the cloth neatly balanced on his shoulder, wincing a little from the weight and from however far he'd had to carry it, staring hard and straight at my wife the whole time she fooled with him, as if he hoped to peer clear through to her soul. His eyes were dark and brooding and hollowed out some. He was like no person either my wife or me had ever seen before.

"Yes," he said, "but suffering of what kind?"

"Worse than I hope forever to carry, I'll tell you that," my wife said. "But why are you asking me these questions? I like your cloth and if the price is right I mean to buy it."

"You can only buy my cloth with love," he said.

We began right then to understand that he was some kind of oddity. He was not like anybody we'd ever seen and he didn't come from around here. He'd come from a place we'd never heard of, and if that was the East, or wherever, then he was welcome to it.

"Love?" she said. "Love? There's *love* and there's *love*, mister. What kind are you talking about?" She hitched a head my way, rolling her eyes, as if to indicate that if it was *passionate* love he was talking about then he'd first have to do something with me. He'd have to get me off my simmer and onto full boil. That's what she was telling him, with this mischief in her eyes.

I put down my pitchfork about here, and strolled nearer. I liked seeing my wife dealing with difficult situations. I didn't want to miss anything. My life with that woman has been packed with the unusual. Unusual circumstances, she calls them. Any time she's ever gone out anywhere without me, whether for a day or an hour or for five minutes, she's come back with whopping good stories about what she's seen and heard and what's happened to her. She's come back with reports on these unusual circumstances, these little adventures in which so many people have done so many extraordinary things or behaved in such fabulous or foolish ways. So what was rare this time, I thought, was that it had come visiting. She hadn't had to go out and find it.

"Hold these," my wife told me. And she put this washtub of clothes in my hands, and went back to hanging wet pieces on the line, which is what she'd been doing when this man with the bolt of cloth ventured up into our yard.

"Love," she told him. "You tell me what kind I need, if I'm to buy that cloth. I got good ears and I'm listening."

The man watched her stick clothespins in her mouth, slap out a good wide sheet, and string it up. He watched her hang two of these, plus a mess of towels, and get her mouth full again before he spoke. He looked about the unhappiest I've ever seen any man look. He didn't have any joy in him. I wondered why he didn't put down that heavy bolt of cloth, and why he didn't step around into a spot of shade. The sun was lick-killing bright in that yard. I was worried he'd faint.

"The ordinary kind," he said. "Your ordinary kind of love will buy this cloth."

My wife flapped her wash and laughed. He was really tickling her. She was having herself a wonderful time.

"What's ordinary?" she said. "I've never known no *ordinary* love."

He jumped right in. He got excited just for a second.

"The kind such as might exist between the closest friends," he said. "The kind such as might exist between a man and his wife or between parents and children or for that matter the love a boy might have for his dog. That kind of love."

"I've got that," she said. "I've had all three. Last year this time

I had me a fourth, but it got run over. Up on the road there, by the tall trees, by a man in a car who didn't even stop."

"That would have been your cat," he said. "I don't know much about cats."

I put down the washtub. My wife let her arms drop. We looked at him, wondering how he knew about that cat. Then I laughed, for I figured someone down the road must have told him of my wife's mourning over that cat. She'd dug it a grave under the grapevine and said sweet words over it. She sorely missed that cat.

"What's wrong with loving cats?" she asked him. "Or beasts of the fields? I'm surprised at you."

The man shifted his burden and worked one shoe into the ground. He stared off at the horizon. He looked like he knew he'd said something he shouldn't.

She pushed me out of the way. She wanted to get nearer to him. She had something more to say.

"Now listen to me," she said. "I've loved lots of things in my life. Lots and lots. *Him!*" she said (pointing at me), "*it*" (pointing to our house), "*them!*" (pointing to the flower beds), "*that!*" (pointing to the sky), "*those*" (pointing to the woods), "*this*" (pointing to the ground)—"practically *everything!* There isn't any of it I've hated, and not much I've been indifferent to. Including cats. So put that in your pipe and smoke it."

Then swooping up her arms and laughing hard, making it plain she bore no grudge but wasn't just fooling.

Funny thing was, hearing her say it, I felt the same way. *It, them, that, those*—they were all beautiful. I couldn't deny it was love I was feeling.

The man with the cloth had turned each way she'd pointed. He'd staggered a time or two but he'd kept up. In fact, it struck me that he'd got a little ahead of her. That he knew where her arm was next going. Some trickle of pleasure was showing in his face. And something else was happening, something I'd never seen. He had his face lifted up to this burning sun. It was big and orange, that sun, and scorching-hot, but he was staring smack into it. He wasn't blinking or squinting. His eyes were wide open.

Madness or miracle, I couldn't tell which.

He strode over to a parcel of good grass.

"I believe you mean it," he said. "How much could you use?"

He placed the bolt of white cloth down on the grass and pulled out shiny scissors from his back pocket.

"I bet he's blind," I whispered to my wife. "I bet he's got false eyes."

My wife shushed me. She wasn't listening. She had her excitement hat on; her *unusual circumstances* look. He was offering free cloth for love, ordinary love, and she figured she'd go along with the gag.

How much?

"Oh," she said, "maybe eight yards. Maybe ten. It depends on how many windows I end up doing, plus what hang I want, plus the pleating I'm after."

"You mean to make these curtains yourself?" he asked. He was already down on his knees, smoothing the bolt. Getting set to roll it out.

"Why, sure," she said. "I don't know who else would do it for me. I don't know who else I would ask."

He nodded soberly, not thinking about it. "That's so," he said casually. "Mend your own fences first." He was perspiring in the sun, and dishevelled, as though he'd been on the road a long time. His shoes had big holes in them and you could see the blistered soles of his feet, but he had an air of exhilaration now. His hair fell down over his eyes and he shoved the dark locks back. I got the impression that some days he went a long time between customers; that he didn't find cause to give away this cloth every day.

He got a fair bit unrolled. It certainly did look like prime goods, once you saw it spread out on the grass in that long expanse.

"It's so pretty!" my wife said. "Heaven help me, but I think it is *prettier* than grass!"

"It's pretty, all right," he said. "It's a wingdinger. Just tell me when to stop," he said. "Just shout yoo-hoo."

"Hold up a minute," she said. "I don't want to get greedy. I don't want you rolling off more than we can afford."

"You can afford it," he said.

He kept unrolling. He was up past the well house by now, whipping it off fast, though the bolt didn't appear to be getting any smaller. My wife had both hands up over her mouth. Half of her wanted to run into the house and get her purse so she could pay; the other half wanted to stay and watch this man unfurl his beautiful cloth. She whipped around to me, all agitated.

"I believe he means it," she said. "He means us to have this cloth. What do I do?"

I shook my head. This was her territory. It was the kind of adventure constant to her nature and necessary to her well-being.

"Honey," I said, "you deal with it."

The sun was bright over everything. It was whipping-hot. There wasn't much wind but I could hear the clothes flapping on the line. A woodpecker had himself a pole somewhere and I could hear him pecking. The sky was wavy blue. The trees seemed to be swaying.

He was up by the front porch now, still unrolling. It surprised us both that he could move so fast.

"Yoo-hoo," my wife said. It was no more than a peep, the sound you might make if a butterfly lands on your hand.

"Wait," he said. "One thing. One question I meant to ask. All this talk of love, your *it*, your *those* and *them*, it slipped my mind."

"Let's hear it," my wife said. "Ask away." It seemed to me that she spoke out of a trance. That she was as dazzled as I was.

"You two got no children," he said. "Why is that? You're out here on this nice farm, and no children to your name. Why is that?"

We hadn't expected this query from him. It did something to the light in the yard and how we saw it. It was as if some giant dark bird had fluttered between us and the sun. Without knowing it, we sidled closer to each other. We fumbled for the other's hand. We stared off every which way. No one on our road had asked that question in a long, long time; they hadn't asked it in some years.

"We're not able," we said. Both of us spoke at the same time. It seemed to me that it was my wife's voice which carried; mine was someplace down in my chest, and dropping, as if it meant to crawl on the ground.

"We're not able," we said. That time it came out pure, without any grief to bind it. It came out the way we long ago learned how to say it.

"Oh," he said. "I see." He mumbled something else. He kicked the ground and took a little walk back and forth. He seemed angry, though not at us. "Wouldn't you know it?" he said. "Wouldn't you know it?"

He swore a time or two. He kicked the ground. He surely didn't like it.

"We're over that now," my wife said. "We're past that caring."

"I bet you are," he said. "You're past that little misfortune."

He took to unrolling his bolt again, working with his back to the sun. Down on his knees, scrambling, smoothing the material. Sweating and huffing. He was past the front porch now, and still going, getting on toward that edge where the high weeds grew.

"About here, do you think?" he asked.

He'd rolled off about fifty yards.

My wife and I slowly shook our heads, not knowing what to think.

"Say the word," he told us. "I can give you more if more is what you want."

"I'd say you were giving us too much," my wife said. "I'd say we don't need nearly that much."

"Never mind that," he said. "I'm feeling generous today."

He nudged the cloth with his fingers and rolled off a few yards more. He would have gone on unwinding his cloth had the weeds not stopped him. He stood and looked back over the great length he had unwound.

"Looks like a long white road, don't it?" he said. "You could walk that road and your feet never get dirty."

My wife clenched my hand; it was what we'd both been thinking.

Snip-snip-snip. He began snipping. His scissors raced over the material. *Snip-snip-snip.* The cloth was sheared clear and clean of his bolt, yet it seemed to me the size of that bolt hadn't lessened any. My wife saw it too.

"He's got cloth for all eternity," she said. "He could unroll that cloth till doomsday."

The man laughed. We were whispering this, but way up by

the weeds he heard us. "There's doom and there's doom," he said. "*Which* doomsday?"

I had the notion he'd gone through more than one. That he knew the picture from both sides.

"It *is* smart as grass," he said. "Smarter. It never needs watering." He chuckled at that, spinning both arms. Dancing a little. "You could make *nighties* out of this," he said. "New bedsheets. Transform your whole bedroom."

My wife made a face. She wasn't too pleased, talking *nighties* with another man.

Innocence without heartbreak, I thought. That's what we're coming to.

He nicely rolled up the cloth he'd sheared off and presented it to my wife. "I hope you like it," he said. "No complaints yet. Maybe you can make yourself a nice dress as well. Maybe two or three. Make him some shirts. I think you'll find there's plenty here."

"Goodness, it's light," she said.

"Not if you've been carrying it long as I have," he said. He pulled a blue bandanna from his pocket and wiped his face and neck. He ran his hand through his hair and slicked it back. He looked up at the sky. His dark eyes seemed to have cleared up some. They looked less broody now. "Gets hot," he said, "working in this sun. But a nice day. I'm glad I found you folks home."

"Oh, we're most always home," my wife said.

I had to laugh at that. My wife almost never *is* home. She's forever gallivanting over the countryside, checking up on this person and that, taking them her soups and jams and breads.

"We're homebodies, us two."

She kept fingering the cloth and sighing over it. She held it up against her cheek and with her eyes closed rested herself on it. The man hoisted his own bolt back on his shoulder; he seemed ready to be going. I looked at my wife's closed lids, at the soft look she had.

I got trembly, fearful of what might happen if that cloth didn't work out.

"Now look," I said to him, "what's wrong with this cloth? Is it going to rot inside a week? Tomorrow is some *other* stranger going to knock on our door saying we owe him a hundred or five hundred dollars for this cloth? Mister, I don't understand you," I said.

He hadn't bothered with me before; now he looked me dead in the eye. "I can't help being a stranger," he said. "If you never set eyes on me before, I guess that's what I would have to be. Don't you like strangers? Don't you trust them?"

My wife jumped in. Her face was fiery, like she thought I had wounded him. "We like strangers just fine," she said. "We've helped out many a one. No, I can't say our door has ever been closed to whoever it is comes by. Strangers can sit in our kitchen just the same as our friends."

He smiled at her but kept his stern look for me. "As to your questions," he said, "You're worried about the golden goose, I can see that. Fair enough. No, your cloth will not rot. It will not shred, fade, or tear. Nor will it ever need cleaning, either. This cloth requires no upkeep whatsoever. Though a sound heart helps. A sweet disposition, too. Innocence without heartbreak, as I told you. And your wife, if it's her making the curtains or making herself a dress, she will find it to be an amazingly easy cloth to work with. It will practically do the job itself. No, I don't believe you will ever find you have any reason to complain of the quality of that cloth."

My wife had it up to her face again. She had her face sunk in it.

"Goodness," she said, "it's *soft!* It smells so fresh. It's like someone singing a song to me."

The man laughed. "It *is* soft," he said. "But it can't sing a note, or has never been known to."

It was my wife singing. She had this little hum under the breath.

"This is the most wonderful cloth in the world," she said.

He nodded. "I can't argue with you on that score," he said. Then he turned again to me. "I believe your wife is satisfied," he said. "But if you have any doubts, if you're worried someone is going to knock on your door tomorrow asking you for a hundred or five hundred dollars, I suppose I could write you up a guarantee. I could give you a Paid in Full."

He was making me feel ashamed of myself. They both were. "No, no," I said, "if she's satisfied then I am. And I can see she's tickled pink. No, I beg your pardon. I meant no offence."

"No offence taken," he said.

But his eyes clouded a token. He gazed off at our road and up along the stand of trees and his eyes kept roaming until they snagged the sun. He kept his eyes there, unblinking, open, staring at the sun. I could see the red orbs reflected in his eyes.

"There is one thing," he said.

I caught my breath and felt my wife catch hers. The hitch? A hitch, after all? Coming so late?

We waited.

He shuffled his feet. He brought out his bandanna and wiped his face again. He stared at the ground.

"Should you ever stop loving," he said, "you shall lose this cloth and all else. You shall wake up one morning and it and all else will no longer be where you left it. It will all be gone and you will not know where you are. You will not know what to do with yourself. You will wish you'd never been born."

My wife's eyes went saucer-size.

He had us in some kind of spell.

Hocus-pocus, I thought. He is telling us some kind of hocus-pocus. Yet I felt my skin shudder; I felt the goose bumps rise.

"That's it?" my wife said. "That's the only catch?"

He shrugged. "That's it," he said. "Not much, is it? Not a whisper of menace for a pair such as yourselves."

My wife's eyes were gauzed over; there was a wetness in them.

"Hold on," she said. "Don't you be leaving yet. Hold this, honey."

She put the cloth in my arms. Then she hastened over to the well, pitched the bucket down, and drew it up running over with fresh water.

"Here," she said, coming back with a good dipperful. "Here's a nice drink of cool water. You need it on a day like this."

The man drank. He held the dipper in both hands, with the tips of his fingers, and drained the dipper dry, then wiped his chin with the back of a hand.

"I did indeed," he said. "That's very tasty water. I thank you."

"That's good water," she said. "That well has been here lo a hundred years. You could stay on for supper," she said. "It's getting on toward that time and I have a fine stew on the stove, with plenty to spare."

"That's kind of you," he said back, "and I'm grateful. But I'd best pass on up your road while there's still daylight left, and see who else might have need of this cloth."

My wife is not normally a demonstrative woman, not in public. Certainly not with strangers. You could have knocked me over with a feather when she up and kissed him full on the mouth, with a nice hug to boot.

"There's payment," she said, "if our money's no good."

He blushed, trying to hide his pleasure. It seemed to me she had him wrapped around her little finger . . . or the other way around.

"You kiss like a woman," he said. "Like one who knows what kissing is for, and can't hardly stop herself."

It was my wife's turn to blush.

I took hold of her hand and held her down to grass, because it seemed to me another kiss or two and she'd fly right away with him.

He walked across the yard and up by the well house, leaving by the same route he had come. Heading for the road. At the turn, he spun around and waved.

"You could try the Hopkins place!" my wife called. "There's a fat woman down that road got a sea of troubles. She could surely use some of that cloth."

He smiled and again waved. Then we saw his head and his bolt of white cloth bobbing along the weeds as he took the dips and rises in the road. Then he went on out of sight.

"There's that man with some horses down that road!" my wife called. "You be careful of him!"

It seemed we heard some sound come back, but whether it was his voice we couldn't say.

My wife and I stood a long time in the yard, me holding the dipper and watching her, while she held her own bolt of cloth in her arms, staring off to where he'd last been.

Then she sighed dreamily and went inside.

I went on down to the barn and looked after the animals. Getting my feeding done. I talked a spell to them. Talking to animals is soothing to me, and they like it too. They pretend to stare at the walls or the floor as they're munching their feed down, but I know they listen to me. We had us an *unusual circumstances* chat.

"That man with the cloth," I said. "Maybe you can tell me what you make of him."

Thirty minutes later I heard my wife excitedly calling me. She was standing out on the back doorstep, with this incredulous look.

"I've finished," she said. "I've finished the windows. *Nine* windows. It beats me how."

I started up to the house. Her voice was all shaky. Her face flushed, flinging her arms about. Then she got this new look on.

"Wait!" she said. "Stay there! Give me ten minutes!"

And she flung herself back inside, banging the door. I laughed. It always gave me a kick how she ordered me around.

I got the milk pail down under the cow. Before I'd touched and drained all four teats she was calling again.

"Come look, come look, oh come look!"

She was standing in the open doorway, with the kitchen to her back. Behind her, through the windows, I could see the streak of a red sunset and how it lit up the swing of trees. But I wasn't looking there. I was looking at her. Looking and swallowing hard and trying to remember how a body produced human speech. I had never thought of white as a colour she could wear. White, it pales her some. It leaves her undefined and washes out what parts I like best. But she looked beautiful now. In her new dress she struck me down to my bootstraps. She made my chest break.

"Do you like it?" she said.

I went running up to her. I was up against her, hugging her and lifting her before she'd even had a chance to get set. I'd never held on so tight or been held so tight back.

Truth is, it was the strangest thing. Like we were both so innocent we hadn't yet shot up out of new ground.

"Come see the curtains," she whispered. "Come see the new

sheets. Come see what else I've made. You'll see it all. You'll see how our home has been transformed."

I crept inside. There was something holy about it. About it and about us and about those rooms and the whole wide world. Something radiant. Like you had to put your foot down easy and hold it down or you'd float on up.

"That's it," she said. "That's how I feel too."

That night in bed, trying to figure it out, we wondered how Ella Mae down the road had done. How the people all along our road had made out.

"No worry," my wife said. "He'll have found a bonanza around here. There's heaps of decent people in this neck of the woods."

"Wonder where he is now?" we said.

"Wonder where he goes next?"

"Where he gets that cloth?"

"Who he *is?*"

We couldn't get to sleep, wondering about that.

The
Blue
Baby

THERE WAS A TIME down in North Carolina when nothing ever happened.

There was the time up north in the Yukon when a man I knew locked up another man I knew inside a freezer and the man froze.

There were those times and there were other times.

I don't know which times to tell you about.

There was the time when I was twelve and riding a bicycle around and around a small shrub in the backyard and the front tire hit a brick and the bicycle crumpled beneath me and I broke a tooth and she did not care.

I am convinced she did not care.

So there was that time too.

There were the times she would bounce me on her knees and ask, Who do you love most, him or me? You didn't remember him or anything about him, but there were those times she asked that. He was like your nickel which rolled between the floor-boards into the utter, unreachable darkness of the world. He was like that. Who do you love most, him or me? And though you knew the answer you never said a word, not one. You would only hang your head and wait for the knee-ride to begin again. She would stop the ride to take your face in her hands and ask that. And though you knew the answer, knew it to the innermost ache of your heart, you never said a word, not one.

You couldn't say, Ride me, mama. You could only squint at the thin darkness between the floorboards and wonder what else over the long years had fallen between those cracks.

Him or me?

For years and years she asked this and you always knew but never answered, and now you are here by her bedside and still you can't.

So there were those times. Some of the times were good times, but they do not belong here. I don't know where they belong.

Here is another one. Sometimes on a dark night you could stand under a tree in front of your house and see two naked fat people in the upstairs room in the house across the street.

I thought, If only they knew how ugly they are.

I thought, Why do they do that?

I thought, Why don't they turn off that light?

The fat man up there lived in another place, lived across the river, and I thought he should stay in the place he came from.

My friends on that street would gather under that tree and they would say, Oh baby, look at them go, and you never could get your friends away from that tree. Shut up, they would say, what's eating you?

My mother was a friend of this woman. She was to be seen in this woman's company, in this fat woman's company, she was to be seen with them. I wondered whether my mother knew what went on up there with this fat couple, and why, when she went out on double dates, she had to go out with people like that.

He had a car, that's why.

On Saturday nights they went to dances together in a place called Edgewater.

I stand corrected on this one small matter. I said "car" but it was not a car. His was a stingy little truck, dusty and black, with narrow, balding tires and corncobs and empty fertilizer sacks in the rear. When they went out to these dances the fat woman would sit up under the fat man's arms and my mother would sit in the cab on her date's lap, her head folded up against the ceiling, and all four would be hooting with laughter.

That was one time.

There was that time I broke a tooth falling against a brick while riding my bicycle around and around this little shrub and my mother said, Now no girl will ever marry you, but I knew she didn't care. She hardly even looked, scarcely even glanced at me, because I wasn't bleeding.

I got hit in the jaw once with a baseball, there was that time.

I pulled long worms out of my behind, there were those times, and I didn't tell her.

There was the time a dentist, my first dentist, took out an aching tooth, the wrong tooth, with a pair of garage pliers and charged two dollars.

You could see those worms up in white circles on my cheeks and across my shoulders and people would look at you, they'd say, Look at that boy, he has worms.

You took a folded note to the store one time which you were not supposed to read, but you read it and it said, Give him head lice powder, I will pay you later.

You stole a nickel from her purse one time and it rolled between the floorboards and you have not yet confessed that.

You were such a nice little boy, so sweet and good.

You had to sit on a board when you got a haircut. You'd see the barber pick up the board and sling it up over the arms of the chair and you wanted to hit him.

You put a penny in the weight machine in front of the drug-store and got your fortune told. You would put in the penny or one of your friends would, and then that friend would step up on the scale with you or you would step up beside him, step up care-fully, not to jiggle or the red cover would slam down over the numbers, and then one of you would step off, step carefully off, not to jiggle, and the numbers would roll back to reveal your own true weight, although both of you had the same fortune.

For two years I never weighed more or less than eighty-seven pounds. There was that time.

Women—young girls, ladies—would come to the door and they would ask, Is So-and-So here? Where is So-and-So? But you weren't supposed to tell them, even if you knew, because So-and-So had washed his hands of these women, was done with them, yet they wouldn't leave him alone.

Policemen knocked on the door, too, they too wanted to know where So-and-So was.

So-and-So was in trouble with women, with the law, with the family and with everyone else, and what you heard was he was no good, he was mean, he cared about no one, he would as soon hit you as look at you, but he was my mother's brother and she was ever defending him and hiding him and if anyone didn't like it they could go climb a pole.

You had to go to the store to buy your mother's Kotex, because no one else would or no one else was around, and that was terri-ble. The storekeeper would say, Speak up, boy, and you would again grumble the word. He would put the Kotex up on the counter and everyone would stare at it, would say this or that, they'd look at me, look me over closely, then the storekeeper would wrap the box in brown paper like a slab of meat and take your money and go away rubbing it between his fingers.

Sometimes a strange dog would come up and follow you for a bit, follow you home even, even stand scratching at the door, but you never knew whose dog it was or what name you could call it except Dog or what means you could devise to make it stay.

Mrs. Whitfield next door refused to return any hit ball which landed in her yard.

The one pecan tree in this place I am talking about was surrounded by a high fence and you could not reach the limbs even with poles and no matter how hard or long you tried.

At night you threw rocks at the light hanging from a cable supported by poles at either side of the gravel street and when you hit it you ran, because Mrs. Whitfield would be calling the law.

The policemen patrolled these streets like beings from another side of the world.

A boy my age jumped or fell from the water tower at the edge of town, there was that time.

There was the time a car was parked in the same alley that ran behind our house, with a hose hooked up from the exhaust to a window, but only the woman died. The man with her had awakened in the night, had changed his mind and fled. She was some other man's wife and her blouse was open and below the waist she had nothing on except her green shoes. My mother said to us all, she said, What kind of scum would leave her like that?

The town smelled. It smelled because of the paper mills and sometimes a black haze would cover the sky and you would have to hold your nose.

Those fat, naked people in the room upstairs, you would see them drink from a bottle sometimes. You would see them with their arms around each other and then a hand would reach down to the window sill and pick up the bottle.

You would see the light bulb hanging from their ceiling and a fly strip dangling to catch the flies.

A body was discovered one summer in a stream called the Dye Ditch, the stream you had to cross to reach grammar school, but you went down to look at that place in the ditch where the body was discovered but no one was there, no corpse was there, and after a while you didn't hear anyone speak of it and you never knew who it was had been stabbed in that ditch. The ditch was deep, with steep clay walls, the walls always wet, wet and smooth and perfect, but clay was not a thing you knew to do anything with. You found a shoe in the woods just up from the bank, a shoe with the tongue missing, and you said, This was the stabbed man's shoe and you asked yourself why So-and-So had done it, because of some woman, most likely.

Some days the ditch water was one colour, some days another colour, vile colours, and at other times it was a mix of many.

You couldn't dam up that stream although you spent endless days trying, and you put your bare foot in the stabbed man's shoes but you still didn't know why or how it had happened.

You were such a nice little boy. You were so nice. You tried making biscuits once, as a surprise for your mother when she came in from work, but you forgot to mix lard in, and the salt and baking powder, and the biscuits didn't rise, and when she came in you'd forgotten to wipe up the flour from the table and floor.

She would sit you on her knees and hold your shoulders as she bounced you up and down and she would say, Which do you love best, him or me?

You were swinging on a tree-rope by the Dye Ditch, swinging high, into the limbs, and you let go and flew and when you landed a rusty nail came up all the way through your foot and as you hobbled the half-mile home you were amazed that it hurt so little and bled so little, and when you got home your brother pulled out the nail with pliers and your mother rubbed burning iodine over the wound and said, Be sure you wear clean socks for the next little while.

Three streets were paved, all others were gravel, and all of the streets were named after U.S. presidents. There was an uptown called Rosemary and a downtown called Downtown, and uptown was bigger, while Downtown was dying, was dead, but was the place you had to go through if you wanted for whatever reason to cross the river.

Across the river was nothing, it was death across the river. The fat man had come from across the river, so had my mother when she was fourteen and fleeing death, which was exactly how she spoke of it. Oh, honey, it was death on that farm.

He was down between the cracks, my father was, that's where he was.

There was another time, an early time, when I walked with my grandfather across the fields and when he stopped to pick up soil and crumble it and let it sift between his fingers I would pick up soil and do the same.

Your grandfather let you walk down the rows with him, he let you hold the plough, and he said, Just let the mule do the work, but you couldn't hold the plough handles and the reins at the same time and the plough blade kept riding up out of the ground. When you came to the end of a row the mule would stop and your grandfather would look at both of you, look and flap his hat against his leg, and say, Now let's see which of you has the better sense. You stood behind your grandfather's chair in the evenings and combed his balding head, but your grandmother said, I've got enough plates to get to the table, why should I get theirs? Why can't she come and take away these that are hers and leave me with those that are mine?

No one asked her to marry that drinker.

Didn't we tell her sixteen was too young?

She made her own bed. There ain't one on their daddy's side ever had pot to pee in or knew what pot was for.

So there was the time she came and packed your goods, your brother and sister's goods, in a paper sack, and took you to town for the first time. The town was only seven miles away, but it was the first time and it was quite a town. It had a downtown called Downtown and an uptown called Rosemary, and she had two up-stairs rooms downtown on Monroe Street, and you had to be very quiet up there because the woman who lived below lived alone below and she was so stupid she thought every sound meant a thief was coming to steal her money.

She had a blue baby, this baby with an enormous blue head, and all of the light bulbs in her rooms were blue so that you wouldn't know she had a blue baby.

Every day for five days in the week, sometimes six, your mother left for work before daylight, you would hear the car out on the street honk for her, you would hear the car door slam, hear the engine, the roll of tires, and she would be gone. You would hear her moving softly about you, you would feel her tucking you in, then she would be gone. You went to school that first week and for five days stood in the woods watching the children at play outside, then the bell would ring and they would go inside, and when the yard had cleared you would tramp through the woods back home, you would dawdle at the Dye Ditch and check where you could and could not jump it and be amazed at all the vile colours, you would sit on the bank and grieve and tell yourself that tomorrow you would go inside with them. Then you would sneak up the stairs and never make a sound all day, just you and the blue baby and the baby's mother in that silent house. You would sit at the table drawing rings of water on the yellow top. At the end of the day your mother would come in with a bag of groceries, come in with a sweater looped over one arm, come in with cotton fuzz in her hair, and she would say, How do you like your new school, is it a nice school? How do you like your new friends?

She would sit you on her knees and bounce you and say, How is my handsome man today?

You were such a good little boy.

On Fridays you got up early to deliver the local paper and the people would not pay, they would say, It is not worth my nickel, and you kept returning but they rarely would pay, although they did not tell you to stop delivering their paper and if you did stop they would call the editor, they would say, Where's my paper?

There was the time I knocked on one door and my uncle So-and-So answered without his clothes on and he said, You haven't seen me, you don't know where I am, and he gave me a dollar.

The blue baby died and went to heaven, but the woman downstairs did not change her light bulbs.

On Mondays you would take your mother's white blouse and black skirt to the cleaners and on Saturdays you would see her wearing these. You would see her in heels, her legs in nice stockings, her mouth red, and she would say, How do I look?

She would say, Say hello to Monty, but you wouldn't.

She would say, He's so cute when he's pouting, and that would make you grin.

She would say, I'll be home early, but you stayed up late with your head pressed against the window and she never came, no, she never.

There was the time she said, You smell like four dead cats in a trunk, why don't you wash? And she flung your clothes off and scraped at your knees, elbows and heels, she twisted a cloth up in your ears, she said, This crust will never come off, and when she had your skin pink and burning she said, Your father is coming, you want to look nice for him, don't you?

But he didn't come, and I put back on my dirty clothes and hid under the house until past bedtime, until past the time she'd stopped walking the street and calling my name, and then I went in and would talk to no one.

There was the time she said, I want the three of you out of this house, I want you out this minute, if I don't get a minute's peace I will stab myself with these scissors. So she dressed you and your brother in identical Little Boy Blue short-pant suits with straps that came over the shoulder, and she washed your faces and necks and ears and slicked your hair down with water. She gave your sister thirty-six cents from her red purse and she said, Take them to see the moving picture show at the People's Theater and don't you dare come back until the picture is over. My sister said, mama, how will we know when the picture is over? and my mother said, When the rest of the audience gets up to leave that's when you leave, and not a second before. So we trooped down to the movie, hurrying to get there because we couldn't imagine what it might be like to see a moving picture show. We entered in the dark and sat in seats at the very rear, while up on the screen you saw the back of a man's head and a woman with her head thrown back and they were kissing. We sat on the edge of our seats, holding hands, my sister in the middle and telling us not to kick our legs, as the man got into a jeep and drove off, not returning the wave of the woman who was running after him, and he got smaller and smaller in his jeep as the music got louder, and then we saw tears slide down the woman's face and she collapsed to her knees in the muddy road and in the next second the theatre lights were rising and everyone was getting up. They were getting up, they were all leaving.

On the way home the three of us bawled and my sister said it wasn't worth thirty-six cents, it wasn't worth nothing and mama must be crazy.

So that was that time and that is why I have hated movies to this day.

You weighed eighty-seven pounds for so many of those years.

You wore socks so stiff with filth you could barely work your feet into them in the morning. Your nose ran, always ran, and you wiped the snot on your sleeves until they turned stiff also, from cuff to elbow.

You would feel this tickling movement, this wriggling motion, while you sat on the toilet, and you'd stand up and wrench yourself over and there would be this long worm coming out of your behind. You couldn't believe it that first time, but here it was, proof that worms were living inside you, and it made you ache with the shame that if worms did, lived inside you, then what else could?

You will tell no one. You would be walking down the street and you'd feel it, feel the worm, and you'd reach a hand inside your britches and pull the worm all the way out and you'd think it never was going to stop coming.

Who do you love best, him or me?

There was the time all this ended, but you never knew when it was that time was, so it was as though that time never ended, which is one reason to think about it. I think about it because it ended, but never really ended, that is why I think about it.

They were always washing your ears.

They were always saying, Tie your shoelaces.

You were always being shoved one way or another by one person or another and you never gained an ounce through so many years.

We got home from the moving picture show fifteen minutes after we left and our mother was sitting in her slip in the kitchen chair, with her eyes closed and both wrists up white in her lap and her feet in a pan of water.

Cotton fluff was in her hair.

One year you asked your mother whatever happened to that fat old guy with the truck who went with that woman across the street, and she didn't know who you meant. Some days later, while washing her hair over a white bowl, she suddenly clapped her hands and said, Oh him, they are not going together any longer, it was never serious anyhow. It's just that he treated her decently and he wasn't a tightwad, and he liked good fun. Why are you asking about something like that?

Why are you? Sometimes I find myself thinking you are a strange little boy.

You're odd. That's how you strike me sometimes.

I think about it now because now she lies in this bed with tubes up her nose and tubes attached to her shaved head and she's holding my hand, or rather her hand is limp in mine and you can't hear her breathe. You can't see her chest rise and her lids never move. Her fingers are silent in mine.

You think of the man you knew who was locked up in the freezer in the Yukon and how he froze.

You think of the freezer and of opening the door, but when the door is opened after all of these years all you see is the freezer empty and the frosty tumble of air.

You think of these things and of those times.

Who do you love?

She has been this way for an hour or more, not moving, and so have I, the two of us here, neither of us moving and nothing happening, her hand cold in mine and the night darkening and I still haven't answered.

Early Obscenities in the Life of the World's Foremost Authority on Heidegger

In this one house lives this young girl who possesses a necklace made of living lizards. She has stitched seven lizards head against tail, employing the best silk thread and a craftful hand. She has only to swallow, or twist her head, or herself lunge into sudden movement, to make these lizards swish in frantic laps around her neck. Cordelia is convinced the racing lizards empower her with otherworldly abilities. So long as they are racing, she can clamp her eyes shut and squeeze her every muscle and utterly focus her every thought—and thus tell you what you are doing, what is going on at your house, if you have the ill fortune to live within the vicinity.

THE CHILD SAID, "I can get no purchase on my self. I feel the affliction of a lifetime living with you, and this bears down upon my fat shoulders like a curse." The child did indeed imagine her shoulders to be unsightly. She often envied those tall skinny creatures who rammed fingers down their throats and vomited up everything they had eaten—behind tree and shrub and in secret toilets all over the place.

"True," the child said. "I'm out of patience with the lot of you. Why don't you go away and die?"

She felt like being insolent. Why not? It was how she felt. She felt it would bring her great pleasure to strike every adult who came into range over their heads with brickbats and barge poles.

These statements earned the child a long black stare from her mother, the one adult at the moment who shared space with her.

"Truly," the girl said, finishing lamely. "You're such a pill."

Her mother did not bat an eye. She had heard all this before. The child should be locked away inside an airless vault, as her father often said. She should be chained to a cyclone fence, like a vicious dog.

Lunch, which they had before them, consisted solely of muffins. The muffins were a leftover from the previous evening, because this vileness had been going on a good while now. At breakfast this morning (with that *other fool*, the child might have thought), they had both erupted from their chairs at the same moment. Heading off into different rooms, onto different floors where, if God were merciful, they could avoid seeing each other's face. Ever, each had thought. Ever again. Even a creak in the floorboards, occasioned by the others' pacing, made their stomachs churn.

"Eat your muffins," the child's mother said. "I'm sure they are tasty."

"Why wouldn't they be?" the child asked. "What makes you think you're the only one who can bake muffins?"

The child's mother said nothing. She had thoughts, however. Who *is* this child? Where did she *come* from? The cross little bitch must have been swapped with mine, in the cradle.

The mother dared not look at her. If she looked, she would sink the butter knife into her child's heart.

"Eat your muffin," she said.

The girl had baked the muffins the previous evening, while a truce of sorts had prevailed. Everyone calm for a change. The mother had beaten the eggs. They had formed a united front against the evils of the world. The truce had been broken when the wrong person—not once, but twice—opened the oven door. The recipe the girl had used called for thirty minutes' baking time. The mother reasoned that in thirty minutes the muffins would burn, or certainly dry out. They would be inedible. But the child had to learn she couldn't trust everything in print (*Damn that Heidegger*, she might have thought), so she had not intervened. If the muffins shrivelled up like black ants in their tin, and black smoke poured from the oven, so much better the lesson.

It was the woman's husband and the child's father who brought the house down. If you wanted a source for these present difficulties, there it was. If you wanted blame, there was blame.

Sauntering through, whistling an inane show tune, he had opened the oven door. Twice. He was hungry, he said. He had had no lunch. "Too busy," he said. "No breakfast either, as I recall."

"You had it," his wife had said. "You had three fried eggs and eight slices of bacon. I cooked it myself."

"You're kidding. All that?"

The child had found this exchange—so typical—typically disgusting. She had decided—the second time he opened the oven door—she could do nothing in this house without their interference. She was their doormat, their sponge. They entered her room without knocking. They had this and that to say about what she wore. They said her room stank. If they came across her sitting in a chair, quietly absorbed in a book, they would flip that book to its cover, breathe deeply, and say, "Not that creep again."

They hated her hair. "Purple! My God, even your scalp is purple!"

They never forked over a dime. They harped on how skinny she was ("Pure *bone!* And those *rags* you wear!"), and wondered why she sealed herself away in the bathroom as often as she did.

"Christ, you'd think you had a lover in there. You'd think you were married to the bathroom, or to that Heidegger creep."

So he was the one who pulled the muffins from the oven before they were ready. He was the one who sat down at the kitchen table, with a ton of butter, and ate the child's muffins.

Pronouncing them delicious, delicious.

They had watched him eat, watched him wet his thumbs and press those thumbs against crumbs, and watched him suck those crumbs into his mouth.

Both had thought this disgusting.

It was the one moment, in the whole adventure of these muffins, when the child and her mother had seen eye to eye, or acknowledged any sense of their blood-attachment one to the other. It was the one moment in weeks when they had looked at each other with anything resembling fondness.

They watched, with utter disgust, as he patted his lips and rubbed his tummy.

Such scrawny lips, each thought. Such a big, ugly tummy.

They watched him rise from the table and stroll away in supreme satisfaction, again whistling that inane—that totally ludicrous—show tune. Something about a dame. Something about there being nothing like a dame. About there being not anyone here who cooked, or looked, or shook, like a dame.

His plate left there on the table. His napkin flung into the butter dish. His Scotch glass smeared with butter.

"Delicious!"

That is what he had said.

What she had said, the child had said, what his daughter had said to the mother, was this: "Why did you marry that pig? Why did you marry such a thick, insensitive person? He's an animal! What could you possibly have been thinking?"

The child's mother took exception to this characterization of the one man in her life to whom she was married. *This* jerk.

"He's a jerk!" the daughter said.

The mother recoiled. She had had quite enough of this behaviour.

"It is not up to *you*," she said, "to tell *me* what I should or should not have done. Young lady. Young lady, you can just watch your mouth."

But the young lady, the child, was still mad about the oven door, and mad at the number of muffins he had eaten, and mad because . . . well, because she was mad all the time now. She had been mad through all the time she could remember. Plus, she had *wanted* to use a ready-mix. It was not *her* idea to crack open all those eggs and dribble slime everywhere. It was not *her* idea to measure out all that flour and sift it everywhere, and search hours through the cupboard for the thousand ingredients, and now be left with all those filthy dishes which she—*she*—would be expected to clean.

No. All she had said at the start, wanting some relief or pause from the troublesome Mr. Heidegger—and this said on a whim, not even thinking about it—was: "I think I will make muffins."

It was her mother, wanting to be *together* with her, to hone up this absurd mother-daughter relationship—wanting to be *pals*— who had come up with all those other crazy ideas.

"Oh, not those mixes, dear. Let's do these muffins from *scratch*."

Now look, just look, how it all had turned out.

So what the child said was this:

"He's *selfish*," she said. "He's a *drunk!* Did you see all that Scotch he belted back? He's *stupid*, too."

"Young lady," the mother said. "Now you just—"

"He *is!* Didn't you tell me he had to sit for his bar exam three times? And then, didn't you say, he only passed by the skin of his teeth?"

The mother's lips coiled. "We were talking about muffins," she said.

"Yeah, muffins," the child said. "Well, how does he come off talking to me about grades, grades, and telling me that my 'precious Heidegger' wouldn't last a minute in a courtroom, when he was such a dumbo himself?"

At this remark, the mother flung her own venom at the luckless child.

"You will not talk about him like that," the mother said. "You will not talk to *me*, like that. Who is it, do you think, who puts shoes on your feet and provides a roof over your head, and works twenty hours a day seeing to your every requirement? Who? Young lady. Who was it around here who for your last birthday bought you the bound eighty volumes of the lifetime work of that shit, Heidegger, that you can't get your nose out of? And as for grades, who is it around here who spends half her time on the telephone talking to imbecile friends with purple hair who look like they were eaten for lunch? Who is it spends the whole of her time locked up in the toilet, and won't say boo to her parents, and has not looked at a book—other than that shitty Heidegger—in a full year? Who? Just answer me that."

"Oh, fuck off!" the child said.

And the mother, shocked, went running to find her husband, to tell him what their daughter had told her to do.

"'—Fuck off'! Yes. I couldn't believe my ears."

Afterwards—after slammed doors and the disappearance of everyone into whatever private, airless space could be found—afterwards, the two parents cornering the child, looming over her, screaming about how a certain somebody in this house could go and live on the moon, go and live on the streets, if she couldn't show a certain respect. Yes! If she was going to be so rebellious, and have such a dirty mouth, and not respect *any*thing, or anyone, and go around with hair looking like *that*, and live with her precious Heidegger in this stinking room, and get so upset about goddamn *muffins*, then she could hit the streets, *live* on the streets, be as one with all the garbage and filth out there. *Eat* garbage, *be* garbage, and see, young lady, how she liked *that*.

Whereupon the girl, this child, decided she had had enough.

Quite enough, thank you.

She told them both to fuck off. Shouted this at them, and flung her eighty Heidegger volumes to the floor, and told them to touch her if they dared. "Hit me," she said, "and I'll have the police on your tails before you can blink."

Which words shocked them more than anything: their mouths open in surprise, because. . . . Well, for God's sake, who had even been *thinking* of hitting anyone around here? Hit her? For God's sake, nobody *ever* hits anybody around here.

Violence has no place in *this* house.

Jesus Christ.

Can you believe it?

Has the child lost her mind?

But the child, having issued that threat, wasn't waiting around to witness any of these befuddled considerations.

No, she had fled into the bathroom as fast as she could get there, and once behind lock and key, had repeatedly thrust her fingers down her throat. She had bent at the sink and tensed her body to the full power of its loathing, and racked her insides, doing her best to vomit up anything that might be down there. Saying to herself over and over, How can two people *hate* me *so much?*

How can they hate *every*one, and every*thing* . . . so much?

Purple hair, Heidegger, my smell, my room, rings in the ear or nose, the navel, the telephone, street people, muffin mix, lizards, my clothes, my posture, God—God, just *every*thing!

The child there, fingers down her throat, trying to retch it all up.

But finding no release in this. None at all. Because she was the one around here who hadn't eaten a single bite during the past twenty-four hours—which was why she had thought to bake the muffins in the first place—and in consequence of this starving of herself nothing could be raked up. Nothing. Except the *taste* of bile. Unless you were to count this stringy mucus clinging to her lips.

Well, let it hang.

Damnit, just let it hang.

So that was last night. That was what went on around here last night. *All* night, no one sleeping a wink.

Now here they are, mother and child, come to the new day, and doing their best to muddle through this muffin lunch.

To put *that* nasty episode behind them.

As for the muffins, those that the husband had not eaten remained in their open baking tin on the table all that night, and have been there all this morning. Stale and dry as can be, although who is going to admit or confess to that?

No one. They are inedible, but the mother feels she must eat them. Because her daughter made them, with the best of hearts, and the only way they can survive this evil, she feels, and she can win back her daughter's love, is to eat the damn things. At the least, to nibble. To put the good face on that terrible night. To *forget* all the horrible things they said to each other, and the poor child left to hide away in the bathroom behind lock and key, where she can retch her eyes out.

Because that's what has been going on around here.

The mother has been coming to this recognition over the recent months, and she can believe it now.

You only have to look at the child's gaunt face, at the skinny body, at those sunken eyes, the pale skin, her *bones*—to realize that something very suspicious has been going on around here.

Although she wishes just once she had thought to peek through the keyhole, just to be sure. Because with a thing like this you don't want just to blurt it out, since there could be a thousand reasons the child locks herself up in there.

It could be that she goes in there only to read the eighty volumes of that loathsome fuckhead Heidegger.

How is it, the mother wonders, that a child of hers has come up with this ridiculous obsession? How does she come by the *brains* for it, just to mention that? Because her husband certainly does not have them, an overflow of brains, and they never ran in her family either.

Yet one has to go on. To persevere. Despite the fact that all three of them are now furious with each other, and what each really feels like doing is like not lifting a hand to do *any*thing, or making *any* amends, because all you really feel like doing, and what you most want to do, is to seal yourself away in a corner, and *die*.

Yes, die, because it is all so hopeless.

That, at any rate, is how the mother feels, here seated at the table with her daughter and their stale muffin lunch.

Nor can she get past this present loathing and fury that she feels for her prick husband.

The child tells her to "fuck off"—well, really, it is just the way children talk these days—and she goes running to him—such a dishrag—and the whole thing spirals into utter insanity.

A minute later, the child has locked herself in the bathroom again, puking her eyes out.

And while she's in there doing this, they are at each other's throats.

"I didn't tell you to go in there and totally undermine her self-respect. I didn't tell you to threaten her, and stand over her like an ogre, and say she would have to go live on the streets! You had no business speaking of garbage, and saying she was garbage, and that she was not wanted around here, and that we didn't love her and would prefer—really prefer—that she had never been born."

"I didn't say that," the husband said. "I at no time said she was garbage, or that we wanted her living with garbage on the street, or that we didn't love her. I clearly recall, for that matter, that you called me to go and reason with her, talk to her, and instill some form of sanity into this madhouse. I distinctly recall that. And I recall, too, that you were the party who made that statement about her hair, which was what really enraged her, whereas I have had no trouble whatsoever in coming to terms with her purple hair, and in fact, rather like it."

"God!" the mother said. "God, you are such a liar. Such a hypocrite and weak little worm and dense fool that I wonder why I ever married you. Why I have ever let you touch me or—Not that that side of this marriage has ever been so great, you know. No, you're hardly the big-time, big-shot lover you think you are, no matter how many show tunes you go around singing with that imbecilic smirk none of us can stand. Dames! *Dames!*"

"Oh, really. Oh, really!" the husband said. "Well, baby, you can just fuck off! You can read my lips, can't you? What am I saying? I am saying _____! Did you get it? Fuck off!"

Well, then. Here they sit, mother and child.

"Eat your muffin," the mother says.

The child raises her eyes and looks at her mother, eating hers.

"If you don't mind," the child says, "I think I will just quietly sit here and drink this *fabulous* tea, and read my *fabulous* Heidegger. *If you don't mind!*"

The mother's eyes close, her hands tighten into small fists, and some seconds pass before she is able to muster the bright smile.

"Why don't you read some of it aloud to me?" she says. "I really would be interested."

They listen a moment to each other's breathing.

This, the child thinks, is parental love of a new dimension. This is motherhood truly hitting a new low.

What, the mother is thinking, have I got myself into?

"You won't understand a word," the child says. "You will find it too intellectual."

The mother is crying. She feels hot maternal tears filling her lashes.

"That in itself might be a relief. Please. I won't say a word."

"All *right!*" the child says. "But try to understand. Try to wake *up!* This is about *being!* This is about the *forgetfulness* of being within the 'essential sphere of oblivion'! Are you with me?"

The mother is all ears. Her daughter's words are pure and total nonsense but she fully intends, in this moment, through every inch of her being—forgotten or otherwise—to be the world's finest mother.

The child begins reading.

Volume 74, the complete, annotated Heidegger.

And despite all that has gone on around here over these recent hours, it would be incorrect of you to assume that the voice the child employs is anything other than precise, clear, and confident. *Gorgeous* stuff.

This girl truly loves her Heidegger.

To see the mother's rapt face, to note the attention she gives every word, and how her tears pour, and how her expression of grave affliction so soon is dispelled and a radiant smile replaces those tears and how her hands ride her pounding heart, you would swear this woman—this mother—loves him, too.

The Heart Must from Its Breaking

The Postman

THIS IS HOW IT HAPPENED that morning at the church. Timmons was speaking on a topic that had us all giggling, "What You Do When and If You Get To Heaven and Find It Empty," and we were all there and saw it. How suddenly before Timmons got wound up good the wood doors burst open and there in the sunlight was someone or something, like a fast-spinning wheel made up of gold, though it couldn't have been gold and was probably some funny trick of the light. Anyway, there it was, and beckoning. Must have been beckoning, or calling somehow, because two children got up from their seats at the front and quiet as you please marched right out to him—to him or it—and went through the door, and that was the last any of us ever saw them. Then a second later that other kid—Tiny Peterson was his name—went out too, but his mama was in time to save him. Now I'd lie about it if I could or if I knew how, but it was all so quiet and quick and then over that I wouldn't know how to improve on the actual happening. Out that door and then swallowed up, those two kids, and that's all there was to it.

The Dead Woman's Sister

He can say that's all if he wants to. Roger Deering sees an affair like this the same way he sees his job, which I would remind you is delivering mail. He drops it through the box, if he can be troubled to come up the path, and then he's gone. What he's left you with don't matter spit to him. But I live in that house now, my sister's house, and I can tell you the story don't end there.

They were my sister's children, Agnes and Cluey. Sister was home in bed sick so I'd taken little Agnes and Cluey to church to hear Timmons give what we hoped would be a good one, and right after the second song, with Timmons hardly begun, Cluey, who was on my left, stood up and whispered "Excuse me," and brushed by my knees, then Agnes on my right stood up, mumbled "Me too," and they went on down the row, scraping by people, getting funny looks, and then going on down the aisle pretty as you please. I thought Cluey had to go to the bathroom. He was always doing that, never going when you told him to and it embarrassed me. But you do get tired of telling a boy to wait wait wait when he's squirming and crossing his legs, trying to hold it in. I don't mean he was doing it that day, I'm only saying that's what I thought he got up for. He'd been nice as pie the whole time, both of them, both while walking along with me to church and while sitting there waiting for Timmons to get primed. So I was in a good mood and bearing them no malice, though they were a long shot from being my favourite nieces and nephews. Sister had been ailing for some while and they were feeling dopey about that, we all were. That was the day Sister died, in fact the very minute, some said. Some said they'd looked at their watches when that door burst open and Cluey and Agnes went out never to be seen again and that very second three blocks over was the very second Sister passed on. It was close, that's all I'm saying, and my skin shivers saying that much, especially when I remember about the blood. But I'm not saying anything about the blood on Sister's window, being content to leave that to the likes of Hank Sparrow who is still dunning me for that ten dollars. I don't like to think any of it is the truth, for I'm living in Sister's house now and I know sometimes I hear her and that she hears me. Sister dies and her two children disappear the same minute and it does make you think. Though I didn't see any whirling light or gold spinning at the door. I felt a draft, that's all. Like most people with any sense I thought the wind had blown it open, and when people say to me there wasn't any wind that day I just look through them, since any fool knows a gust can come up. Still, it's strange. I can't think what happened to the children. No one wanted them. I couldn't, and Sister wasn't able. Their daddy couldn't have come and got them because none of us hardly remembered who their daddy was, or wanted to, because even in his best of days he hadn't been what you'd call a solid citizen. He wasn't right in the head, and not much in the body either, and even Sister knew that. So she had her hard times, raising that pair without a hand from him who hadn't been seen I think in nine years when all this happened. No aunts or uncles would have come for them. We don't have kidnappers around here. No, it defies explanation and I've given up trying. When

Sister wakes me calling in the night I sit up in bed and answer back and we go on talking that way until her spirit quietens.

I hope Cluey and Agnes are all right, wherever they are, that's all I hope. I don't agree with those who say they're long-since dead, nor those who say they're in heaven either. Timmons might.

The Preacher

Sure they're dead. I don't know how, or how come, or why, not having the divine intervention on it, but you can't tell me two children dressed for church and without penny or snotrag between them are going to get out of this town without anyone knowing it. There are just two ways for entering or leaving and that's by the one street that leads off to Scotland Neck at one end and Enfield at the other, and they didn't go either of those ways. Couldn't have, because a hundred people rocking on their porches that fine Sunday when they should have been at Spring Level hearing my sermon on "The Empty Hell" would have noted their progress and likely turned them around.

So they're dead. Yep, and their bones plucked by now. Dust to dust and the Lord's will abideth.

Somebody picked them up right off the churchgrounds, I'd say, right there at the door, and spooked them away. Why I don't know. They were ordinary children, no better or worse than most. Funny things go on in this town the same as they do anyplace else and I figure those two are buried this minute down in somebody's cellar or in a backyard where a thousand things hidden go on day in and day out. I've preached till I'm blue in the face, the same as one or two other ministers have, and it's done no good. Not a lick. You can't stamp out the devil's work for he's like a mad dog once he gets going. That's what it was, of course. The old devil keeping his hand in. If it hadn't been those two children it would have been something worse.

We searched the woods, every rock, weed and clover. Nothing. Not a hint.

About that door. I saw *something* but *what* is something else. It wasn't gold, though. It was more like a giant black shadow had spun up over the stairs and filled the doorway. I remember remarking to myself at the time: It's got so dark in here so suddenly I'm going to have difficulty reading my text. I was going to ask Minnie at the organ to turn more light on, when Cluey and Agnes got up and distracted me. A second later it was light again. If I'd known what was to happen I would have called out. But who knew? That's how you know it's the devil's work, I say, because you don't. You just don't. You never will. Ask Minnie. She'll tell you the same.

Minnie the Organist

I will not. But I was at the organ. I didn't want to be, having a bad cold, but I was. They couldn't get anybody else. My nose was runny, I told them, and I had aches—but so what? "Minnie, now Minnie, you come on down." So I did. Yet it's the same story every time and nobody even bothering to keep up. I've heard cows mooing in a meadow had more rhythm and feeling than the people in that church. But I saw nothing. Saw and heard nothing. No light or gold. No shadow. No children either. It takes a lot in that church to make me turn around. Back trouble, leg trouble, I wore a neck brace for ten years. I keep my back to that lot and that's how I like it. One time a curtain caught fire back there when Orson Johnson—the cross-eyed one—was playing with matches. I looked around then. That's about the only time.

Orson

I'm the one she's talking about. What I wished I'd done that day was burn the whole building down. But I didn't and I growed up and I was there the day those two walked out. There whittling on a stick with this Fobisher knife I have. With the wife and hoping it would wind up early, though I knew it wouldn't, so I could go home and have dinner, maybe grab some shut-eye. But, yes, I saw them, and I felt my neck crawl too, before they ever stood up, because something was behind me. Maybe not at the door, but behind me certainly. My skin froze and I remember gripping my wife's wrist I got that scared. I thought it was Death back there, Death calling, and He was going to lay his cold hand over my shoulder and speed me on off. "What date is it?" I asked my wife. "How long we been married?" Now I don't know why I said this, but I know it scared her too, though she just kept shooshing me. I didn't want to die. Hell, it seemed to me I'd only started living. But "shoosh" she says, so I shoosh. I shoosh right up; I couldn't have said another word anyway. I sat there with my knees knocking, waiting for Death's hand to grab me. Then I see the kids coming down the aisle. They got their faces scrubbed and that ramrod aunt of theirs, Gladys, she had slapped some worn duds on them and got their hair combed. Death's hold on me seemed to loosen a bit and I thought how I might slip out and ask them how their mother was doing—whether she was still in her sickbed or out of danger yet, that sort of thing—maybe slip them a quarter because I'd always felt pity for those kids—and I tried to move, to wiggle out the side and sort of slink to the back door, but what it was I found was I couldn't move. I couldn't stir a muscle. And a second later my hair stood up on my head because a voice was hissing in my ear. "Don't go," it said. "Don't go, Orson, it will get you too."

Though I didn't think then that "too" business was including the kids. I might have got up if I'd known that. I might have headed them off, tried to save them. If anyone could have. I don't know. Oh, they're dead, no question of that. I think they were likely dead before nightfall. Maybe within the minute. It's too bad too, especially with their mother going that same day.

Delilah Johnson

I felt Orson stiffen beside me. He looked like death warmed over and he started jabbering beside me, shivering so hard he was rattling the whole row. I put my hand down between his legs and pinched his thigh hard as I could but he didn't even blink. He was trying to get out. So I put my hand up where his man parts were and I squeezed real hard and told him to hush up. "Hush up, Orson, stop playing the fool"—something like that. He was freezing cold. He had sweat beads on his brow an inch thick. I brought my heel down on his foot, trying to get him quiet, then I heard him say "Death, Death, Death." And "Don't go, don't go." He didn't know he was talking. I saw Aaron Spelling, in front of us, lean over and say to Therma that Orson Johnson had a briar in his behind. Therma turned and looked at us. Her mouth popped open. Because Orson was such a sight. I got my hand away real quick from where it was; I just clamped my fingernails into his thigh and kept them there the rest of the service.

Later on we had to get the doctor in, I'd hurt him so and the infection must have lasted a month.

I didn't notice the kids; I had my hands full with Orson.

It was three whole days in fact before I so much as heard of the children gone missing or dead and of their mother's death.

The Nurse's Tale

I was nursing Tory when she took her final breath. By her bedside I was with a teacup in my lap and watching the window because I thought I'd heard something running around out there. Like a galloping horse it was. But my legs were bothering me, and my sides, so I didn't take the trouble to go to the window and see. I sat sipping my tea, listening to the galloping horse.

It was a day like many another one up to that time except that the house was empty, it being a Sunday, and other than that horse. A few minutes before, when I got up to get my tea, I'd put my head down on Tory's chest. I was always doing that, couldn't help it, because although I've sat with hundreds of sick people I'd never heard a heart like hers. It was like water sloshing around in a bowl; she hardly had no regular heartbeat is what I'm saying. So I'd put my head down over her chest and listen to it slosh like that.

I couldn't see how a human being could live with a heartbeat like that.

The horse it keeps right on galloping. Now and then I'd catch a whir at the window, whitish, so I knew it wasn't no dark horse. Then all at once my blood just stops, because something has caught hold of me. I look down at my wrist and there's the queerest hand I ever saw. Thin and shrunk and mostly bones. The hand

is all it was in that second, and I shrieked. The china cup fell to
the floor and broke. Saucer too. Tea I splashed all over me, so I
afterwards had to go in and soak my dress in cold water. There
were the long red nails though. A vile colour, but Gladys said
Tory liked it. That she wouldn't feel comfortable in bed, sick like
that, without her nails painted, because how would you feel to be
in bed like she was and looking like death, in case anybody came
in. So let's keep her looking civilized, Gladys said, and one or the
other of us kept her nails freshly painted. So after my minute of
fright I knew it was Tory's hand, her who hadn't moved a twitch
in three months, suddenly sitting up with a grip like steel on my
arm. It was practically the first sign of life I'd seen in her in the
whole time I'd been minding her. She was sitting bolt up, with
her gown straps down at her elbows so her poor little bosom, the
most puckered, shrivelled little breasts I ever hope to see, was
exposed to the full eyes of the world.

She had her eyes locked on the window.

And there went the horse again, gallop, gallop.

I got hold of myself, got her hand off me, and stooped down
over her. I was about to say, "Now, little lady, let's get that gown
up over your bosom before you catch your death"—but then
that word got caught in my throat so I said nothing. And I'm
glad I didn't or I might of missed what she said. Her eyes were on
fire and she was grabbing at something. At the very air, it seemed
to me. "You'll not get my children!" she said. "No, you'll not get
them!" Well, my skin crawled. I don't know why, don't know to
this day. Just the way she was crying it. "You'll not get them, not
my Cluey and Agnes!" She was screeching that out now, as
frightened—but as brave too—as any soul I hope to see. "*You
can't have my children!*" On and on like that. And she was twisting around in bed, flailing her arms, striking at something with

her poor little fists. *"No, you can't!"* she said. Then this even worse look come over her face and for the longest time she wasn't making human sounds at all. Half-animal, I thought. Like something caught in a trap. I thought she'd finally bit the noose—that her mind had gone. I kept trying to get that gown up over her breast works—you never knew who would come barging into that house without knocking or breathing a word, even her sister has crept in sometimes and scared me out of my wits. And she's fighting me, not letting me get her back down in the bed. She's scratching and yelling and kicking—her whose legs the doctor claimed were paralysed—and she's moaning and biting. Then she shrieks, *"Run! Run! Oh, children, run!"* And this perfect horror comes over her face, pure agony it is, and torture worse than I've ever known a body to feel. *"No!"* she screams, *"No! Please! Please don't!"* and the next second her breath flies out, her eyes roll up, and she sags down like a broken baby in my arms. I put her head back on the pillow and fluff it some. I pull her straps back up and smooth out her gown over her chest's flatness. I pat the comforter up around her neck. I get her hair looking straight. I close her eyes, first the left then the right just as they say you ought to do, and I root in my purse and dig out two pennies. I go in and wash them off and dry them on my dress, and I put them nicely over her eyes. Then I sit watching her, trembling more than I ever have. Wondering what has gone on and thinking how I'm going to have to tell her sister and those poor children when they come in from the church. Not once giving mind to that broken china on the floor. I reckon I never did. I reckon someone else must have come in and cleared that mess up. Maybe Gladys did. Or maybe not. I plumb can't guess, because one second I'm there sitting looking at my hands in my lap and the next second I'm thinking, What about that galloping horse? Because I don't hear it any more. No, it's so quiet you can hear a pin drop. And I hear it too. Pins dropping, that's what I think. This shiver comes over me. I have the funny feeling I'm not alone in the room: that there's me, a dead person, and something else. I look over at the bed and what do I see? Well, it's empty. Tory ain't there. I hear more of these pins dropping and they seem to be coming from the window so I look there. And what I see is this: it is Tory, come back to some strange form of life, and sliding up over, over the sill and out of that window. That's right, just gone. And I guess I fainted then, that being the first of my faints. The next time I open my eyes my sight is on that window again and this time Tory is coming back through it, sliding along, and her little breasts are naked again, she's all cut up, and blood has soaked through her and she's leaving a trail of it every inch she comes. "Help me, Rosie," she says. Well, that's what I'm there for. So I get her up easy as kittens—she hardly weighs an ounce —and I get her back to bed. "They're safe," she says. I say, "Good." I say a lot of comforting words like that. "Don't let anyone see me like this," she says. "I'm black and blue from head to toe." It's the truth too, she sure is. "Have Gladys quietly bury me," she says. "Closed coffin. Can you promise that?" I said sure. She patted my hand then, poor thing, as though I was the one to be comforted. Then she slips away. She slips away smiling. So I get the pennies back on. I straighten the covers. Then I sit back in the chair and faint away a second time. I'm just waking up when Gladys comes in from church to tell me that Agnes and Cluey have gone and there's been a mighty mess at the church and some are saying the children are dead or gone up to heaven. I pass out the third time. I can't help it. I fold down to the floor like a limp rag and I don't know what else is going on till there is a policeman or a doctor at my elbow, I don't know which.

Officer Sam

It was me, Sam Clive. Clive, C-L-I-V-E. Officer Sam Clive. I wasn't there in any official capacity. I lived then just two doors down from Tory and that day I felt in my bones how something was wrong. I was out in my yard mowing and this funny feeling come over me. I looked up and it seemed to be coming from her house. It was shut up tight, the house was, but there was this whirring disc in the sky. A flying whatayacallit I at first thought. Anyway, it seemed to sink down in the woods just behind her place. So I strolled over. I saw curtains fluttering at her sickroom window and I was brought up real short by that—because that window had always been closed. Every day, winter and summer, on account of Tory was holding on by such a thin thread. Heart trouble, kidneys, pneumonia—the whole shebang. I stepped closer, not wanting to be nosy and more because of this eerie feeling I had. Well, I saw those curtains were dripping blood. It was pouring right off that cloth and down the boards, that blood. And I thought I saw something sliding up over the sill the minute I come up. Flutter, flutter. It was the curtains I guess. Though I don't recollect it being a windy day. But that blood, heck, you can still see where it dribbled down the side of the house, because they never painted it over. They painted the rest of the house, the sister did after she got it, but for reasons known only to them they painted up to the blood and stopped right there. Anyhow, I hurried on over. I looked through the window and there was this fat nurse down in a heap on the floor beside this broken china and Tory in the bed with bright pennies over her eyes.

The House Painter

I done the paint job. I give the old gal a good price and me and one other, my half-brother who was helping me then, we went at it. White, of course, that was the only colour she'd have. And she wanted two coats, one put on vertical and one crossways. I said why. She said her daddy told her when she was a kid that's how you put paint on if you wanted a thing to stand up to the elements more'n a year or two. I said I'd never heard that. I said to Tom Earl, Have you ever heard that? and he said, No, no he hadn't. She said, Well, that's how she wanted it and if I wouldn't or couldn't do it or didn't think I was able then she reckoned I wasn't the only painter in town and a lot of them cheaper'n me. Ha! I said. I said it's going to cost you extra. She said, I don't see why. I said, Because, Miss Gladys, it will take me a good sight longer painting this house the fool way you want it. You can't hardly git no speed painting vertical because the natural way is to go crosswise following the lay of the grain. She said it might be natural to a durn fool like me but that weren't how her daddy done it and I could do it and at the price quoted or I could shove off and go out and stick somebody else. So I got the message. Two coats? I said. Two coats, she said, Hank Sparrow, can't you do that neither? I shook my head a time or two. There weren't any way I was going to make one red cent out of it. I'd be doing well just covering wages and gitting the paint paid for. But her sister had passed on and hide nor hair of her kin had been seen, those two children, so I said, well, it won't hurt me none to do this woman a favour.

I got Tom Earl and him and me took at it. It went right smooth and we did the same top job we always did. Till we got to that window. I brushed the paint over them dark red streaks and said to Tom Earl, Well, it'll take a second coat, but that ought to do her. But when it dried, even after the third and fourth coat, them blood streaks were still there same as they were when we started. Tom Earl said, Well, she ain't going to pay, you know that, until we get these streaks covered over. I looked at him and I said, You're right there, you done spoke a big mouthful. And I went out to the truck and got me my tools. Got me my hammer and chisels, my blowtorch too: one way or the other I was going to git that blood removed.

Well, she comes running. She has got her head up in a towel, one shoe off and the other one on, and she's dripping water, but still she comes running. What are you doing, what are you doing, she keeps asking, are you going to take hammer to my house or burn it down? Is this what you call painting? she says. So I looked at Tom Earl and he's no help, he just shrugs his shoulders. I look to her and say I've painted and I've painted and it's still there. What is? she says. Hank Sparrow, are you trying to two-bit me? No'm, I say, but there's something peculiar going on here. There sure is, she says, and it's you two with no more sense that a cat has pigeons. Now, hold on a minute, I say. So I take her round the house and I show her how we've put on a good seven coats minimum. But still that blood where your sister crawled up over the ledge. You leave my sister out of this, she says. She says, Hank Sparrow, I have known you Sparrows all my life and there has never been one of you didn't try to weasel out of work and didn't lie with every breath scored. Now give me that brush, she says.

Tom Earl and me we give it to her. We coat it up good and we wrap a little tissue over the handle so she won't get none on her hand, and we tell her to go to it. We stand back picking our teeth and poking each other, laughing, because one, the way she held that brush in both hands with her tongue between her teeth and bent over like she was meaning to pick up dimes, and two, because we knew it was a lost cause and no way in hell that paint was going to do it.

See there? She said. See there? Now is that covered or isn't it?

Give it a minute, we said. You give them streaks about two minutes and your eyes will pop out.

Well, she stood right there with us, insulting us up one side and down the other every inch of the way. But we took it. We said nothing hard back to her. We knowed she was going to get the surprise of her life and be walking over hot coals to beg pardon. And in two minutes, sure as rainwater, those streaks were back. They looked fresh brand-new, even brighter.

She went back and stood under the tree studying it, thinking her and distance would make a difference.

It's this paint, she said. This is shoddy paint you're using.

Well, we saw there was no end to it. So we got her in the truck between us, her with her hair still up in this green towel, and we drove down to the hardware. She got Henry Gordon pinned in the corner not knowing which way to turn, but no matter how hard she pinned him he kept telling her that the paint we had was the best paint made and there weren't none no better including what went on the mayor's own house. I'll see about this, she said. And danged if she didn't call the distributor, long-distance, charging it to Henry. What is the best paint made? she said. And he said the very one we'd put on her house. She slammed down that phone. All right, she said, but Henry Gordon you have sold these two so-called working men a bad mix. I want another. Help yourself, Henry told her. She marches in his stockroom, says eenymeenyminymoe over the cans, and comes out with one. All four of us now go back to her house. She has me git the lid off and she dabs over that blood again, so thick it just trickles down to the ground. We wait. She is now fit to be tied. I have lost a dear sister, she says, and lost my precious niece and nephew, and now you are telling me I've got to live with the curse of this blood?

We said it looked like it. Every one of us did, jumping right in with it. Because that blood was coming right back up. It was coming up bright as ever.

Well, I never, she says.

So we go inside and stand in her kitchen and she gives each of us a co-cola. It surpasses meaning, she said. I don't understand it. I don't guess I'm meant to.

We said, Yesmam.

All right then, she said, I will just have to leave it there. It's meant to be left there. It's meant to be some kind of sign or signal. A symbol.

We didn't argue with her. I didn't even raise a hand when she said she was holding back ten dollars' paint money because I never finished the house. There was something spooky about that place. All I wanted was to git shut of it. Me and Tom Earl took her cash and I give him some and me and him went out drinking.

The Painter's Apprentice

He drank. I didn't because I was only thirteen and the law wouldn't have it. But I knew Cluey, had seen him around, and that Agnes too because she was always at his heels, and I'd heard the stories of how the woman had died and Cluey and Agnes had gone up in thin air. I had beat up some on Cluey, being something of a bully in them days. I had bloodied his nose once and left him sobbing. I remember it and know it was him because he threw a rock at me and got me on the kneecap. And because of what he said. "My daddy will git you," he said. I was nice enough not to say "What daddy?" And I was glad I didn't. Because that night something tripped me up as I was walking home along the Dye Ditch, and I fell off into that ditch and broke my left leg. It was somebody there all right, that's all I'm saying, and it warn't Cluey or any other thing with two legs. It tripped me up, then it put a hand in my back, and I went tumbling over. I was with Tiny Peterson. He can tell you.

Tiny

It's every word true. But what I want to get to is that church. Timmons was being his usual assy self, playing up like he was doing a cameo role for Rin-Tin-Tin, yammering on about emptiness this and emptiness that, when the wood doors burst open. I was already turned around, trying to smack at a little girl back there, when Cluey come by me. I had my legs up high and he couldn't get past. So I dropped my legs. I'd just got them back up when his little sister tapped my knee. "Excuse me," she said. "Me and him are going out to see my daddy. That's him at the door."

I raised up high in my seat and looked again at that door. People behind me started hissing but I didn't care. There was something in that door all right, but it wasn't hardly human. It didn't have two arms and two legs and it didn't have a face either. But it was beckoning. I saw Cluey and Agnes walk into the thing, whatever it was, and then they simply were not there any more. There was nothing. I thought it was a vision. Timmons just then got his smart voice back and was saying something about "Heaven is empty." The empty heaven, something like that. I admit it.

Goose bumps rose high on my arm as a kitchen window. I was really scared. Now, why I did it I don't know to this day, but I went running out after them. I figured that if maybe their daddy was out there then maybe mine was too and he might save me from my empty heaven. I went flying out. I sped out over everybody's knees and trampled on feet and the next second I was outside in the yard. Cluey and Agnes couldn't have been five seconds in front of me. And what I saw there gave me a chill I can feel to this minute. There was this woman there in a white gown which was down to her waist so I could see her nipples and these real wizened breasts. I reckon to this day it's why I like big-bosomed women. But what she was doing was struggling with this creature. Creature is what he was, make no mistake about that. She had her arms and legs wrapped around him, pulling and tugging and chewing—pure out-and-out screeching—while the creature thing was trying to throw her off and still hold on to poor Cluey and Agnes who by this time were just bawling. They were just bawling. The creature was dragging them along and that woman was up on the creature's back, riding him, biting into the thing's neck, punching and clawing. Well, it let go of the children. It gave a great howl and tore the woman off itself and practically bent her double. I mean it had her with her back across his knees and it was slamming her down all the while she screamed, "Run! Run! Oh, children, run!" And they streaked off. I've never seen nothing tear away so fast. "Run! Run!" she cried. And they did and it was about this time that I heard this galloping, and a great white horse came out of the woods. The prettiest horse I ever will see. It galloped up to the children and slowed down and Cluey swung on its back, then got Agnes up there with him, and that horse took off full speed, faster than I'd think a horse could. Then gone, just flying. The creature still had the woman. He slammed her down one last time and from where I was, hiding behind the tree, I could hear it: her back snap.

Snap, like that, and the creature flung her down. It let out a great roar—of hatred, of pure madness at being thwarted, I don't know which—and then it took off too. But in the wrong way, not after the children. It seemed to me, the longer I looked at it run, that the closer it came to having human form. It had arms and legs and a face, though that face looked a million years old and like it hated everything alive.

That's all I saw. My own momma came out then and fixed her finger over my ear and nearly wrung it off. "Git yourself back in yonder," she said, "and don't you move one muscle less'n I tell you you can. When I git home I mean to put stick to your britches and you are going to wish you'd never been born."

I whimpered some, though not because of her ear twists or any threats she made. I never told anyone till now. Hell with them.

Tiny Peterson's Mother

I thought when I went out and tweaked his ear that the sobbing Tiny was doing wasn't on account of that ear. He was snow-white and trembling and it was all I could do to hold him up. If I hadn't been so mad and set in my ways I would have known he'd seen something. It warn't no way for me to behave, whether it's to your own flesh or another's—but my husband had run out on me again and I imagine that had something to do with it.

But I'm sorry for it. I think it was the last time I wrung that boy's ear.

The Farmer's Husband

The horse came by my place. I was out on the porch rocking away when it come by. Mary was in her chair with peas in her lap, shelling them. It was white, that horse was, it had two riders. They were up in the hills though. They were out a good far piece. There was something unnatural about it, I thought that. About how fast that horse was running, how it didn't get slowed down none by tree or brush. I said to Mary how I'd never seen no horse like that, not around here. Not anywhere else either, I reckon. My dog was down between my legs and he got up and took off after them. About a quarter hour later he come back whimpering, his tail drawed up under his legs. He went under the house and moaned. It took me two days to git that dog out.

Mary, the Farmer

See that horse? He told me. And pointed off. I went on shelling my peas.

Don't you have one iota of sense, I told him. That there is the supernatural.

The Doctor

You are all looking at me. Keep looking, then. You've always come to me with your aches and pains, now you're coming to me with this—is that it? I've told you my end before. I've never held anything back, and I won't now. Yes, I signed the certificate. She'd been slipping a long time and we'd all expected her death. I spent more time than most worrying about her. I said to her one day, "Tory," I said, "my medicines are doing you no good. I know you are in terrible pain all day and we both know you haven't got long. If you've a mind to, and want me to, and realize I am only raising this issue because I am aware of your misery, then I could give you something to help you go out easy and gentle and without the smallest pain."

She always told me she'd think on it. She'd let me know, she said. Then one day, after I'd given her every painkiller I could and none of it was helping her the slightest bit, I raised the question again.

"I'd like to go off, doctor," she said, "in a nice and swoony dream just as you describe. But I can't go yet. I've got to hold on for my children's sake because I know one day he is coming back. I've got to stay and save them from him, if I can."

I knew, of course, who she was talking about. You can't live here as long as I have without knowing that. But I said, "Tory, if he *does* come back, we will take care of his hide. You don't have to worry about his harming your kids."

"You don't understand," she said. "There will not be a single thing a living soul can do. No," she said, "I will have to take care of this myself, if I'm able. But I thank you."

I don't read anything special into these remarks. It tells us something of her spirit, I suppose, and confirms her love for that pair. Anything else, I'd discount. All this ghostly stuff. She died a natural death, that's what my certificate says. But yet, she was black and blue. Some bones broken. Someone's skin under her fingernails. Blood you couldn't remove from window and floor, and not her own blood either, as the lab tests showed. And not a blood we could type. But there are reasonable, logical explanations. There always are. Let this woman and her children rest in peace, I say. Let these stories stop right here.

Saks Fifth Avenue

A WOMAN CALLED ME UP on the telephone. She was going to give me twenty thousand dollars, she said. I said come right over, I'm not doing anything this evening. Then I went back into the living room where my wife was, seated on the sofa with her nail files and paint, painting her nails. I wanted to keep it to myself for a bit. I strolled around, pawing the knick-knacks, glancing now and then at myself in the mirror. I was feeling pretty breezy.

Twenty thousand, I thought. Holy Christ!

Those knick-knacks were really dusty; I had to go in and wash my hands. While I was in there, in the bathroom, I splashed on a little cologne and smiled at myself. There are going to be some changes around here, is what I told myself. These old mirror tiles got to go.

The old lady looked up. She'd finished her left hand, which she always does first, God knows why. Her nails were the vilest colour I ever saw—dried blood. What they call Songbird Red in the ads. Songbird Red: how about that? It's her favourite colour for nails. Also, she says it protects them, and keeps her from chewing.

So she looked up. "You're smirking," she said. "God, I hate it when you smirk. Why don't you go get us a beer?"

I went into the kitchen and got the beer.

"Thanks," she said. "You look like you swallowed a monkey. It's disgusting. You disgust me, Cecil." She folded her fingers over and blew on the songbirds. Then she fluttered her fingers. I watched her do it. That's a pretty sexy act, that nail-blowing act. It's about as sexy as anything I can imagine. Seeing old Coolie blow on her nails is enough to make me forgive her for all of her sins, including how she talks to me.

Coolie, I forgive you.

Coolie, you set my heart a-racing.

Coolie, let's go to bed.

Silly, but that's how it is. I was really feeling mellowed out.

"Well?" she said. "Why the honey-licking grin? Why don't you take a walk? Polish your shoes, do something! You're full of yourself this evening. God knows why, after the way you behaved last night."

She said a lot of stuff like that. Once she gets going you never know when she's going to wind down. I figure she doesn't even hear herself. She talks to her mother—to her mother and her girl-friends—that same way. They never slow down. They don't even hear each other.

"Stop pacing, Cecil," she said.

I got out my shoes and the polish box. We keep the polish—the white and the neutral, blacks and reds and tans, and a tin of Arctic Dubbin that must have been in there fifteen years—in a thick white cardboard box that says "Saks Fifth Avenue." I always look at that box. I try to figure out what must have come in that box. How we came to have it. It's one of the mysteries of my life, that box. I look at it and sometimes wonder if old Coolie hasn't had a life I don't know about.

That's deep, deep business, but I get that way sometimes. I can be watching TV for instance, the old prime time, and right out of the blue that thought will come to me: how'd we get that box? Where did it come from? What was in it? Sometimes I'll look up and find the show ending, and I've been thinking about that box the whole hour.

"Can you believe it!" Coolie will say. "Why do they show trash like that? Wasn't that the most impossible crap you ever saw?"

"I don't know, Coolie," I say. "That car chase was pretty good."

She gives me this level gaze. "You are totally without taste," she says. "They make this crap for imbeciles like you."

I mention this box business as an example of the kind of secret life that some of us have. How you can pass old Joe Blow on the street, have a conversation with him, even a real interesting one, and then you walk away wondering what the heck either of you said.

I mean we don't even hear each other.

So I got out the box. I couldn't decide which pair needed doing, the loafers or the old cowboy boots. None of them really needed it. What the loafers needed was new heels.

"These heels are worn down," I told Coolie. "Look at these heels."

She didn't look.

"How long have I had these shoes?" I asked her. "I bet I had these shoes a good ten years. Did I ever ask you where this Saks box came from? That one's going to drive me crazy if I don't figure it out."

"Would you shut up?" said Coolie. "Would you please hush your mouth?"

She'd gone back to painting her other fingers. She had her tongue between her lips and sat all bunched over, scrunched up tight, with her right hand spread out over her knees and this look of utter concentration on her face. I'd noticed that tongue before. Usually she's biting down on it with her teeth, the upper lip curled back, but tonight she just had it hanging there. Squinting, because she had her contacts out. She was wearing this pink gown I got for her one Christmas Eve at K-Mart, and she had it flung back away from her knees so no paint would get on it. None of that Songbird Red.

It had already got pretty grimy, that gown. I don't think she's washed it once. I find this odd, and maybe a little bit out of character, her always wearing that filthy gown, because she's got this idea she's the sharpest dresser in town. "And on my budget!"—is what she's always saying.

"Would you stop looking at me!" she says now. "Would you stop it! Would you put a lid on it!"

What I figure is it's just like Coolie is. It's how she talks. Say when she's with her girlfriends or with her mother, she doesn't hear herself or them. They don't either. I've never understood a word, not a word, any of them have said. You come into the room and they are all eating cake and clattering cups and all going at once. Not even a pause for breath. It beats me. I'm really fascinated by it.

"What did they say?" I'll ask her once everyone has gone. "What were you talking about?"

She'll give me her withering look. "Oh you're such a dope," she'll say. "Oh, Cecil, you are the world's prize dope. Don't concern yourself. Go on with your life. Go out and rake the yard."

Maybe I am a dope. Maybe they do hear each other. But I got my doubts. I'm going to hold on to my doubts. I figure it's like that gown. She doesn't *know* how grimy that gown is. To her, all that dirt is invisible. She'd be mortally offended if I took a notion to drop hints. "*Are you calling me dirty, Cecil! Are you saying I am un-clean!*" No, she grabs that gown off the hook every evening, she whips it on and comes running downstairs, and that's the end of it.

"Damnit, Cecil!" she says now. "Stop staring! Haven't I told you? I'm going to throw this bottle at you!"

That bottle. That little bottle of nail polish. What I really wanted was for that bottle to spill over, dribble over her knees and down her leg and spot the carpet. Spot it real nice. Then when people ask me what colour that carpet is I could say, well, some of it is Songbird Red. Some of it is.

Coolie would kill me, but I'd say it anyhow.

A little drama, you see, is what I wanted. A bit of cold, hard action. For if old Coolie accidentally knocked over that polish she'd leap up screeching, turning over tables and slamming the knick-knacks about, and go on flapping her arms for a full ten minutes.

That's how Coolie is. Pretty high-strung. I love it when old Coolie goes into her screeching routine.

Those little bottles are insane. That's what I think. Big white cap built like a finger, with a nail two inches long. Painted Song-bird Red. Dried blood. Quite a knick-knack itself, that bottle. I sat there watching her dab the colour on her nails, wondering how many of those little bottles it would take to paint the house. How *long* it would take, using that stupid brush. What the house would look like done up in a dynamite dried blood. Songbird Red.

About fifty million, I thought.

Take about twenty-seven years.

Coolie flipped the gown up over her knees. Groaned. She fig-ured I had been staring at her naked knees. Getting an eyeful of the famous Coolie legs. Getting ideas.

"Last night," she said. "Last night. We just won't speak of last night."

She gave me this long look. Long, *mean* and intense. "No," that look said. "Last night is not to be spoken of. We'd best, both of us, forget last night."

She was right, too. Last night we'd had a bit of erotica around here. A dab of it. Pretty high-powered stuff, too, for a while. Kissing and fondling—hell, *rapture*, if you want to know the truth.

"Kiss me, Cecil! Kiss me till my mouth bursts into flames!"

A *hot* time, I'm saying, and straight out of right field. She came in at five, said, "Cecil, mix us a drink." At ten after, she said, "Lead the way." A minute later there's that "mouth-into-flames" line. And no doubt about it, either. Sparks all over the place. Erotic *art*, for God's sake. Then the phone rings. Coolie snatches it up. "Not now!" she says. She starts to slam it back down and is already rolling into me, but the voice is chattering on. "What?" says Coolie. "What?" And she's got that phone back at her ear. "Six glasses for fourteen ninety-five? Long-stemmed! Gold-rimmed! That's unheard-of! You're sure?"

But not only glassware, it seems.

"Fur coats at half price! *Shoes!* Did you say *shoes!*"

I roll away. Reach for something to read. There's *Redbook*. Well, by God, I'll read *Redbook*—that's what I say to myself. It's a jam-packed issue, too. I could spend a month just turning the pages.

"Blues and greens!" Coolie says. "They've got them in blues and greens! At twelve-eighty-*eight*! Jesus, mother!"

So I get up. I have a long shower. I go downstairs and make myself a roast beef. I have four or five hard drinks. I sponge the counter. Get the garbage taken out. Read the paper.

"I've got to go, mother," I hear Coolie saying. "Cecil's sulking."

Half an hour later they are still going strong. Not even hearing each other.

Well, it's getting dark. It's way *past* dark. Heck, in another minute or two it will be morning. But they are still going at it.

So I get dressed. I get on the old cowboy boots and go for a walk. All over the neighbourhood. Maybe ten or twelve miles. When I get back old Coolie is standing in the open doorway. She's got on her grimy robe. She's patting her foot.

"You son of a bitch!" she says. And she whirls and strides away.

No. We best not speak of last night. We best let that sleeping dog stay where he is.

What I say is: thank God for the nail polish. That little act, for the moment, has taken care of both our emotional needs. I checked my watch. The woman on the phone had said she'd be over about eight. Give or take a few minutes. She'd be bringing the money with her. Every last dollar.

I was thinking I might mention this to Coolie. I was thinking she might want to run a comb through her hair. Maybe step into that hotshot pantsuit she got at Zeller's. Got for practically nothing, I might add. What they did was they had this big flashing green light went off every hour, and if you were one of the first five thousand to rush over in the next five minutes then you could get this great pantsuit for practically nothing. The "Green-Light Special," they called it. Coolie got two of them, one black and the other a kind of orange. I hadn't seen her wearing that black one yet. I figured it either didn't fit—too tight in the hips is what it usually was—or she was saving it for something special. Tonight it might be just what the doctor ordered. She'd want to look snazzy for that woman coming over with the money.

I was going to say something along these lines, but Coolie beat me to the punch. She got in her two bits first.

"Supper tonight was terrible," she said. "You can't do casseroles. I wish you wouldn't even try. Your cooking has sure gone downhill. I've been sitting here thinking of what you cook and what I let go into my stomach, and the whole thing makes me sick. I can't bear to think of it. Christ, for once can't you follow a recipe?"

My face went a little hard at this. I'm touchy about my cooking. There was nothing wrong with my casserole.

Anyway, she ate it. Had seconds, too.

"I mean it," she said. "If I eat another casserole in this house I will puke. I will. I think I will die."

She started that nail-blowing act again. She'd put on a second coat.

Bless you, Coolie, I thought. You are such a wizard.

She straightened her two hands up in front of her face, flipped them over, flipped them back, then shot out her arms and bent her wrists and squinted long-range at those fingers. Then she shook them.

She kept on doing that.

I shaded my face and watched. It was better than TV. It had prime time beat by a mile. I was thinking of bones. Thinking of a woman's bones and how old Coolie could fold her hands down until they practically lay alongside her wrists. Fold them back the same. Supple as a shoe rag.

Well, they are contortionists, that's what they are.

Wizards, from head to toe.

"God, you make me sick," Coolie said. "I don't know what I am to do with you. My mother's right, you know. You know what she said? Only the other day she said to me, "Coolie, what your husband needs is a pacemaker. A good pacemaker, secondhand." Seriously, that's what she said. "Otherwise," she said, "otherwise, someone is going to mistake him for dead. You're going to come home one day from work and find men in white coats rolling him out of there." It's true, too, Cecil. You're going to be mistaken for the dead."

She said that, but she wasn't looking at me. First she was looking at the bottle, then at her feet, then at the nail polish again. She was trying to figure out whether she wanted to paint her toes. She couldn't decide. Should I or should I not? She has this little argument with herself about once a week. Sometimes the toenails win and sometimes they lose.

"What do you think?" she said. "Should I?"

If I say don't, then she will paint them. If I say do, she will look at me as if I've lost my mind. If I hem and haw over the question, then she's liable to storm out. Or sulk. She's liable to say I'm the most offensive, scatterbrained, illogical, indecisive and demented person who ever drew a human breath. She'll wonder aloud why she bothers to talk to me.

What I say is: talk away. I'm not listening. I'm not hearing a word you're saying.

What *are* you saying, Coolie? Lay it on me, sweetheart.

Tonight I really wasn't listening. Coolie's toenails, painted or not, lovely as they are, weren't something I felt like dwelling on. I was looking out our front window. We had the curtains back and I was looking out there. It was dark, but I still thought I could see him. I could see the boy out there plain as day, just as I'd seen him earlier. This little kid. Maybe three years old. Certainly no older than that. I had been going about the room, straightening up things, getting rid of what Coolie calls the clutter, and there he was. This little kid walking by. He had on this blue sunsuit and this white shirt with a funny collar, and these little sandals—thongs, I guess they are. They were flip-flopping up and down and once or twice he'd lift his feet and they'd fall off. He had on this kind of hat, but even so you could see he had a nice head of golden hair. And this fine fair skin. The sun was shining on him and I swear he seemed to be glowing. He was about the prettiest kid I ever saw. But that's not why I kept looking. He had these two adults with him, what I would say were his parents. Nice-looking pair, young, maybe thirty. Both had on white slacks and the man wore one of those soft-knit shirts with an alligator over the pocket. The woman had on this wide-brimmed hat, white, very stylish. I wondered what they were doing strolling the side-walk in our neighbourhood. They didn't seem to fit in. We don't get many parents with young children out here. We don't have any nearby schools, or day-care centres, and no playgrounds. We got one park but the benches are all broken. No, young parents come out here looking over the real estate, and right away they know they want no part of it. You can't blame them. But I was talking about that kid. The reason I was watching that kid was because of the golf bag. It was a real one, I mean, slung over his shoulder, about the size of a loaf of French bread. And it was a good one, I could see that. That kid's parents were not fooling around. This golf bag was made of finest leather, and it had about eight to ten putts—irons, whatever they're called—stuck in it. Protruding from the bag, you know, like a dozen gleaming metal heads. Expensive, I could see that. Two hundred smackers, mini-mum, I'd say. And heavy, too, because that little kid could hardly carry it. He kept trying to drag it along the sidewalk, but the par-ents wouldn't have it. First you'd hear the father, then the mother, then the father again.

"Carry the bag," the father would say.

Then the mother: "Carry the bag, Buster. Keep it up high on your shoulder."

It took them ten minutes just to pass my house.

"Don't drag the bag, Buster."

They were pretty angry. They were trying to stay calm but you could see they wanted to swat him.

"Pick up the bag, Buster."

Finally, the kid stopped. Just stopped. You could see he didn't mean to take another step. He threw down the bag. He sailed off his hat about ten feet up the street. He gave his parents this dark look.

"What are you doing, Buster?" they said. "Come on, Buster."

"I'm golfing," he said. "Me and him are golfing." And he gave me this lidded, dark look. He'd seen me all right. He had my number. He then sorted through his clubs and took out the one he liked best. A big iron. He swung it around a time or two, getting the feel of it. His legs looked rubbery. He looked like a good breeze would send him flying. But he was cute. He was the cutest kid I ever saw. Then he got out this yellow golf ball and got out a tee and put the ball on it. The ball kept rolling off, but finally he managed. He stood up straight, on his tippy-toes, and got the club swung way back over his shoulder.

"Stand back!" he said. "Watch out!"

I had the side of my face pressed up against the window. Christ, I was barely breathing. He was really going to hit that son of a bitch. He was going to hit it hard. He was going to maul that bastard. He had his tongue between his teeth and this look of terrible wrath on his face and he was going to knock holy shit out of that stupid ball.

His father rushed up and grabbed him from behind just as he was swinging. "Wait," he said. "That's not how you do it. Let me show you." And the kid was trapped. He had to do it the way his father said. "Back up. Widen your stance. Don't hold it like a baseball bat. This club isn't an axe. And your swing? Haven't I told you how to swing?"

"Listen to your father, Buster," the mother kept saying. "Listen to your father."

The kid crumpled. He just folded up. He squatted down on the sidewalk and the father had to keep yanking him up.

"Damn you. Buster!"

The kid wailed. He wailed and wailed. He squirmed and wriggled. He grabbed the ball and flung it into my hedge. He kicked at the golfing bag. He clamped his teeth into the father's arm.

The father yanked up the kid and tucked him under his arm. The kid yelled. Oh boy, how he squalled. The mother scooped up the clubs. The three of them went on out of sight. But I heard that wailing a long time. I still could.

So that's what was going through my mind as I stared out our black window. That kid. Old Buster.

"Stand back! Watch out!"

Coolie, I noticed, was giving me the once-over. She wasn't saying anything just yet, though she was looking hard. I had these two shoes I'd been shining, up in my hands. One on each hand and I figured, from the way Coolie was staring, that I must have been waving these shoes about. Slapping golf balls. Kicking at the father. I didn't know for sure, but that's what I figured.

"I worry about you," she said. "I really do. There are times, Cecil, when I know you don't have a brain in your head. You're just not all here. You're off God knows where."

She meant it, too. There was a different sound in the air. A different note struck. She'd made a new turn in the way she regarded me. What she said came from some more distant, more objective place. I even figured I knew what she was thinking: *Maybe one day we had something, this crackpot and me. Now God help us.*

That's what I figured.

So I decided I wouldn't mention just yet the lady with the money. When she came, I'd spread it out on the floor. Every dollar. Coolie could do with it whatever she wanted.

So I sat there smiling, pondering things. Considering that Saks box. Old Buster. Talking about shoes. "See these loafers," I said. "Look at these heels. It isn't healthy walking around in heels like this. What I think I'll do is go down to the shoe repair tomorrow and get me a new set put on. Maybe even throw these out, buy a new pair. What do you think?"

Coolie was eyeing me hard. Her jaw was set and she had her squint locked in; her mouth twitched; I could see her sucking in her breath. She looked old. I swear to hell she looked older than me. Yet I never felt so old as what I knew she felt, looking at me.

She wouldn't have called it age. She would have called it something that happened to us a long time ago. A decision we made.

I put the shoes down. I went over and closed the drapes.

Coolie whipped the cap over the polish bottle. No toe painting tonight.

"You are the most boring creature who ever lived," she said. "I sometimes wonder what it would be like to be you and to have your mind and to have to go through life with the mind-boggling triviality of thought that you have. How do you do it? I know these are extraordinary times and that there is no end to the bizarre, low creatures that exist on this planet, but how in God's name do you do it? In your shoes I would jump off the first cliff I came to. I would go over head first. As Christ is my witness, I certainly would. Now would you put away your stupid shoe stuff? Would you stop fondling that stupid Saks box? Don't leave it for me to pick up. You can go to the repair shop or go to the moon or take a flying leap, I don't care. Cecil, I really don't. First your casseroles and now your shoes. Did you think you were conducting an orchestra? You're going to drive me out of my mind, Cecil. You really are."

Old Coolie is a killer. She knows how to get you right between the eyes, when being got is the last thing you want. If you blink, there it comes again.

I threw up my hands. "I surrender," I said. "You got me cornered, officer. Just read me my rights."

She covered her face. She sat a moment on the sofa's edge, shaking her head. Moaning a little.

But she came out of it smiling. Still shaking her head, but smiling now. Old Coolie's smile knocks me out.

She padded over on her naked feet and for a second clung to me, patting my head. She worked her warm face up under my neck. "A child," she said, in a low, husky voice. "You're like a little child."

I knew that voice: Veronica Lake.

Old Coolie the sorcerer.

I gave her a tight hug. Her body stiffened and she pulled away. "Get me another beer," she said. "Another pound or two, why the Christ not!"

She flung herself down on the sofa and her fingers went *snap snap*.

"And bring it in a glass this time," she said. "I'm not an animal yet."

Ah, Coolie, you're a demon.

Coolie, sweetheart, you're a dream.

In the kitchen, opening the bottle, pouring the beer into a fake-crystal glass with a golden rim, I have these thoughts. I am thinking of that Saks box and trying to set a date for when it first showed up in the house. Five years or ten—the time flows together. It isn't my box, it isn't Coolie's, it belongs to neither of us.

Maybe it was just here; maybe it goes with the house. It's just a box, goddamnit, anyway. I am looking at the leftover casserole on the table and trying to figure whether I should put it away or throw it out. I give it a sniff. It smells okay. All the right stuff has gone into it. I get out the book and flip it open to the recipe. I run a finger down what's printed there. The page is greasy and stained and it has an aroma, too. I've found a lot of goodness in that page. With minor variations, I've made this casserole a hundred times.

Maybe, I think, that's where the trouble is.

I can hear Coolie at the dining table. I can hear what Coolie is saying. What she'll say tomorrow, if I can't mend my ways. "This dish tastes like manure. This dish is horrible. But spoon me another teensy helping. I've got to eat. A person has to live."

We don't hear each other any more. I wonder why it is I am hearing that.

Habit: me with my dishes, Coolie with her words.

What I am mostly wondering about, as I stand there, is what we'd do if we had us a kid. What we would have done, way back when.

I wonder whether that kid would be like me, God help him . . . or like Coolie, God help her.

I wonder what that kid would look like.

And how old that kid would be now.

If we had us a kid I'd get that kid alone when Coolie was out of the house and I'd sit that kid down and we'd figure out a few things. We'd figure out where that Saks box came from and what came in it. We'd figure out a thousand things like that. I'd have the kid with me in the kitchen and I'd say, "Flip to page 248, kid, and let's see what goes into the old casserole tonight." And the kid would do it because me and that kid were tight as twins. The kid would slice up the onions and sauté them over a slow fire. "What next, kid?" I'd say. And the kid would dice the tomatoes and slice up the green peppers and mince a few dozen cloves of garlic. We'd pour in the olive oil. "Is that enough, kid?" I'd say, and the kid would say, "No, dad, I think that dish needs another cup or so." And I'd watch the kid pour it in. We'd stir the bastard around. I'd say, "Get me that bottle of white wine, kid," and the kid would get it and we'd smile and have us a little swig. Then before we got skunked we'd cube the shoulder of veal, forgotten until now, and we'd throw that into the skillet and brown the son of a bitch just right. We'd salt it and pepper it and butter it and I'd say, "How's that, kid?" "Just right, dad," my kid would say. "Mmmm-mmmm, I can't wait!" We'd join everything together in a big clay pot and then cover it and drop the heat to low and we'd let that bastard cook for a good two hours and fifteen minutes.

We'd stand over it, drooling.

"What's that, kid?" I'd ask. "What fine dish do we have here?"

"We have *spezzatino di vitello*," the kid would say. "We've got the best spezzatino di vitello any dad and his kid ever cooked up on the face of this earth."

"Bet your ass, kid," I'd say.

Then we'd light the fourteen candles and call old Coolie in. We'd install her at the table head on plump cushions and spread a lacy serviette over her lap. We'd hum her a few notes from a nice Puccini opera as we ladled up spezzatino di vitello on her plate. We'd click our heels as we poured her a robust wine in the table's tallest, most glittering glass.

"Eat and be merry," we'd say.

That's what we'd do, me and the kid.

I brought in Coolie her glass of beer, pulling up the side table so she could get at it without disturbing herself. She was stretched out on the sofa with one pillow over her face and another tucked between her legs.

"I would have ordered it from China," she said, "if I had known you were going to take all day. What in the name of God were you doing back there?"

Having me a kid, I thought to say. But I stayed quiet. All hell would break loose if I said that. Coolie would fly up screeching. She'd come at me like a bat out to suck blood. To suck it and ladle it on her nails. Songbird Red.

Coolie sipped at her beer. "It's not cold," she said. "It's gone flat."

I turned on a lamp or two.

"But far be it from me to complain," she said. "That's right. Run up the bills."

I tried my loafers out. Tested the shine. They were buffed up to a nice gleam all around. They looked pretty good, although my heels sank down into the floor. It was like walking on eggs, kind of curvy, I mean. I wondered how I'd ever let them get run-down like that.

I rolled the TV up, got it going, then settled down into my chair.

"I'm not watching that junk," Coolie said.

I got up and turned the TV off. It made a sizzling sound, like fat in a frying pan. It always does. That TV, I thought, it's got a mind of its own.

Coolie took the pillow off her face and jammed it under her head. I watched her toes go through their ABCs.

"Last night," she said. "Where did you go last night?"

"Bowling," I said.

She snatched herself up, glaring. "You son of a bitch," she said. "You haven't been bowling in twenty years."

Old Coolie: I find nothing in life so buoyant to me as her abuse.

Something else got her attention. She leaped up and stalked over to the wall. She stayed there the longest time, gravely studying the floor, one hand under her chin.

"You missed a spot," she said. "Did the vacuum break down? You missed this whole area."

I don't hear you, I thought. Coolie, I don't hear a word you're saying.

"Come here," she said.

I went over.

She pointed.

"That's dirt," she said. "Now that is what I call genuine dirt. That's *dirt*, Cecil. Were you planning on putting in a field of corn?"

I laughed. Old Coolie and her corn: to hear her tell it I've put in a thousand acres in the living room alone. I started off after the vacuum. Coolie brushed by me, racing fast. "No, no," she said, "don't tax yourself. I know some things are just beyond you."

She wrestled out the vacuum and got the spot cleaned to her satisfaction. But her gown got caught in the suction—she shrieked. It was nearly ripped off her.

"It's trying to tell you something, Coolie," I said. "It's maybe telling you that gown needs a little attention."

This remark went past her. But it gave me this little idea. I figured that tomorrow while she was out at work I'd soak it in the Ivory Snow. I'd soak it for about nine hours.

"You're right about that floor," I said. "Heck, I can see the difference. Heck, a person could eat off it now."

"*You* eat off it, Cecil. Not me."

"Spezzatino di vitello," I said. "A fine floor dish."

She ignored this. She flung herself down on the sofa, groaned, then leaped up again. She got the TV going. "Anything is better than your company," she said. "I'm worn out, just knowing you're here."

I put her nail polish away, up on the mantel where she keeps it, behind the brass deer.

I put the cowboy boots back in the closet.

I gathered up the shoe-polish stuff and put it into the Saks box and stored it away.

Saks, it said. Saks Fifth Avenue. It said this on the top and on all four sides, in a nice black script. Flaring across, black on white. Pretty sharp. But where did we get it? When? What had come in this box?

"Now, kid," I said, "this one is for you to figure out. You get no sleep tonight until you figure it out."

"Okay, dad."

I must have said this aloud, or something like it, for Coolie was calling me. She had her "yell" button pushed. You'd have thought she'd just busted her kneecap up against a fire hydrant.

"You silly old bastard," she said. "What are you doing? Why are you in there mumbling to yourself? I thought someone was with you. Get in here. There's a movie on."

I came back in smiling, and took my chair.

The old TV music was getting zippy. It was really going.

"Look at that!" Coolie said, bolting up. "Can you believe it? What rubbish!"

It was some guy up in an old two-seater, two-engine plane, in pretty bad weather. In black and white this one was—how I like it best. This guy was out on wet storm-tossed wing, slipping and sliding. Squirming along. Dana Andrews it was. Dana? I wasn't sure. He looked a bit like Dana. Fog or clouds—this white stuff —kept swirling across his face. But getting blacker all the time. Whoever he was, he meant business. He wasn't out for a Sunday stroll. He was up to something, out on that wing. *Zap! Zap!* Lightning was flashing all across the sky. Jagged, bristling bolts. *Crack!* Another one. There went a propeller. The camera came in on this guy's face—it wasn't Dana, too bad—and you could see he was worried. He was desperate. But squirming along. Then we got another shot. He had this knife sticking out of his back. A delicate—what I would say was definitely a feminine—item. That knife. Pearl handle. Oodles of blood.

When the wings tilted you could see the raging sea, and swollen ice caps beyond.

"Oh God!" cried Coolie, slapping her head. "I can't believe this! Who do they think we are!"

The old music was really waltzing; it was jitterbugging to beat the band.

The man on the wing was shouting at someone as he crawled. You couldn't hear what he was saying. The wind just whistled it away. It doesn't matter. People don't hear you anyway. We heard something though. Yep. There it went. That old prop. It ripped away and plunged whining into the sea.

Coolie was twisting about. Shrieking. She had herself tied up in knots. "Get on with it, man! Shake that load out of your britches."

I kept getting a glimpse of this white hand at the bottom of the screen.

Coolie kicked her foot out at the man. At Dana. Maybe it was Dana. He had Dana's lips. That way of measuring things.

"Will he save her?" Coolie asked. "Christ, this is a new low even for them!"

Save what *her*, I wondered. Save *who?*

Oh. That hand.

My mind was drifting a bit. The "Pick Pix of the Week" was

sailing by me. Hold the phone, I was thinking. Hold that phone. Because I was thinking of that kid. My kitchen ace. Of kids, with maybe that Saks box thrown in. What if we had us *two* kids living here, I thought. A boy and a girl. Say we had a girl to match up with my kitchen ace. Brother and sister. Say that girl kid was named . . . well, what? There is Louise, after my mother. Louise Proffit. Now that's not bad. A girl can get along with a calling card like that. Or Celeste. Suppose we call her Celeste. Or Cynthia. How about Cynthia? Clea? Clea would be all right. That's a thought. Nothing wrong with Clea. Wait a minute though. Hold the phone. Clea Proffit? That's no good. What that is is a joke. Clear profit, get it? Actually, it isn't that bad. It's joky, but has a certain style. Class. Clea Proffit, attorney-at-law. Clea Proffit, brain surgeon. Something like that. Secretary-general, United Nations. Heck, she'd be about twelve now, old Clea would. Maybe the oldest. Say she's the oldest. Though she still sucks her thumb. Probably always will. Who cares. Clea, darling, you can suck your thumb.

"All right, daddy."

Christ yes, I was really getting into it. I could *hear* old Clea.

"Whatever you say, daddy."

Beautiful voice. Clea Proffit, star of stage and screen.

All right, this is how it is. This is how it would be. While the kid and me are out in the kitchen getting a bead on dinner, sipping the wine, talking about that box, Clea is in here keeping Coolie company. Talking away. Having a fine chat. Neither hearing the other, of course, but . . . well, she'd have nice long hair, Clea would, maybe golden like that boy with the golf clubs. A perky little nose. Beautiful eyes, a lively face. Creamy complexion. Bit of a mess around the lips just now because she's been out in the kitchen checking out our dish. Saying "Ummmm good!" Now she's in here. Chatting. Smart as a whip. "Too many missiles, mama. Too many warheads. Stamp out the warheads." Coolie's plaiting her hair. Yes. Talking shop. "No, no, mama. Allende was a *good* man. He was a *good* man." Pretty but not too pretty. She'd have my looks and Coolie's character. She'd have Coolie's screech if ever something riled her. "No, no, mama. The Tomb of the Unknown is a *symbol*; it isn't a Communist plot." Good at her books. No trouble to anyone. A free spirit. She'd have friends, about a hundred. They'd always be over, smushing the cushions, emptying the fridge. Playing records. Whispering, giggling. She'd have this best friend, a wee, waifish, reddish-haired creature named Prissy. No, named Scarlet. She and that Scarlet kid would be always together. Chattering away, not hearing each other. "No, no, Scarlet. Turkey *claims* Cyprus. That's where they are trying to stamp out the Kurds." But they'd hear me and my kitchen ace when we called them in to dinner.

"Soup's on! Come get your spezzatino di vitello!"

And Coolie would roar, "Not *again*! I *hate* spezzatino di vitello! I can't *stand* spezzatino di vitello! Spezzatino makes me *sick*!"

But my daughter and little Scarlet would go to her. They'd bring her around. They'd say, "Yes, you do, mama. Yes you do. You know you love spezzatino di vitello. We all do. Our spezzatino is delicious."

"I know," Coolie would whisper. "I adore it. I just can't admit it to *him*."

That's what I was thinking as I watched the black and white. These were bad thoughts. Depressing thoughts. I hadn't had thoughts like this in a month of Sundays—which isn't so long, now I think of it.

"Are you listening, Cecil!" Coolie cried. "Are you *alert* to this! Can you believe it!"

The music thundered.

The plane was burning.

One wing had fallen off.

A girl was dangling in the sky. The man was holding her by one arm. His grip slipping inch by inch. The poor girl was weeping. Weeping and screeching. She reminded me of Coolie. Coolie, too, was accustomed to seeing life from this woman's point of view. You could see sharks circling in the water below. Lightning flashing. The careening plane a black line of smoke. The girl in the sky, wriggling. She was terrified. The wind throwing her about. She had on this flimsy dress that looked a bit like Coolie's gown. Flapping about. Shredding. Now and then the music would drop so you could hear their speech. Their gasps. Their hard breath. The lick of flames fast approaching. Hold on, the man kept saying. Hold tight. The girl was getting more naked by the minute. Pretty soon we were going to have us an X-rated movie. She was trying to tell him something, though you couldn't make it out. The music boomed in each time we went to her. But she seemed to be saying something about that knife. Yes, the knife, for the camera kept swaying to the knife in old Dana's back. "Forgive me," she was saying. "Forgive me, my lover, my pet. My lamb."

Coolie, I forgive you.

Coolie, you set my heart a-racing.

Coolie, let's climb into bed.

"Hush up," said Coolie. "Be quiet. I'm listening to this."

The other wing fell off.

The fuselage cracked in half.

The music crashed in. The scene faded to black.

"Jesus help us," said Coolie in a moan. She was wrenching about on the sofa, her eyes closed, a pillow clenched under her chin. Old Coolie loves her movies. "What's the point!" she yelled to the TV. "Jesus, I hate these miserable endings. Do they live or die? Are you morons? Do you think *we* are?"

Just then I heard the doorbell ring. Coolie didn't notice. She had her hands up over her ears now, watching the quivering screen.

Bing-pong!—there went the bell again. I took the time to check myself in the mirror. I smoothed back my hair. Put on my polished shoes.

I walked on out to the front door and swung it open.

She was dressed in a belted coat so immaculate it seemed to shimmer, and sheer white stockings the same colour, and I never got to notice her shoes because she was speaking to me, her hair swept back on both sides and her face so pale, white, and clean she looked the twin of her pristine garments.

"It's all here," she said, "every last penny. I'm glad you let me bring it out this evening. I tell you, it will be a load off my mind, getting rid of this money. We don't usually handle so much."

She had a nice voice, on the soft side. Silver earrings gleamed from her lobes and there was a silk scarf, not exactly white, circling her throat. She was about my height and her hair had a reddish tinge. She had this fine leather satchel strapped to one arm.

She was younger than I had figured.

She had a sweet shape.

An easy, comfortable way of looking you in the eye.

"No trouble, I hope," I said. "I wouldn't want you to go to any extra trouble on my account."

"No trouble at all," she said.

I asked if she wanted to come inside. Maybe take off that coat, meet the wife, have a quiet chat. She said no. No, she had to run. She had plans, she said. The evening was still young.

I peeked around her. There was a small shiny car by the curb, with someone sitting in it.

"Do you want to count it?" she said.

I told her no, no point in that.

I took the satchel.

"Do I have to sign for it?" I asked. "The old John Henry? Are there any strings attached? Is there anything I ought to know about this money?"

"No," she said. "It's yours. It's yours and that's all there is to it."

She was a nice girl with a nice sweet voice and she had these remarkable eyes, clear as rainwater.

I had no trouble hearing her.

"We were wondering," she said—hesitating, not wanting to pry—"we were wondering what you intend doing with it."

"Do with it?" I said. "I don't know."

"Well . . . good night then."

"There's this kid," I said. "Down in Nigeria."

"Oh yes?"

"He's been getting fifty cents a week. I've been sending him that much. Now I might raise it to a dollar."

"We hoped you'd do something like that," she said.

She was turning to go. She had this handbag strapped over her shoulder, not white exactly but more the colour of that scarf, and she was digging into it. She brought out a pair of high heels.

"Do you figure a dollar is enough?" I asked.

She slowed her steps. I could see her mulling this over. Fifty cents or a dollar—it was an important question.

"I *suppose* so," she said. "You have to keep these things in pro-portion."

I could see that little kid with his hand out, stretching all across the continent. Those big eyes. The scabs. The spindly legs. Named

Lopé, I think. Lopé something-or-other. Something like that.

Lopé Proffit. It killed me every time I thought of that kid.

"Hell," I said, "I might make it *two* dollars! What the hell."

She leaned up against the porch post, taking off her low business heels and sliding the new ones on. Then she pitched the lows into her handbag and snapped it shut.

"Wait a minute," I said. "There's another one down in Peru. Peru, of all places. Can you beat that? A little girl this one is. Pathetic-looking, but the energy she has! These stick legs, sores all over her body—pus!—and her feet turned in so you know she'll never be much of a runner. Never a golfer. Millet and rice, that's what she eats. Not much of that, either. The flies! She's got a thousand flies buzzing all over. On her mouth too, feeding on those sores. Giving itch to the scabs. Lice in her hair. But what stamina! Christ, my heart bleeds. Marjula her name is. Marjula, what kind of name is that? But I like it. Christ, Marjula is plenty good enough for me. Hard *h*, you get it? Hula, a real hula girl. Take ten of our kids over here just to hold her down, and I'm including that kid with the golf clubs and the golden hair. 'Watch out! Stand back! Don't get in my way!' That's what old Marjula is always saying. It's the message I get. What do you think? Am I on the right track? I think five dollars a week myself. Five, just until she learns how to count. Maybe hook her up with that Nigeria fella. Get something going. Lopé and Marjula. What do you think? I could call it my 'Green-Light Special,' what's coming at them this week from our neck of the woods. Would that knock out her eyes? Shoo away them flies? An orphan, you know. No mama, no daddy. Scabby like him. Big protruding belly. But she's ours now, old Coolie's and mine. Did I say five? Forget five. I say ten, minimum, and that's cheap, my bargain this week. Am I on the right track? Am I talking sense?"

She had got down the steps and out onto the walk. She looked pretty sharp in her high heels. She was a pretty handsome woman, what you'd call a bit of all right.

"It's a question of their *perspective*," she said. "You can't raise false expectations. That would never do."

This baffled me. I wondered how it was she thought any of us lived. How any of us had survived.

"Clear up the drinking water," I said. "Buy *real* milk. Speed that up. Hey, I got it. Another water buffalo!"

She laughed. It was a good, high, hard laugh, lots of enjoyment in it. I forgave her all her sins.

"I hear you," she said. "You're coming in loud and clear. It's your money. All yours. Ta ta."

She went on down the path, that coat shimmering. It was nicely cut, that coat, beautifully form-fitting. She had wonderful legs, a strong stride.

"Going dancing?" I said.

She swirled. She gave a little rat-tat-tat to the pavement. "You bet!" she said. "All night long!"

The man in the car grinned and waved.

"So long."

I walked into the living room with the satchel of money.

"It isn't over," Coolie said without turning around.

She meant the movie. The man from the airplane and the woman in the tattered dress were up in the Andes somewhere. Snow all over. I wondered how they had survived the crash. But I granted them that. Funny things happen in this world.

"Where've you been?" Coolie said. "You missed the best part."

These two were hugging each other. Trembling. They looked pretty beaten. It was cold up there. The highest peak, old Clea would say, this side of Asia. Snow swirling every which way. They were trying to talk but their teeth were chattering too hard.

"She's his wife," Coolie said.

Now they were trying to get a fire going. They scooped out a deep hole in the snow. They scratched up a few twigs. They crouched down inside the hole. He got out his matches. They studied each other over the flame. They got this dark, serious look in their eyes. You could see it happening: the desire swelling up. The music, too. They were crying. Suddenly they slammed into each other, moaning and twisting, driving at each other's lips and throat, as the snow dropped over them like huge wafers. The matches got kicked over with snow. They got kicked farther. Not that this pair noticed or cared. They were going at it. You can't say no to such desire. You can't say no, I guess, whether you're in the Andes, at the Proffit house, or on a bridge in Venice.

Coolie didn't agree. Her face was up at the screen. She was shaking her fists and yelling at them. "Build the fire!" she said. "Oh, you suckers, build the fire! You'll die, damn you!"

Snow blanketed the screen. You could just peer through it to see that human beings were there.

"They won't die, Coolie," I said. "it's only a movie."

I started spreading the money out over the carpet.

I started counting the money.

Art

I TOLD THE WOMAN I wanted that bunch down near the pine grove by the rippling stream.

Where the cow is? she asked.

I told her yep, that was the spot.

She said I'd have to wait until the milking was done.

The cow mooed a time or two as we waited. It was all very peaceful.

How much if you throw in the maiden? I asked.

Without the cow? she asked, or *with*?

Both would be nice, I said.

But it turned out a Not for Sale sign had already gone up on the girl. Too bad. It was sweet enough with her out of the picture, but not quite the same.

I took my cut bunch of flowers and plodded on behind the cow over to the next field. I wanted a horse too, if I could get one cheap.

Any horses? I asked.

Not today, they said.

Strawberries?

Not the season, I was told.

At home, I threw out the old bunch and put the new crop in a vase by the picture window so the wife might marvel at them when she came in from her hard day's grind.

I staked the cow out front where the grass was still doing pretty well.

It was touch-and-go whether we'd be able to do the milking ourselves. It would be rough without a shed or stall.

Oh, hand-painted! the wife said when she came in.

I propped her up in the easy chair and put up her feet. She looked a trifle wind-blown.

Hard day? I asked.

So-so, she said.

I mixed up a gin and tonic, nice as I knew how, and lugged that in.

A touch flat, she said, but the lemon wedge has a nice effect.

I pointed out the cow, which was tranquilly grazing.

Sweet, she said. Very sweet. What a lovely idea.

I put on the stereo for her.

That needle needs redoing, she observed. The tip needs retouching, I mean.

It will have to wait until tomorrow, I told her.

She gave me a sorrowful look, though one without any dire reproach in it. She pecked me a benign one on the cheek. A little wet. I wiped it off before it could do any damage.

The flowers were a good thought, she said. I appreciate the flowers.

Well, you know how it is, I said. What I meant was that one did the best one could—though I didn't really have to tell her that. It was what she was always telling me.

She was snoozing away in the chair as I tiptoed off to bed. I was beginning to flake a little myself. Needed a good touch-up job from an expert.

We all do, I guess. The dampness, the mildew, the rot—it gets into the system somehow.

Not much to be done about it, however.

I thought about the cow. Wondered if I hadn't made a mistake on that. Without the maiden to milk her, there didn't seem to be much *point* in having a cow. Go back tomorrow, I thought. Offer a good price for the maiden, the stream, and the whole damned field.

Of course, I could go the other way: find a nice seascape somewhere. Hang that up.

Well, sleep on it, I thought.

The wife slipped into bed about two in the morning. That's approximate. The paint job on the hour hand wasn't holding up very well. The undercoating was beginning to show through on the entire clock face, and a big crack was developing down in the six o'clock area.

Shoddy goods, I thought. Shoddy artisanship.

Still, we'd been around a bit. Undated, unsigned, but somewhere in the nineteenth century was my guess. It was hard to remember. I just wished the painter had been more careful. I wished he'd given me more chest, and made the bed less rumpled.

Sorry, baby, she said. Sorry I waked you.

She whispered something else, which I couldn't hear, and settled down far away on her side of the bed. I waited for her to roll into me and embrace me. I waited for her warmth, but she remained where she was and I thought all this very strange.

What's wrong? I said.

She stayed very quiet and did not move. I could feel her holding herself in place, could hear her shallow, irregular breathing, and I caught the sweep of one arm as she brought it up to cover her face. She started shivering.

I am so sorry, she said. I am so sorry. She said that over and over.

Tell me what's wrong, I said.

No, she said, please don't touch me, please don't, please don't even think about touching me. She went on like this for some seconds, her voice rising, growing in alarm, and I thought to myself, Well, I have done something to upset her, I must have said or done something unforgivable, and I lay there with my eyes open wide, trying to think what it might be.

I am so sorry, she said. So very very sorry.

I reached for her hand, out of that hurting need we have for warmth and reassurance, and it was then that I found her hand had gone all wet and muddy and smeary.

Don't! she said, oh please don't, I don't want you to hurt yourself!

Her voice was wan and low and she had a catch in her voice and a note of forlorn panic. I lifted my hand away quickly from her wetness, though not quickly enough for I knew the damage already had been done. The tips of my fingers were moist and cold, and the pain, bad enough but not yet severe, was slowly seeping up my arm.

My drink spilled, she said. She snapped that out so I would know.

Christ, I thought. Oh, Jesus Christ. God help us.

I shifted quickly away to the far side of the bed, my side, away from her, far as I could get, for I was frightened now and all I could think was that I must get away from her, I must not let her wetness touch me any more than it had.

Yes, she said shivering, do that, stay there, you must try and save yourself, oh darling I am so sorry.

We lay in the darkness, on our backs, separated by all that distance, yet I could still feel her warmth and her tremors and I knew there was nothing I could do to save her.

Her wonderful scent was already going and her weight on the bed was already decreasing.

I slithered up high on the sheets, keeping my body away from her, and ran my good hand through her hair and down around her warm neck and brought my face up against hers.

I know it hurts, I said. You're being so brave.

Do you hurt much? she said. I am so terribly, terribly sorry. I was dozing in the chair and opened my eyes and saw the dark shape of the cow out on the lawn and for an instant I didn't know what it was and it scared me. I hope I haven't hurt you. I've always loved you and the life we had in here. My own wounds aren't so bad now. I don't feel much of anything any more. I know the water has gone all through me and how frightful I must look to you. Oh please forgive me, it hurts and I'm afraid I can't think straight.

I couldn't look at her. I looked down at my own hand and saw that the stain had spread. It had spread up to my elbow and in a small puddle where my arm lay, but it seemed to have stopped there. I couldn't look at her. I knew her agony must be very great and I marvelled a little that she was being so brave for I knew that in such circumstances I would be weak and angry and able to think only of myself.

Water damage, I thought, that's the hardest part to come to terms with. The fear that's over you like a curse. Every day you think you've reconciled yourself to it and come to terms with how susceptible you are, and unprotected you are, and then something else happens. But you never think you will do it to yourself.

Oil stands up best, I thought. Oh holy Christ why couldn't we have been done in oil.

You get confident, you get to thinking what a good life you have, so you go out and buy yourself flowers and a goddamn cow.

I wish I could kiss you, she moaned. I wish I could.

My good hand was already behind her neck and I wanted to bring my head down on her breasts and put my hand there too. I wanted to close my eyes and stroke her all over and lose myself in the last sweetness I'd ever know.

I will too, I thought. I'll do it.

Although I tried, I couldn't, not all over, so I stroked my hand through her hair and rolled my head over till my lips gently touched hers.

She sobbed and broke away.

It's too much, she said. I'm going to cry. I am, I know I am.

Don't, I said. Don't. If you do that will be the end of you.

The tears burst and I spun above her, wrenching inside, gripping the sheet and wiping it furiously about her eyes.

I can't stop it! she said. It's no use. It burns so much but I can't stop it, it's so sad but I've got to cry!

She kept on crying.

Soon there was just a smear of muddled colour on the pillow where her face had been, and then the pillow was washing away.

The moisture spread, reaching out and touching me, filling the bed until at last it and I collapsed on the floor.

Yet the stain continued widening.

I had the curious feeling that people were already coming in, that someone already was disassembling our frame, pressing us flat, saying, Well here's one we can throw out. You can see how the house, the cow, etc., have all bled together. You can't recognize the woman any more, or see that this once was a bed and . . . well it's all a big puddle except those flowers. Flowers are a dime a dozen but these are pretty good, we could snip out the flowers, I guess, give them their own small frame. Might fetch a dollar or two, what do you say?

The Birth Control King of the Upper Volta

THE MOST EXTRAORDINARY THING happened to me today. I woke up and discovered I had lost yesterday. Amazing! Not a slither, parcel or dot of it remained. Yes! The sun was dazzling bright, my entire room was lit up like a storefront. I stretched, I yawned, I kicked off my sheets: Oh, lovely, lovely! is what I said.

Absolutely. That's how innocent I was.

And here I am forty-seven years old. You'd think I would have had a hint.

Dogs outside my window were having a romp. Squealing, yowling—how I had slept through their hubbub was more than I could imagine. Yet I felt wonderfully excited. Renewed, you might say. "What a dreamy day!" That's exactly what I said to myself— and right away set about performing my exercises. A somersault. Another one. Nothing broke, thank goodness. My room is so small I have to do these flip-flops on a pinhead. But the exhilaration!—I truly felt superb, even while lifting my barbells. Twenty, thirty, this is too easy, I told myself—add more weight! Add a ton. I slid on the ton. Ten, twenty, thirty—no trouble at all. I could have gone on all day pressing these feathers, with barely a pause for breath.

"Oh you're fit," I said, laughing, addressing my form in the mirror. "You're in peak condition, Adlai!" I pulled on my pants, scooped back my hair. Washed my face and neck in the little sink, eager to run down to breakfast. "Eat a horse, Adlai," I said, "yes, you could. What an appetite you've worked up! Hurry up, now!"

Ah, what a babe. What an innocent. For it was then, hustling through the door, that I made the discovery. The beautiful calendar hanging by the nail drew my eye. And why not, for pictured there was my sweetheart, Greta Gustafsson. I always notice her, entering or leaving. Sultry woman, she'd mope—she'd scratch out my eyes—if I didn't. Everyone needs noticing, is what Greta would say. "What a beauty you are," I said, rubbing my cheek against this image. Kissing her bare shoulders. Greta moaned. I moaned also. "Good morning, my darling," I said. "Sleep well, my beauty?" She lowered her eyes. This morning she seemed preoccupied—seemed distant. My heart ached. Greta deserved better than I could give her. She deserved, at the least, a silver frame, a wall with a good view. Yet as it is there is hardly room for myself. For my footlocker and narrow bed. The walls!—stretch out your arms and there you have it. And so ugly! Uneven and fly-specked—filthy!—with immense zigzags cracking all about.

"No, the door," I said, smoothing down her hair, "the door is best for you, beautiful Greta. Don't complain. Don't scold. Things will be looking up for us once I get that job with the Pole. Give me a smile, darling. What would you like for breakfast, my

honey? Say the word and I shall get it." I kissed her eyes. Greta
likes that. She purred. Oh Greta adores eye-kissing. My perfect
Greta.

But wait, for here's the news. Drawing back, I happened to
glance at the calendar dates. Mercy! "What's this?" I asked myself.
Impossible. But yes, there it was. Yesterday didn't exist—had disappeared! Had become, I mean, today. What *do* I mean? I mean
at that very second I discovered there had been no August ten in
my life. The bold red type was clearly announcing itself: August
nine—full moon. August eleven—anniversary of Blondin's crossing of Niagara Falls on a tightrope wire. So the little historical
note informed me. But no August ten. Gone. *"God help me!"* I
cried. *"I've lost yesterday! What happened to the tenth?"* Greta giggled. Then she saw my stricken face and fell quiet.

One whole day! I thought. Jesus God!

I stumbled out into the hall. Voices floated up from the dining-room, jibber-jabber, everyone talking at once, the way they
always do. Slurp-slurp—you'd think I slept above a hog pen. Jibber-jabber, slurp-slurp—what imps!

"I say," I called, "what's the date down there?"

Silence. Not a word. You'd think I had dropped a giant brickbat on their heads. And out of the stillness came Mergentoire's
sprightly reply: "Wednesday! It's Wednesday, you ape!"

Ape? Ape? What had got into sweet Mergentoire?

"Idiot!" I screeched. "Get control of yourself, woman. The
date, what's the *date?*"

More silence. Utter stealth, you'd have thought. One would
have sworn the entire table had fallen asleep. Then Mergentoire's
voice again, laughing this time, shrill as a rat. "The eleventh, you
rogue! Wednesday the eleventh. The day Blondin went across
Niagara on a tightrope!"

Then the clatter of dishes once more, and everyone else shouting up the hideous message too. Chomping away on pancakes, scraping back their chairs—where's the butter, who's got the milk jug, *oops!*—that sort of thing. All the confusion and turmoil, the belching and bellyaching you get when twenty hard-hat labourers are trying to gulp down their protein before rushing off to their jobs. No shilly-shallying, I mean, quick-quick, sorry old mate, got to run!

What a waste of man and woman's best hour. My old mam and I, we would sit for hours about the breakfast table, munching carrot sticks, dipping our bread into tea, perusing the journals and up-to-date magazines, rattling the tabloids.

—*Ah, son, here's another one.*

—Another one, my mam?

—Guinea-Bissau, this one's called. How many does that make, son?

—I don't know, my mam. What's your guess?

—I count forty-one, son. Forty-one since your old daddy went into the field.

—That's a lot of emerging nations, my mam! That's a whole hodgepodge full! Oh, they are really carving it up. What do you think old daddy would say, my mam?

—He'd say 'Roll me over, dear. Roll me over in my grave and throw another white right on top of me.'

—Tell me about it, my mam.

—It was the Upper Volta that broke your old dad's heart. Oh, son, when they let the Upper Volta go they as much as put a dagger through his chest.

—Cold-blooded murder, my mam?

—That's right, son. It was a mean, depraved act and who's to reap the whirlwind now?

—Us, my mam?

—That's the bite of it, son. But eat your carrots, Adlai, they don't grow on trees and a boy needs to hoard up his strength.

I went back into my room, thinking about poor old mam and all the black African hordes yet to sweep down. Crossing the water on rafts and matchstick canoes, beaming their great white teeth and kicking their great black legs, all to gobble up our jobs and steal our women and make a garbage hole of our neighbourhoods. "Not yet, my mam," I wanted to tell her. "Adlai is holding on. Old Adlai's got the biceps and the brawn, he's got the willpower: you won't find him kissing no woolly hair."

I could see old mam nodding her approval even as I stared with remorse and disbelief at my calendar's lost date. Where was yesterday? Old mam would say the blacks had got it, just as they'd take away anything else I'd be foolish enough to leave lying about.

—That's right, son, they got it. They'll take the shoes off your feet if you don't lace them up tight!

Greta Gustafsson gave me her alluring smile. I swayed in close, putting the kiss of sin into her smouldering eyes.

"*I vunt to be alone,*" she whispered, turning away.

My heart skipped; it always puts me in a torture, seeing Greta in her moods.

"But Greta!" I whined.

"*Yoo lust a day,*" she murmured, resentful and hurt. "*They are my days too and I hold yoo responsible.*"

I dropped down on my narrow bed. Scrunching up my toes, for there was not enough room for my feet between it and the wall. Something fishy going on here is what I thought. Adlai, you've got to use your wits if you intend to figure this one out.

Days, I thought—as you would have yourself—just don't disappear.

I consulted my diary, lying open on the footlocker table. Lying open to August ten. To the day that had never been. "7:00—wake up, lazy-bones! Exercise. Wash. 7:30—Pancakes with the gang, mmmmm! 8-6:00 p.m.—job, ughh (but don't complain!). 7:00 p.m.—Talk to the pole. 8:00—Home. Dust room. Wipe sink. Exercise. Bedtime snack. Shut-eye. (And no messing about with Greta.)

"Oh there's monkey business afoot here, Adlai," I said—for it looked to me as if I'd had a very busy day. And why not?—a thousand irons in the fire, things to get done, people to see! Life to *live!* My old mam, looking at my diary, would have patted my head. She would have said, "That's dreamy, son. That's top marks. How you get it all done is beyond me. Oh yes, you're a chop off the old block."

So.

So I'd say myself.

Yet I was blotto. I had not even the fumes, not even the ashes, of my past day. Zero.

Greta was sulking, giving me first one cold shoulder and then the other. Drop dead, is what Greta was saying. What a disappointment you are. What a rathead. "You expect too much of me, Greta," I told her. "I do the best I can." But she flounced her hair and thrust out her chin and drew the cloak of gloom over herself.

A *hard* woman. A *tough* woman. Just, I thought, like old mam.

So I forgave her. I decided she was right to be mad. I had let her down. I had promised her she would be safe with me. That I had what it took to keep a good woman happy.

A newshawker was shouting his headlines out on the street, and I rushed to the window. "You!" I yelled, "what's the date?"

His startled black face sought to find mine.

"August eleventh, boss," he said.

The dogs were still fighting in the dirt, squealing and yowling and spinning in a fury.

"Are those mongrels yours, boy?" I asked.

"Not mine, boss."

The dogs momentarily ceased their yowling to blink up at me. Then they went back to it with renewed ferocity.

"Well then," I asked the boy, "what's the news today?" And he held up his grim headlines to me:

SUMMIT TALKS COLLAPSE

AUTO-MAKERS LAY OFF ANOTHER 30,000

INFLATION HITS NEW HIGH

My world, I thought, and still there.

"That all, boss?" asked the black face.

And when I didn't answer immediately, he did a little soft-shoe.

It seemed to me I'd seen him before—him or his twin—standing in the line-up to receive his dole, wearing butter-yellow shoes, a red eyepatch, a watch-chain long as his arm—and streaming off in his big Rolls-Royce with three boisterous women white as white eggs and laughing like mud-flaps.

But was this true or was it my old daddy sending his vision across the licking water?

"Listen, kid," I called, "did I buy a paper off you yesterday?"

His black face grinned up at me over his watermelon. "Not off me, boss. I'm fresh brand-new in the country, first day on the job." He danced a swift jig along the pavement, playing a mean tune with his harmonica comb. "I aims to make my fortune, boss," he chirped. "Me and my fourteen brothers looking no way but up. We got a toe-hold on progress. Gonna git our relatives in. From here on out de sky is de limit!"

I slammed my window down on this strapping young grinner, and proceeded to do one hundred push-ups—a few headstands —to work the vitriol out of my system. It had been the vitriol that had slammed down my old daddy and made his gums bleed. That had turned him boots up.

—What killed him, my mam?

—Vitriol, son. When the blacks painted up their bodies and screamed their heebie-jeebies he was filled up with vitriol and flung himself into the first river.

—What was he doing there, my mam, in the distant Upper Volta?

—Selling birth control to the Roman Catholics, son. No easy job.

Greta was breathing hard. Clenching her fists as she strode this way and that. Hissing. Stopping me cold with her hot fury. I knew what was on her mind. She wanted me stepping up in the world. Wanted me out of my red suspenders and into top hats. She wanted me to call up the Pole, find out about that job. I stole a look at her, wondering. Trying to figure out what it is about women. Why they drive their men so hard. Why they can't be satisfied. It crossed my mind that I wasn't cut out for a go-getter like Greta. That I'd be better off with some redhead lounging back in a bikini on a leopard-skin rug, selling fertilizer to farmers. With someone all bosom and legs who would say, "I'm for my man, right or wrong. My man is a macho-doctor, good for what ails me." But I didn't think this long. Greta was my heart's need, my solace, my joy. Without her I'd be swinging on vines.

So I stepped out into the hall to make my call.

Mergentoire, I noticed, had put up a new sign: Don't Hog the Phone. This was tacked up beside another one that said No Calls After 8 P.M. And another one, dripping blood, that said This Means You.

"The Pole here," the Pole's voice shrieked in my ear. "Speak up!"

But there was thunder overhead. Then the thunder was rumbling down from the third floor, down the stairs, driving towards me. "Out of my way, fat man!" came the nasty cry. Wong, the slant-eye. I shrank back, hugging the wall. His yellow face whirled past, bumping me—hurling himself off to his job. Late again. This Chinaman, one more of the numberless hordes. "Fat men!" he screeched. "Always fat men! Never looking where they're going! Always hogging the phone!" He clattered on down, flinging back more abuse.

A big country like that, you'd think they'd stay in their rice fields.

The Pole was shouting, too. "Who is it? Speak up! I haven't got all day!"

I gave him my name.

"Oh," he said. "Oh, it's you! The nincompoop! What's on your mind, nincompoop? Why are you bothering me?"

Hold on here, I said to myself. Why is the Pole addressing me in this unseemly fashion? What gives? It had been my impression that the Pole, more than most, held me in high regard. Respected my talents. Why otherwise would he have been trying to give me a job?

"If it's about that job," he now was saying, "you can blow it out of your stove-pipe. I told you yesterday. I've hired someone else. I got some foreign bird at half the pay. Strong! Eight feet tall! Can't speak a word of English. But I'll work the stink off him, don't worry about that!"

And before I could get my wits raked clean the rascal had hung up.

Poles, I thought: what can you say about Poles?

I thought, What a relief! Changing jobs, what a nuisance that would have been! I mopped my brow, thinking, What a close call!

Anyway, I told myself, I like the job I've got. I'm happy. Greta's happy, what's the worry?

I slouched back into my room, feeling pretty good.

"It's the Pole's bad luck," I told Greta. "He missed a good bet. Hiring me was his golden opportunity."

Greta wasn't talking to me. She had put on one of her hats, the one with feathers. Plumed like a cavalier. Scooped low, the brim shading one eye. String of pearls at her throat, as if she intended going someplace.

Well, I didn't mind. I liked to see Greta all dressed up.

But she had fire in her eyes—a torrid spitball.

"*Rats!*" she hissed—or something like that.

Her shoulders arched back as she paced, pivoting her hips. I watched those hips, those eyes, stole glances at her flat chest. She looked so luscious, so mysterious—so magnificent and sure of herself.

I wanted to hug and hold her, to weep in her thighs.

But I put the brave face on. "That Pole," I said, "he must have been out of his mind to think I wanted his soft job. Me, at a desk! What a laugh. None of that white-collar malarkey for me. I like being outside breathing in the fresh air. Hauling those rocks. Working in rain, wind, snow. Working up a good sweat in the hard freeze. A man's work, that's what I'm cut out for."

Greta's cruel veil of derision fluttered down.

I could swear my old mam walked right into the room. She stood not a foot away, shaking a finger.

—It keeps a body fit, my mam. In tune with nature. It's nice being out there where only the fittest survive. It's educational, old mam. Not a day goes by I don't tip my hat to old Darwin the theorizer.

—So long as you don't get the heebie-jeebies, son. That's what done in your daddy. That and the vitriol.

—I've heard it said he was a drinker too, my mam.

—Envy, son. The envy and malice of small minds. It was the envy of him that spread that story.

—And womanizing, my mam? Was he a womanizer, as I've heard?

She sat down on my bed, spreading her hands palms up on her lap. She had a spot of soot on her chin, and watery eyes. I reached over and brushed away the soot. Her hair had a singed odour, as if she'd fallen head first into a smoker's flame.

—Womanizing won't kill a person, son. There are some as would say it's what keeps a body going. But your daddy wasn't like that. And if he had been, it isn't likely he would ever have touched black. Now listen to me, Adlai. You listen good. Three thousand nautical miles separated your daddy in the Upper Volta from us where we were, not to mention umpteen years—but your daddy's eyes were always looking back home. He kept his heart and his eyes dead set on us. On me and you. He put love first, but he knew he had that. Had our love and our trust. But he was a committed man. An obsessed man. I've told you a thousand times: your daddy had a mission to protect us, and others like us. Our very way of life. And he went with my blessings. I remember the day he left I said to him, 'Go and do it, Humpter, and do it well, and always know you have me here thumping my feet for every success you have.' Humpter, that was my secret pet name for him. Every time I would call him Humpter he would blush.

Yes, and I would too, for we were just newlyweds, you see. We still had the rice in our hair. But I knew my duty. And he knew his. So he pecked his mouth to my cheek and said to me, 'You're the one woman every man dreams of! You know a man's duty comes first!' —and then he shook my shoulder, and left. It was so beautiful, so beautiful the way he said it that I broke down and cried.

—Did I cry too, my mam? I asked. But old mam was gazing off into the blue, as if she were back there with him, and didn't answer me straight-out.

—What's that, son? What did you say?

She had a clump of mud down on her knee, and I brushed this off. Her old skin was leathery and brown and there seemed to be mites running in her hair. This, or some trickery in the air.

She was giving my walls and the room the hard-eye.

—Is this the best you can do, son? Why this room is hardly bigger than a burying hole. And look there! You've tracked dirt all over the floor. Don't you ever clean up?

—Down on my knees, mam, every evening. Down with soap and rag, just like you.

For old mam always had; she'd liked a place clean.

—Not *last* evening, son.

—No, old mam. Something must have come up.

—Excuses won't get you into paradise, Adlai. I'm only glad your daddy isn't here to see it. And that! she said, pointing. Who is that? That smoky-looking temptress up on your door?

I made way to introduce my sweetheart, Greta, but old mam was having none of it. "*Shame, baby, shame!*" she was saying. She stretched back groaning on the bed, letting her feet flop over the edge. She still wore the same ankle-high work boots that had mesmerized me in my childhood. They had the rot of thirty years messing about with turnips and spuds, a lifetime of kicking at grass and dandelion. The laces were covered with mould. The socks on her thin bones were both shoved down.

Old mam closed her eyes.

—Are you going to take a nap, my mam?

Greta was hissing at me to get that woman—"that *voh-mahn*" —out of here.

—I never shut my eyes in the daytime, mam sadly replied. No, nor sleep in the night-time either, if you want to know the truth.

—Why not, my mam?

She reached up—as though dreaming—and with a small sob stroked bent fingers across my cheek.

—From worrying about you, son, the way I never had to worry about your daddy, though I'm pained to say it.

—Why's that, my mam?

I crouched down, my face only inches from her bird-tracked skin. I was pained, too, and jumping with nerves. My mam looked a thousand years old, all helpless and withery and done in. I wanted to fling myself down across her bosom, and moan. To say, *Old mam, what's happened to us?* For I had lost a day and my life was going nowhere—but where had hers gone? She smelled musty and—well, *mouldy*,—as if she'd been put away in some high cupboard and left there a long time, and now had come down all wizened and crusty.

But I stayed still. I couldn't bring myself to hurt or confuse or embarrass old mam.

—There are moments, son, when I think you don't care about your old mam. Moments when I wonder if you don't think I brought you up wrong. Times when I think you are holding me responsible for so much that goes on in this mean world.

—I'd never think that, I said, half horrified.

—Or that you don't revere your daddy, that you don't uphold his cause.

—No, mam! I cried, how could you think that?

She was gripping my hand tightly, her mouth twitching. Her eyes boring up into mine. Yet she looked so ancient, so feeble, so ahead of or behind her times. Her brow as wrinkled as a scrub-board. The flesh so speckled. It was as though a flock of perky chickens had got loose to scratch at her skin, which sagged down over her bones—but all so thin it was practically translucent.

—Oh, don't look at my face! she suddenly cried out. Don't stare at me like that! I know what you're thinking! Know how you've turned against me! How you've come to hate your own flesh and blood!

This speech utterly amazed me.

—*Me?* I said. *Me,* my mam!

For I'd always thought of us as close. As tight, I'd thought, as nectar and honey.

Mam sobbed. She rolled over, burying her head in the pillow. I eased down on my footlocker, shivering for her. Slowly stroking my hand up and down her backside. Saying, There, there, mam. There, there, good lady.

A fine little weave of bones was about all I could feel.

Her body felt cold. Cold and *icy.* And moist, too. And there arose again that smell, all earthy and wormy, as if she'd washed up from some foul pit or tomb, some ill and dank un-resting place.

—Don't worry, I soothed her. Don't trouble yourself, old mam. It was us together through thick and thin for all of those years. For *so many* years. And I tell you the truth, I never knew one from the other, never knew thick *from* thin, that was how much I knew I could count on your love. True, old mam. And it's how much you can count on mine now.

—Do you mean it, Adlai?

—I do, mam. I sure-as-shooting do.

She clawed at my hand. Grappled my fingers up to her lips, and kissed them. My man, she sobbed. My little man. My comfort in this sick old age.

We had us a good cry.

And I think old mam might have dozed, for I saw her breath slacken, felt her bones soften and smooth out underneath my stroking hand. I might have dozed or daydreamed myself—dappled off on beams of sunlight—for at any rate when I next blinked my eyes back to it the aura in the room seemed to have changed. It seemed as if not just minutes but hours, days, whole weeks had tumbled by.

The dogs were setting up a din outside my window, snarling and yowling.

I could hear Mergentoire at the foot of the stairs, shouting up at me. Get off the pot! Quit slacking! Get a move on! Saying she wasn't holding breakfast all day. Not for the likes of me. Then growling at her son Hedgepolt. Telling him too to shake a leg.

Women. You'd think they were shot from the womb to ferret out wrongdoers and hobnail them to a pristine trail.

What a nag.

Greta was in a huff, down on her knees on the floor, going at the dry mud-tracks with a scrunched-up hat. At *my* mud-tracks, or so it appeared. For they had my hoof-print. But who? How come? Greta throwing up insults at me: *ape* this and *ape* that. She is such a puzzle, Greta is. Aloof much of the time, yet now ready to scratch out my eyes because I had let my own sweet mam walk in and take a moment's rest on my unmade bed.

Isn't Greta funny? I thought. Oh, how I wish I knew what makes Greta tick!

But my stomach was growling; I needed my pancakes fast.

—Mam? You feeling okay?

Mam sat up, wiping her wet cheeks with the back of one frail hand.

—Oh, she said with a brave smile, it was just like in the old days, us having that good cry. It has done my heart good.

—Mine too, my mam.

She patted my head—That's a good lamb!—then hopped up spry as a cat with four legs to catch herself and knowing she would. Time's a battlefield, son, she gaily observed, but them that's got the backbone will whack through it to the other side.

—I'm whacking, mam, I said. I'm whacking hard.

Her eyes lit up; the old colour came back to her cheeks. Yes, you got the backbone, the same as your daddy did. I only hope you got his grit. That you're willing to stand up for what's-what.

—I will, mam. You can count on me.

She came in for a big hug, and I could swear she lifted me right off the floor.

—Don't get me wrong, son, what I was saying earlier. I'm not renouncing any of the ways you were raised. I don't apologize for swat. Right is right, and a mother has got to stick to that. No, it was just your daddy's ghost preying on my mind. Me feeling low, wishing I could be with him. They broke the mould, you know, when they made him.

—He stood tall, that he did.

She stared off, all misty-eyed. Her hands up to her temples, looking back to those days. "Poor man, it was the birth control that sapped him. Think of the pressure he lived under. Imagine the Upper Volta as it was the day he set foot there. Two hundred thousand Roman Catholics reproducing all over the place. They're like dogs, where two drop down ten more will pop up. So that was the RCs. And that's not to mention three million Mossis with the soles of their feet white as yours or mine and every bit as busy. Or half a million Lobis, another half-million Bobis, plus the thousands of itchy Gurunsis. Not one ever having heard of birth control until he came. And everyone black, black, black! The brightest sunshine makes no difference to a continent like that. Daytime or night-time, you'd never know it. That's what so many blacks can do to a country. Your daddy had to walk about with a good Eveready just to tell one black hole from another, and hope he didn't fall in. A woman wanting a baby she'd fall down in a ditch and let the men poke at her. That's all there was to it, so your daddy said. It makes you sick, don't it? Just thinking about it. It does me. But your daddy was no cry-baby. He was not the man to tuck tail under his britches and run. No, he kept plugging. Kept singing the glories of birth control. He knew it was *us*, our very way of life, our very freedoms, that he was defending. He knew all about their matchstick canoes; knew they'd soon be finding their way across the water. That they'd take our jobs, gut our neighbourhoods, throw down and have their mean pleasure with our women!"

She stood trembling, radiant with his memory, yet sickened by the reality of that other vision.

—I know it, my mam. I take my hat off to him the same as I take it off to you.

—So I thumped my foot and said, 'Go to it, Humpter. It's your job and you do it well.'

—He did it too, mam. He sure did.

Mam vacantly nodded, still trapped back there in time with him. I saw her little foot tapping; saw the worship flare in her eyes.

—You were tops too, mam, I said. You kept the home fires burning.

Mam smiled, in a drowsy, far-off way. Her voice went all wispy. "Now and then I'd get a sweet letter from him. 'Chalk up another one,' he'd say—and I'd know he'd saved another white child his rightful spot in the world. Another white boy his freedom. His job, his sweetheart, his neighbourhood. And I'd go down on my knees, saying, 'Bless him, bless him, bless Humpter, for that spot he's saved could be my Adlai's!'"

—He did it too, my mam! He saved my spot! Except for him I bet this very minute some black man would be standing right here where I'm standing. That bed would be his, and the footlocker would be his, my barbells, and probably he'd even have Greta!

But old mam had switched off. She was beginning to have that tuckered-out look again. She seemed to be fading.

—It was always my hope, she said wanly, that one day you'd take up your daddy's mighty cudgel.

My head sagged down. I looked dumbly at my shoes.

—I did, Adlai.

I had been dreading this remark since first she entered. I looked miserably at my dirty thumbnails. Whimpering,

—I'm sorry, my mam.

Mam stared right through me. Her tongue slashed like a lizard's.

—As it is, you haven't even married. You don't even have children.

I saw Greta suck in her breath. Saw her face go scarlet.

—Nary a one, continued mam. No, you've let your spot, and your children's spots, go to some gang of unruly, howling blacks! You've let the blacks take charge!

Old mam, I knew, did not mean to hurt. She was only expressing her disappointment in me. Telling me how my daddy would hang his head.

—But remember I'm whacking, mam! I'm whacking away. I've got Greta! I've got that Pole I was telling you about!

But mam wasn't listening. She was simply smiling her sad understanding at me. Smiling her sad, abandoned hope; letting me see how her dreams and my daddy's dreams had got splattered by the whirlwind. She laughed, trying to lighten both our loads. Thick and thin, she said, it doesn't rain but it pours.

—I'll shape up, I moaned. I'll shape up yet!

Mam was slowly buttoning up her coat. Her fingers were gnarled and spotted. The colour of oatmeal. Nothing but bones. Somehow the soot had got back on her nose. Her hair was like wires. Even as I looked, her fingernails seemed to be growing. Her cheeks were sunken. She had on her favourite coat. The coat was faded and tatty and hung unevenly at her heels. I remembered that coat. She'd got it off some hook at the bingo parlour. She had the little gold locket around her neck. Heart-shaped. My daddy's image would be on one side; I would be on the other. If, unbeknownst to us, some black face hadn't jumped in.

She backed, groaning, out into the hall. Her finger beckoned to me. "Our kind is no more than a spit in the bucket," she said. "You remember that. It's all one big tub out there and what part isn't filled with blacks is stacked up to the brim with Chinese. It's overflowing with Poles and A-rabs and Indians and even Huguenots. That's another bunch your daddy didn't like, them Huguenots. And the whirlwind's coming. But that don't mean we toss in the towel, does it, son?"

—You bet! I said. You bet, my wonderful old mam!

She was already vanishing. Holding up her old Victory fist.

—One more thing, son. Get that tarty woman off your door.

Folding back into the wall, becoming the wall. Stumbling once or twice and then . . . gone. Yes, gone.

Yet I hung in the doorway, hoping for one final glimpse.

—Mam? I whispered. Mam, are you still there?

I ran over and kissed the wall. Put my cheek where her visage had been.

—Mam? I said. Will I see you again?

But she *was* gone. Wall or world, it had swallowed her up. And I stood trembling, pining for a sweet farewell. Longing for one unsullied word of love. Wanting total forgiveness—full recognition—from her.

Afraid—shivering with fear!—that my daddy next would walk in.

Sighing. Unable to admit that what I wanted most was what I never could have. This: that *both* would leave me alone.

And Christ, which way *now* could I turn? For I wasn't out of these woods yet. I spotted Mergentoire at the foot of the stairs, stomping the floor, shaking a spoon.

"I've told you!" she shouted. "Told you and told you! Breakfast this minute or you go hungry!" And spun off.

Hedgepolt, hidden away, was banging on pots and pans.

The dogs were nipping and yowling.

Inside my room Greta was heaping up rage. Barking out her scorn. Quite furious.

"*Kooom* here!" she ordered.

Defiant, sullen, raving Greta. My angry beloved. She'd come down out of her calendar to wipe up mud and listen to the prattle of old mam. To stride the cramped room, to whirl contemptuously about and with guttural, raking voice—dramatic as a blizzard—declare that she had never been so insulted, so humiliated. So violated and abused. "*Like dirt I am treated! Yes? No?*" To ask what kind of flea or toad was I, what creature, what snivelling worm, what formless, horrible, gambolling idiot? *Yes? No?* To ask how *"dot voh-mahn"* could dare invade our privacy, rumple our sheets, question the way we conducted our lives. *"Who is dot death-hag to tell me I shood marry, I shood haf children! How dare she? Und did yoo see dot coat? Dose shoes? It's lunacy, sheer lunacy, und I, Greta Gustafsson, I moost put up with theece!"* To rail at the callousness, the bigotry, the inanity, the perversity—at the dimwitted nature of mankind in its totality and my bloodline in its particulars.

"Vy do I stay with yoo?" she shouted. "Vy do I make myself preet-tee? Vy did I ev-vair koom to theece half mahn, to theece child, theece mental deficient! Vot a place your room izz! Vot a stinkhole! I haf seen shoeboxes big-gair. Me, Greta, who has lived in palaces, who kood haf kings with the krook of my fing-gair!"

"Oh!" she cried, galloping about, thumping her fists against my head, wrenching up and down. "O-o-o-oh! De an-sair is only one. *Une!* Me, I am craze-eee too! Greta is birdbrain!"

This Stockholm beauty, what a flame-thrower! What acid! And how beautiful. How divine. How my heart soared to see her in this mood. Sultry. Passionate. Maddeningly dramatic. I had seen her a hundred times this way on the shimmering screen: breathing this fierce energy, this mystery, this power. A dynamo of unrelenting love. Yielding only *to* love, no matter how fatal. Love came first, above her very life. Her every performance insisting that love *was* life. That every risk was worth the taking. *Mata Hari. Camille. Ninotchka. Wild Orchids. The Blue Sea. The Yellow Bed. Anna Karenina.* Garbo. My very own Garbo. The great Greta Lovisa Gustafsson. Yet never so in my little room. Always the cold shoulder, the blank stare, the senseless smouldering—elusive, self-absorbed, afraid of her shadow! *Above* life.

"Liar!" she now screeched. "*Yoo haf not loved me enough! I haf not vunted your idolization! I haf vunted to be loved as I am! As you haf loved your lunatic old mam! Greta does not vunt to be alone! She does not vunt alvays to be on de door. Hold me, darling!"*

Oh Greta, Greta, Greta. This much I now knew of Greta, as I was coming to know it of myself: every encounter, including those only imagined, is an affair of the soul. Is cutthroat war. The soul is at vigil; it is in a last-ditch battle. It is in armed conflict against the grinning dark, the waiting terror, the foul abyss. It holds off the stinking Hereafter. The soul would defend and preserve our tenuous and fleeting bones. This pitiful, slime-sinking body. Soul is heroic! It goes on warring despite impossible odds of stone and brickbat and the immense conflagration, the high flames that ever sweep around it.

This I find remarkable.

Nothing else in life is so beautiful.

And Greta now accepted this, too. Greta was willing. *"Any-zing!"* she now wept. *"I vill do any-zing to hold your love! Even theece ugliest of rooms, theece flea-box, theece hole, theece dot! Let it be ours! Hold me, Adlai. Hold and kiss and save your demented Greta!"*

Oh, what a speech! My flesh tingled. Bells clanged in a thousand towers. For we were saving ourselves. We were discovering again that one body alone cannot hold back, cannot assuage, bend or diffuse the wicked dark. The vile, thunderous, rampaging dark. One's frame falls apart, bones scatter, flesh flies apart like birds over water, but true love, true life, charges on. The bones explode, they mix with air and water, with air and flower, and when they come down they come down rearranged. Love, dreadful love, slouches in.

And so her lips plunged down on mine. The famous Garbo mouth burned, burned and parted. Our tongues slithered and slid like a hundred snakes uncoiling in a single wet hole. A wet, luscious, heavenly bog. We moaned—exultant! What a picnic!

What a dreamy, wondrous, spine-tingling dark! What ecstasy! For mouth was nice, but mouth wasn't all. We locked limbs, we licked and scratched, we yowled and bit and spun. Howl, spit and claw. What a whimpering, roaring, blood-boiling feast love is! The floor scraped at our elbows. Knees cooked. But our singing flesh went on multiplying. Steel replaced backbone. Fire replaced lips. Hands tugged and stroked, tongues slurped, our hips hummed. *Hmmmmmmmmmm!* Our hearts clanged like a Cyclops's thunderbolts. We crashed against the footlocker, kicked against wall, and came grappling—breathless!—up over it. We slithered as one onto the crumbling bed. The mattress sizzled. Smoke shot from my ears. The roof lifted right out of my skull. And still our tongues went on working. For mouth was nice but mouth wasn't all. Matters got deadly. The hum quickened. EEEEEEEEEEEE!!!

"I want you, Garbo!" I thundered.

"Dun't talk, idiot!"

We romped past passion, past love's fury, and settled in for holy worship of piquant—exquisite—lust. And I thought, as I have always thought: What a treasure woman is! What a world! What a dream-time! Oh, wow, Adlai, how lucky you are!

The first time.

The first time ever.

My baptism.

Soul's immersion.

Thus when it was over I still couldn't believe it. Impossible. Greta had wanted *me?* Pitiful me? I studied her sleeping body, amazed. Her little feet! What extraordinary toes!—like the curved white petals of a flower. Her bent knees and the fingers so softly folded. How fragile she seemed. The chin tucked so childishly into her bosom. Her breath so faint, so sweet, so . . . *not there* . . . that I wanted to convey it into heaven on a quivering rainbow.

This dream had wanted me? Uncanny. No, it was beyond truth. Reality couldn't touch this.

But I touched her—one finger along the ribs—and knew that it had.

"All the news you want!" shouted the black vender. *"Get it here, boss!"*

I went at last down to breakfast.

Mergentoire and her son Hedgepolt sat at the massive table, alone but for each other and a sea of soiled dishes. The steaming atmosphere of daily exhaustion and a mother's eternal, despairing vigilance. What wreckage! Oh the appetite, the furnace-stoking, gut-storming wizardry of twenty hard-hat labourers at their meal! Reaching, sweating, chomping—packing in the fuel. My brusque, unroped companions from the mines, the factories, from field, ditch, and stable; our century's dogly warriors. Our last heroes.

Mergentoire was slumped low, brooding in half-doze, raking a hand idly up and down Hedgepolt's spine. The boy didn't hear me enter; he stayed limp as a rag. Mergentoire's eyes shifted grievously to me. "Here he is," she moaned. "The man who doesn't know what day it is. Who doesn't know today from tomorrow or yesterday from a mile of cotton candy." She looked away dreamily, scratching away at some itch under her bra strap. "How was the funeral?" she asked softly.

My eyebrows went up.

I sat down.

Mergentoire's mood underwent another subtle shifting. She glowered, hoisting a heavy arm in the direction of my room. "I could shoot you," she said, "for what you do up there."

I grinned sheepishly into my lap. My body was still humming:

the hum was silent, but I yet had it. *Ummmmmmm*. Like ripples on a lake when the sky is becalmed.

Mergentoire sighed heavily. "Well," she said, "if there's anything left, feel free to gobble it up."

The bread dish was empty. The fruit dish was too. No eggs, no porridge. The coffee pot had six drops left in it.

I didn't mind. My stomach was motor-boating away but my head was off in dreamland. My thighs still had the quiver.

Mergentoire's voice softened again. "The old lady," she said, "I hope she went happy. I hope she'd made her peace with God."

I was studying Hedgepolt, who had a fly trapped in his hand. He opened his fingers slowly, but the fly remained, as found. In his palm's centre, faintly buzzing, mindlessly grooming its ugly head.

Mergentoire and I stared at the fly. We stared at Hedgepolt as well, though it was the fly we kept returning to.

Hedgepolt poked a finger at the fly. The fly flipped over and lay on its back, unmoving.

"The old lady," murmured Mergentoire. "How did it go?"

But I hardly heard her. What about that? I was thinking, Hedgepolt has a pet fly.

"The funeral, you ape!" growled Mergentoire. "How did it go?"

The fly lifted, banking away.

"Did anyone come? Did she have flowers?"

Whoa, I thought. *Whoa*, Mergentoire. What gives here? For I knew not at all what she was talking about.

Yet, as I blinked at her my confusion, something tapped at my eyelids. A dim, grey shadow lifted on the previous day. The littered table gave way to rain-soaked ground.

Leaning headstones.

A black, snarling sky.

Rain thundering down.

My shoes sloshing through muck.

Wind whistling past my ears like shrieks from a shut-up thing.

Hedgepolt's sticky hand in mine.

Mergentoire saw something too. And looked to see if she could find evidence of it in my trembling hand. In my besotted eyes.

Whoa, I thought. Whoa, Mergentoire. Let's not go too fast.

"I was up all night cleaning his shoes," she said. "Lucky for you he didn't catch cold." She eyed me shrewdly, raking a coil of hair back behind one ear. Tugging her housecoat up to her throat. "Well, I'm not the one to say it, and God forgive me, but what I say is you can count your blessings she's gone."

Whoa, Mergentoire.

"I mean, she was *old*. I mean, she's out of her misery now."

Hedgepolt, I noticed, was now studying me. His mouth opened a little wider. His eyes too. Drool coagulated around his chin.

"Hello, Hedgepolt," I said.

He closed up his hand. The fly had returned.

I can't understand Hedgepolt and here's why: he looks to be every bit of thirty, yet he's still in grammar school. Still wears his trousers rolled to his knees, still has a runny nose. Can usually be found sucking on a filthy dishrag. I call it so; Mergentoire calls it his security cloth.

This morning he didn't have the cloth. His great head was slung out over the table like an ironing board. Studying me, when he should have been training his fly.

"Say good morning, Hedgepolt," Mergentoire told him.

Hedgepolt blinked. His tongue slipped out. Slowly he dipped his head and began licking at a clear spot on the table.

I laughed, though his behaviour made me uneasy. This was

regressive conditioning, it was backsliding. It went against the pact I had with him. Even so, I went on laughing. "Hey, Hedgepolt," I said, "who's your mam?"

His eyes jiggled, he straightened rigidly in his seat—then his arm flopped up to point directly at me.

"Good old Hedgepolt," I warmly murmured. Touched, as I always was, by this odd familial display. Such a good-hearted, agreeable lad, I thought. I leaned over and roughed his hair.

Mergentoire glared.

I ignored her crossness. We all have such days.

"It won't work," she snapped. "It's time you faced up to things. The old lady—"

But I cut her off. "The boy needs a haircut," I said. "He needs to give more attention to his appearance. One of these days old Hedgepolt is going to start thinking of girls."

Mergentoire's face went red. She caught her breath. Her fists bunched up and her close little eyes stared angrily into mine. "Not under my roof he won't," she said heatedly. "Not while I live and breathe!"

Hedgepolt was nodding excitedly, a grand smile on his face.

We had had talks, him and me. I'd set him straight on the birds and the bees.

"Look at him," I said. "He's ready right now. You do want a girlfriend, don't you, Hedgepolt?"

He was nodding as Mergentoire's fist slammed down. She was genuinely fed up now. "Stop saying that!" she cried. "Stop dreaming dreams for my Hedgepolt! Quit giving him expectations!"

I thought, *Ah, that Mergentoire, what a case!* I thought, *Dream the dreams, Hedgepolt. Dare to be God!*

And Mergentoire's face drained. She rose up, clutching a fork, clutching the folds of her loose gown—fit to be tied. You'd think she had stepped right into my head. "So it's God now, is it?" she raged. "It's God you want him to be? When he can't even go to the bathroom by himself!"

I thought, *Small stuff, Mergentoire*. Thought, *Poor Mergentoire*.

For Mergentoire disliked the interest I took in her boy. Hated the care I had taken in grooming this boy for a normal life. It alarmed her, our walks in the moonlight, our talking of birds and bees. The way he hung on my every word. Nor could she admit to herself the long way he'd come, under my wing. *A sea of expectations*, I thought. *A sea for everyone*.

"God!" she shouted. "When he can't even tie his shoes? When he doesn't even know what shoes are for?"

Hedgepolt was crying. His wide thick shoulders shook and actual tears were splashing down. One quivering hand reached for the tablecloth. He tried stuffing that into his mouth. Terrible. Oh, what sounds. I knew he was suffering. I knew the hurt he felt. I ached with him. But a mere six months before this he'd been docile as a turnip patch. Empty. A vacuum. His face had never revealed the faintest expression, beyond a stony watching. He had never cried.

It hurt. But this was progress.

Mergentoire whimpered, embracing him, tugging his head to her bosom. "Don't cry," she whispered, sobbing herself. "Oh, don't cry. Mam's sorry. Mam got out on the wrong side of the bed this morning. Mam's sorry she raised her voice. Forgive your mam? Forgive me, Hedgepolt? Mam would never hurt her Hedgepolt. Mam loves Hedgepolt."

Beautiful. I loved Mergentoire at her mothering.

"Let's see your fly again. Let mam and Adlai see your nice fly."

They went on blubbering. And, yes, I did too. For I was remembering my own old mam. I was back there with her, my head on her bosom. Sobbing. Getting charley horses in my gut from all the ache I was carrying.

—There, there, she'd say. You're thinking of him, aren't you, son? Of the good daddy you've never seen? But don't cry. Don't blubber. You know your daddy has got his work to do. Just as one day you'll have yours.

—Will I, mam?

—Sure you will. Your spot is saved. It's waiting for you.

—Mam? My mam? Did he ever try it out on you?

—Try what, my boy?

—His birth control.

—Oh gracious. Goodness gracious. Of course he did. I was the first.

—But mam!

—It didn't take, son. Otherwise, would I have had you?

—I'm here, am I not, my mam? I'm *real*?

—Oh, you're real, son.

—Are you sorry, my mam? That I'm here?

—Now, son, don't cry! Don't blubber. Hold those shoulders back. Don't you want your daddy to be proud of you?

—Will he be? Will I grow up to fill his fine shoes?

—Oh, I doubt that. There can be only one of him. And there's this to think about: long before you've come of age the black tide will have swept over all of us.

—But my *spot*, my mam!

—I've upset you, haven't I? There, there. Mam's sorry. Give a kiss to your potty, unthinking old mam. Mam got up on the wrong side of the bed today. That's it—give a smile to your old mam.

Dear wonderful mam. Dear comforting mam. She was aged then herself, and her back stiff from weeding spuds. From keeping together house and home. Between my daddy and the bingo I was all she lived for.

—Is that true, mam? Am I your pudding and pie?

—You're it, Adlai. The apple of my eye.

—I wasn't dropped off on your doorstep? By some man on a black horse?

Mam would get cross when I'd ask that. She'd get out what she said was my daddy's old walking stick, and switch my behind.

—Who's been telling you them stories? Putting these tales in your head.

For it was a fact I'd been hearing things. There was talk that mam wasn't all she said she was. That mam had never wed, for one, and that'd I'd come down the chimney like a chimney-black.

—Lies! Lies! Don't listen to them!

But I'd been wondering. Not all I'd heard was going out of both ears.

—They hint that I'm tar-brushed, old mam. That there's a tar-brush somewhere! That there's not smoke without fire!

—Hush! Hush! Don't even whisper it, child. Your daddy is away yonder in the Upper Volta doing his work. You're making his ears burn.

But I'd find myself looking and wondering. For something else was occurring. Putting the heebie-jeebies on me. I'd look at mam's elbows and her knees. I'd look at her hands and feet. I'd examine her skin. I'd catch her with her housecoat undone and I'd think: *that's* strange. For it seemed to me mam's skin was changing. That her flesh was darkening with every day that went by.

—What's happening, my mam? I'd say. What's happening to you?

And mam would cover up her face, she'd shiver and shake.

—It's old age! she'd moan. It's my . . . my Change! It . . . it's from thinking all the dark thoughts of a lifetime! It's . . . from having you!

And I'd laugh. Old mam, what a joker.

But later I'd be looking in mirrors. In bed at night I'd be feeling my hair. A bit *stiff*, I'd think. A bit *wiry*. A bit on the black side.

And next day I'd nag at old mam. I'd say, mam, don't you have a photo of my daddy? Don't you have *one* picture of him?

Mam would thump her chest. "In here," she'd say. "In my heart, that's where your daddy's photo is. And in yours, too, if you had any decency left."

Sweet, dear old mam. Her stick was hard on the behind, but she was ever straight with me.

The dogs' yowling, and not Hedgepolt's weeping, broke up my reverie. They'd come yowling three times around the house and twice up the nettle tree, and now had parked under the dining-room window to kick up dust and yowl all the harder. It was blood-curdling murder out there, with maybe a cat or two mixed in.

I nibbled on a toast scrap from the neighbouring plate. I licked on bacon rind found under the chair.

It didn't matter. Appetite was the last thing I had.

I was remembering a letter I'd received. *Dear Son. My spot's about used up. I'm slipping. Not long left now. Will you come? Can you do that for me?*

I hadn't gone. No, I'd let her dot fade right out.

August eleventh. Anniversary of Blondin's crossing Niagara on a tightrope wire. And mam stretched out in a box on the rain-soaked ground.

"Do you love me, Hedgepolt?" Mergentoire was asking. "Do you love Mergentoire most in the world?" She had his head on her shoulder, was stroking his hair. Her voice soothing, even to me. "Your mam loves *you*," she said. "Adlai loves you too. We are all one big family." Her foot nudged mine under the table. "Tell him, Adlai. Tell him how happy we are."

For Hedgepolt's sake I managed a smile. A nice little nod of the head. "You bet," I said. "She's said a mouthful, son."

Hedgepolt's robe-chewing slackened. His eyes widened. His look swam from her to me. "Brace up, Hedgepolt," I said. "Life has its little monkey-wrenches, but you can follow my example."

And I sat erect, my shoulders back, my expression firm. Pretending I was looking intelligence at him. Happiness, too.

We sat a long time that way.

Strangely, his face shook loose of its idiocy until at last it became one radiant angel's smile.

"*Dad-dee*," he said.

Our jaws dropped. Hedgepolt had never been known to speak before.

"*Dad-dee*," he said again. And his arm flopped towards me. Then with more grace than I could believe he swung it around to point at Mergentoire. "*Mam-mee!*" He patted her head.

Mergentoire's lips quivered. Her eyes glazed over, then moistened. With a deep moan, half sob, half joy, she swooped her arms around him. But Hedgepolt's own arm kept on rising. His face was flushed, his heart pounding; I could see he was getting the hang of speech. "*Gret-ta*," he said. "*Gret-ta Gus-TAFS-son!*" He wheeled about, beaming. Dashing to the window. "*Dogs!*" he cried. "*Brutish, snarling dogs!*"

Mergentoire jumped up. We were both dazed. For a moment we shared an uncomprehending look. Then bliss streamed out of her pores. "*You're cured!*" shouted Mergentoire. "*Oh, Adlai, he's cured! My son is cured!*" She embraced him, lifted him off his

feet, swirled him around. *"My baby! My baby's no baby no more!"*
And she—and both of them—broke off into riotous laughter.
They danced and hugged and jumped on the floor. But Hedgepolt was still wanting to talk. He was stammering in excitement,
wanting to get it all out:

"Shoes!" he crowed. *"Adlai and Hedgepolt get shoes wet? Walk in
muck? See old mother? Throw flower in grave? Kiss old mother goodbye? Walk home in rain? Adlai hold Hedgepolt's hand? . . ."*

He spoke on, radiant. And joy, pure joy, in that moment
seemed to serenade my bones. It seemed to seep up through my
chair and to surge through me like light through a door. And it
went on blazing. It went on rising. It shot up through the long
table, rattling the dishes; it pulsed over our heads, and spun; it
crashed up into the ceiling and went on rising; it crashed through
our very walls and went on splashing and tumbling, whirling like
a fireball through the atmosphere. Even the dogs, vicious that second before, fell silent. Joy rolled on, flooding the universe. And
even then it swept on, shining and beautiful.

We were all in rapture.

"Adlai happy!" screeched Hedgepolt. *"Adlai happy for his old
mother? He happy for Hedgepolt? He happy with world?"*

Hold on, I thought. Adlai, hold on.

For it wasn't mam I saw, or Hedgepolt's glee, or the two of us
reeling over mam's sorrowful grave, or mud on our shoes. These
were but a flick at the eyelids. Joy, purest joy, was shunting these
aside. What I was seeing was deep water and over the mammoth
face of that water legion upon legion of matchstick canoes and
in those canoes a thousand black faces and those faces whooping
delight at me the same as I was whooping it back at them. And
nothing poor mam could do about it. One by one they were crying out, *I'm coming, I'm coming, make way for me! I'm going no*

place but UP UP UP! Oh, look at the Devil running! Flags I saw waving by the hundreds. There were the Upper Volta colours and beside it little Benin and Guinea-Bissau. Over there were Gabon and Cameroon, Ghana and the Ivory Coast. Here came Somalia and Djibouti and Botswana, Nigeria and Malawi and Kenya. And a great chorus was riding the waves: *We coming! We are coming, brother!*

Hold on, I thought. Hold on.

For I could hear myself shouting back, as if from a planet a breath's space removed: *Come on, you polecats! There are spots for all of us!* The Upper Volta ears pricked up. Their eyes did a double-take. *Is that you, boss?* they asked. *Is that you? Is that the king?* And I gave them my biggest wave. *Come on! Come on! Git the lead out!* At this the Mossis, the Lobis, even the itchy Gurunsis scooped their hands into the water, rode the crests of waves, and came crashing forward. *We coming, boss!*

Crashing on past me as I sat rocking in my chair—in my chair or wherever my spot was—delirious in the face of this vision, wondering which was vision and which was real life and finally where it, or they, or even myself, had gone.

Something wet was licking my hand.

My scalp felt tingly.

This day, too, I thought, was slipping away from me. The light seemed eerie. Had I slipped forward into some future year? Adlai, where are you? Adlai is on his tightrope out over the swirling water, balanced between rope and sky, wavering and floundering with his balancing pole. Adlai steering for the river's other shore. Adlai saying, Mam, are you there? Mam, will you forgive me? Adlai falling. Adlai crying. Then only the quivering rope and the crashing water there.

"You've done it, Adlai! Hooray for you!"

What's this? I thought. What's happening now? For Mergentoire was hugging me. Hedgepolt was hugging me. And I was hugging myself, too. I was trembling inside a rapture totally new and strange. What a mystery! Sweat dripped from my nose. Is this happiness? I asked.

I could hear Greta upstairs gaily chirping. Calling to me. "Adlai, come draw my bath. Come up and scrub my back and sit with me."

Mergentoire and Hedgepolt were silent. Their eyes rapt.

The dogs beneath the window were silent. Or gone. I thought I could see them racing as a pack down the long street to another place. Soon, perhaps, to splay off into green countryside.

I closed my eyes.

Peace.

Soul's ascension.

And mam's watchful eye splayed off, too. It went whirling away into the dark.

"Adlai, are you coming?" Greta called.

I had the strangest desire. I wanted to say to Greta, "Go home, honey. There are people at home who have need of you."

But I said nothing. I stayed on. Stayed, I say, as if bolted to my chair, as Hedgepolt's head lay warmly in my lap, and Mergentoire leaned against my knees, emptied of her joyful weeping. I sat on, thinking, So many people in the world depend on you. So many. Even if you're nothing—even if you're no one and you don't know which way to turn or whether turning is a thing you're capable of —even then they do.

Oh, mam, they do.

Painting the Dog

J ACQUES TEAK did all the moneyed people's pooches. This and that party swore to his excellence, you can't go wrong with terrible Jacques Teak, they said. "Why is he terrible?" Charmaine had asked. No manners, they said, first word out of his mouth you'll want to shoot him.

Charmaine's husband, Donald, told her, "Sure, go ahead, call the guy, he can't be that bad, you can handle him. When I get home next week, I'll expect to see one pink pooch. Jesus Christ, I've stumbled over that dog a thousand times."

Donald spoke the truth. Charmaine's white pooch, Monica, was getting lost against the white marble, she was getting stepped on, kicked for a loop. You're strolling along, sipping the Moët et Chandon, and suddenly you're sprawling, oops!

Unmentioned by tactful Donald was, one, his opinion, there was too much marble, forty thousand square feet of marble, a guy could go blind in this house; two, but for her yapping, the pooch Monica would be a pancake by now. "She yaps," he said to her this very morning, "at least you saw that red tongue, otherwise it's a fucking nightmare."

This pooch Monica, bunny-white like the marble, white like the walls, the flooring, carpets, the ceiling, like the sofas and chairs, lampshades, every room, even the whatnots white, this pooch blending in with forty thousand square feet of snowy field, come winter you can't even see the house. Donald was dead on, for those who couldn't hack white this ten-mill Rockcliffe Park palace was a nightmare. How many broken arms, sprained ankles, how many noggins hitting the floor, all on account of that pooch?

Charmaine pouted, she said, "Permission to redirect, your honour." She wasn't without wit, our Charmaine, she wasn't without brains. You had the idea she was just a long-limbed bimbo from Chicoutimi with dyed blond hair who, but for plucky Donald, might still be fitting spectacles in the Sparks Street optical shop. I'd advise you to abandon that image right now.

"I wish you wouldn't use that F word," Charmaine said, and Donald only rolled his eyes at this reproof, he buzzed her lips nicely, gave a nice stroke to her fanny, then out the door, the limo waiting, he's got a plane to catch, for Chrissake. Charmaine had a foul mouth, too, you just had to crank her up with Moët et Chandon.

They got along, Charmaine and Donald. To put it another way, they had respect for each other, they were lovers, pals. You want the truth, they didn't see that much of each other except at special put-aside times, it was a happy marriage, exactly what both desired.

Charmaine sopped up her hurt feelings re the pooch, re their little squabble, she merely yelled out the white window, "Calm down, Donald, I said I would take care of it."

Meaning the dye job.

"Good," Donald shouted back. "He misbehaves, shoot the son of a bitch."

Meaning Jacques Teak.

This was at breakfast, six o'clock, after their usual sweat hour in the Nautilus gym off the bedroom, off and up a few landings, thirty-seven machines of customized chrome, no flab around here, any little jiggle of flesh we are hitting the machines, forgoing the stir-fry, letting only ginseng-and-spirulina shakes power our bones. Lean Charmaine checking in at five-eight, 116 on the scales, a bobsledder, a snowboarder, skydiver, dynamite on the squash court, great instincts on the slopes, powerful feet, trim ankles, a knockout, ask anyone.

Charmaine's in the pink, no question, but doesn't Donald have a point? There's the pooch's feelings to consider, the mutt getting slammed every which way, we don't want her personality undermined, we don't want her developing an attitude. We can take Donald's word for it, the mutt is getting whiny, she's safe only in the slumber hours, her up there on Charmaine and Donald's wraparound bed, the pooch cute as can be as she snoozes away in her very own thousand-buck Prada handbag, that being how she came, a gift from that prince fellow over in St. Moritz, thank you, Prince.

Here that same day came Jacques Teak, driving up in a red Porsche, for Chrissake, not even thinking about going around to the servants' entrance.

"Sure thing," Charmaine could hear him telling Ella the maid, "that's me, the dye man." Then a quick scream, what, has he pinched her fanny?—a flurry of feet, a hard smack, nobody fools with Ella.

But the guy coming right on in, like he's been accustomed to a swanky, high-tone manor like this from the moment of conception, like he lived this minute in one every bit as swell, such grandeur did not discompose Jacques Teak, didn't inhibit him, the guy only saying, in a lilt that expressed his amazement, "What a lot of white marble! Jeez, I needed my binocs just to find the house."

Charmaine hating him from that first minute.

"Carrara marble," she said. "Take the sofa, yes, that's the dog I want painted, Monica, darling, say hello to"—this asshole, she almost said—only correcting herself in the last second—"to Mr. Teak."

"Whoa," said Jacques Teak, "she blends right in, doesn't she? I nearly tripped over the mutt—how many lawsuits you had?"

Charmaine feeling a shiver go through her in that second, a premonition: this day isn't going to be an ordinary day, dire events are to transpire this day. Right that second, intuition told her to march upstairs, get the pistol, load the sucker, strap it to her waist.

But she subdued these rash thoughts, what on earth was the matter with her? "Would you like something to drink, Mr. Teak?" she asked, she will entertain the bastard a minute before getting down to business, she's no snob, just a simple girl from Chicoutimi who got lucky, who knew what she wanted and came equipped with the assets—"Champagne, a glass of Moët et Chandon?"

Charmaine lowers herself onto the down cushions, crosses those amazing legs, she's going informal today, the white leather catsuit, white gold adorning neck and wrists, bare feet because she loves that cool marble next to her flesh, she drinks nothing herself but Moët et Chandon.

"Whatever you're having," said Jacques Teak, looking about, measuring the property value, every newcomer did. Charmaine hated that, not the measuring so much as the very words issuing from his mouth. If a person can't abide the bubbly, if they prefer something else, let them speak right up, such is her view.

"Nifty layout," Jacques Teak said.

Charmaine wanted to sock him.

She'd done this house herself. Well, mostly, well, in concert with the supremo master Gunnar Birkerts. Charmaine was proud of this house, a showplace, you could find it on the pages of a dozen magazines, so it was a tad white, that was the whole idea, Gunnar had agreed with her. We've got to cut, snap, funnel and shape light into the most inaccessible space, Gunnar had said, think "snowy field, Charmaine."

Out there was the sculpture garden, sixteen alabaster nude women in acrobatic flight sixteen feet high around the gushing curved-earth fountain, columns imported from Italy, the pool house there in white marble, a white marble pool the size of a city park, place a value on that, Mr. Teak, Charmaine thought, and I'll bet you won't even be in the ballpark.

"Nifty sculpturi," the man said.

Charmaine dragged a hand through her hair, stifling a groan, wincing at something, maybe at Jacques Teak's voice, which was certainly on the fey side. She didn't cotton to this guy, he was too full of himself, a cockroach, and look at those ringed fingers, those cowboy boots, that blue ascot around his neck, woo, forgive me if I shudder, Mr. Teak.

But there was poor, bedraggled Monica, bunny-white with her pink eyes, her red tongue, hopping into the dye guy's lap, circling to sit, now doing so, and Jacques Teak lifting the pooch's ears, peering about as if he suspected ticks were in there.

"Monica," the man said, "Now, that's not a name I would ever give a dog. What, she's a typist, a porno star? Nice collar, though, a Gucci, I'll bet."

Impossible, who were these friends that had recommended this bug?

But Charmaine got control of herself, she wasn't about to let herself be undone by a lowly pet consultant, a pet stylist, whatever he called himself.

"I got a one-eyed Maltese the near twin," he said, "female just like Monica here, I call her Tessie."

Charmaine barked out a good laugh, you could say it was involuntary, the guy not knowing a Gucci neck collar from a Chanel and saddling a Maltese with such an insipid name, Tessie, my God, practically Victorian. She should have let Donald handle this, Donald have would put this guy in his place, Donald would have taken one look at that ascot, those boots, and kicked this Teak out the door. But Donald liked her to assert herself, Donald would have said she was every bit his equal on any front you could name, and better than him in many respects, his company had even named a tech system in her honour, Charmaine Catalyst 2000, that was the kind of marriage theirs was. No fooling around either, Charmaine had not the least interest in embarking on such as that. So she would just have to take care of this dye thingy, as well as any other domestic issue arising. Just because a woman had a demanding career, meaning the upcoming TV hostessy duty, and had for pride's sake to spend endless hours looking to her own upkeep and to set aside several months annually for a lock-in at the Ashram, that wonderful California boot camp spa, didn't mean you let home issues slide.

Charmaine pressed the button on the white side table, and there instantly was Ella popping through the open French doors, she must have been in the hallway waiting, good girl, Ella. Here Ella came, the face composed, black hair in a Cleopatra cut, white cap on top of her head, skin shaded with whitening a near match of the marble but for those sultry eyes, the buttercup lips, her imprisoned bosom, hipless, the poor thing, but attractive nevertheless in a very striking tight white uniform, quite a maid's ticket, in other words, that uniform being a design of Donald's own genius, with help from a celebrated designer in Paris, France, not that we want to drop names.

Jacques Teak was checking out Ella, legs slung over a carpet yanked from Arabic sands, bleached bone-white by five hundred years of Bedouin sun, six hundred knots per square inch—one boot propped above the other, leering, but that leer a bit phony, a bogus copy, in Charmaine's judgment.

Ella pouring the fizz into two exceptionally tall glasses, finest cut crystal, at one time Charmaine had twenty-four of these beauties, now down to a mere trio, Donald with his big hands couldn't seem to get the hang of holding good crystal, he, after all, being a trucker's boy.

Then, can you imagine, not a pin dropping, Jacques Teak's hand coming up between Ella's legs, stroking over the white stockings, him there smirking at Charmaine for what seems like endless minutes, Ella shock-still in the instant but that Moët et Chandon still pouring, not a drop spilled, Charmaine filled with admiration for the woman even as she thinks, It's time I went upstairs and got that pistol.

"Thank you, Ella, that will be all," Charmaine said, her voice shaky, the girl in the instant retreating, Jacques Teak raising a brow, smiling, disdainful, as he observes Ella's slim-line hips, the streamlined legs, the high breasts, that uniform tight on her, tasteless, you could say, but Donald wasn't any too fond of loose rags on a female, that layered look women had gone in for over the past decade, well, that was just insane unless you were a fatso and had reason to hide it.

Charmaine rising, saying to Jacques Teak, "Excuse me one minute, sir," leaving the room hurriedly, but where has Ella got to, she's nowhere to be seen, just a great expanse of white space, a snowy field, the pooch's little paws going click-click behind her, but suddenly there's the black Cleopatra hair, a silver tray about chest high, Ella's figure emerging from the white wall. "Ella," Charmaine asks, "did I just see what I thought I saw in there, that creep's hands on you?" The girl has tears in her eyes, she says, "No, Miss Charmaine, you did not imagine it," and for a second Charmaine feels witless, she is without volition, as though stranded in a white wilderness, in mountainous snow, but this passes, dear Monica is gnawing at one of her toes.

"Then we shall just have to teach him a lesson," Charmaine tells Ella, and an instant later she is climbing the stairs, here she is in her bedroom, here she is hefting the pistol, she's had lessons, she's the proud owner of a sharpshooter badge made of sapphires and diamonds set in platinum, clip chalcedony, gift of the prince, she can drill that son of a bitch Jacques Teak between the eyes at fifty paces, if she must.

When she reenters, he's there on the sofa, drinking from the bottle, looking her over, licking his lips, Moët et Chandon dripping from his chin. He's saying, "I use an aloe vera dye, best in the business, your mutt will have to be redyed every three weeks, purple, pink, green, blue, whatever you like, you want I should show you paint chips? Say your pooch lives ten years, the net to you will be approximately fifty thou, Jacques Teak don't come cheap. You understand, though, I got a waiting list a mile long, three months minimum before I can touch the mutt, and if you're thinking I might let you jump the queue because of that sexy catsuit you're wearing, because of who you are, you can forget it, Jacques Teak don't do no one no favours."

Charmaine drains her glass, she licks her lips, fans her hair, stares at Jacques Teak the longest time, her eyes squinting, cold, a test to see who will flinch first. But caught up short the next instant because she finds herself suddenly thinking of her mother, missing her childhood in Chicoutimi, even missing those care-free days in the Sparks Street optician's shop. The past is floating in front of her eyes, how amazing, there's no denying we are the custodian of our own lost selves.

The truth is, let's admit it, Charmaine doesn't want to dye her pooch. Monica, bless her, is just fine as she is, she blends into the white marble, you don't see Monica, you trip over the pooch, that's your own trouble, fix your own self up, get your own self dyed, that's what Charmaine is thinking.

"Of course," Jacques Teak is saying, "I'd have to have a hefty advance, and other than colour, it's me who calls the shots."

"Shots? You're calling the shots?"

"Yeah."

"Did you call this one?"

So Charmaine, that instant, shot him.

Afterward, she called Donald's office, she left a message with the secretary, "Tell him we've got a problem." She called the pro-ducer of her upcoming TV show, *Celebrity Pooch*, she told him there might be troubled waters ahead, hold the phone. Then she called the police. She and Ella sat on the sofa drinking a new Moët et Chandon, the pooch between them, all three watching Jacques Teak crawling tragically across the white marble, pretty soon he might reach the hallway, the front door, if he doesn't bleed to death he might even make it outside. If the son of a bitch had been wearing white, if those feet were not painting a crimson trail, in the fullness of the snowy landscape here at Rockcliffe Park they would hardly even have seen him.

All in all, it was kind of beautiful.

"Now," said Ella, another Chicoutimi girl, "to concoct a tale."

Wintering in Victoria

Y ESTERDAY REBECCA JUNE left me, no word of warning, no scenes, I walked in the bedroom and found her packing.

"That's right, jerk," she said. "I'm getting out of your life, you prick, I can't get out of this house fast enough."

Fine, I said, are you taking the kid?

"The kid, the kid, the kid!" she said, "do you even know her name? You bet I'm taking her, she isn't safe here with you!"

What have we done to our women?

Years have gone by since I met one who believed a child was safe with its father.

Not that it bothered me.

I waved them down the hall and out the door, told them if they changed their minds it would be all right with me.

If you want to come back, fine, if you want to make this permanent, fine—no hard feelings on my part.

My wife came running back inside a few minutes later to tell me she'd like to kick me silly, nothing would give her more pleasure.

"Someone," she said, "ought to knock some sense into you

before it's too late. If I was only big enough or strong enough or stupid enough, I'd do it myself. Man, would I give it to you!"

I put down the latest issue of *Swampstump*, got up out of the easy chair and bent over.

Go ahead, I said, this ought to make it easier.

The kid was crying, however.

The kid stood in the open doorway, her coat bunched in her arms, saying, "daddy, daddy, daddy, bye, daddy!"

Something is wrong with me. I was touched but barely enough to tell it.

My wife ran up to her, shook her, picked her up in her arms and said "Don't talk to that s.o.b."

Then they went.

Walking, who knows where or for how long, probably without a dime between them.

Too bad, I thought, it wasn't raining.

Since it wasn't I decided to go out for a while myself. Take a walk, Jake, I told myself, be good for you.

My pal Jack was in his driveway the next block down, polishing his Austin Mini. Across the street Mr. and Mrs. Arthur C. Pole were raking up wet leaves, trying to set fire to them.

Look at those idiots, I said to Jack—wasting perfectly good mulch.

Not that I cared.

Jack threw down his chamois cloth.

"You're my friend," he said, "right?"

Right, I said.

"I can talk to you," he said, "right?"

Right, I said.

"And you'll not take offence, right, you'll not want to punch my head in if I level with you?"

I told him not to worry, we were pals, we had been good friends for a long time, if he had something to say to me to come right out and lay it on me, no hard feelings on my part.

"Okay," he said, "I been wanting to say this to you for some months now."

Go ahead, I said.

"All right," he said, "I will. You've become a big pain, Jake, you've gone wing-wingy on us, nobody can stand your company any more. It isn't that you don't have feelings, no, I'm not claiming that, but nobody can reach you any more, Jake, it's a pain being with you, you've become a first-class down-at-the-heels shit-in-the-mouth and I can't stand the sight of you, I wish to hell I could never see you again." He stopped then and hitched up his pants and glared at me.

I told him I understood, that I wasn't upset, to get it all off his chest right now if it would make him feel better.

"All right, Jake," he said. "The fact is you've become a bloody cipher, a big zero, a big hulking zombie-fish that I get queasy just talking to! For your own sake you ought to seek professional help, talk to your minister, do something about your lousy condition."

Good, I said, I'm glad you told me, Jack, is there any more?

"That about sums it up," he said. "I've talked it over with my wife, I've talked it over with all the guys, and we are all in mutual agreement that we don't want to have anything more to do with you, we wash our hands of you."

Fine by me, I said, and turned and strolled away, not bothered in the least.

In fact, I felt relief—if anything.

I walked down to the billiards hall and broke a rack and dropped in seven balls the rotation way and quit then, hung up my stick, leaving the rest on the table, it's always that cruddy eighth ball that breaks my streak.

I went over to another table and broke another rack and ran seven more.

I felt all right, pretty good, but I can't claim much elation.

I picked up a pot roast from the butcher shop and walked home and put it in a pot with a potato and an onion and put this in the oven on a slow bake.

I thought it might feel pretty good to sit at home and enjoy a good dinner alone with maybe a glass of wine, take off my shoes, maybe afterwards have a quiet snooze.

In the meantime I checked through the mail, got out my chequebook, paid off some old bills.

I figured it cost me twelve thousand and eighty-four dollars a month just to be comfortable.

To have heat, lights, phone, seven rooms, a car and clothes.

The only thing I have even a faint objection to is the bird, a canary, that business of eating like a bird is utter nonsense, I can recall times in the past when I've thought the bird was eating me out of house and home.

But he does the best he can, I don't blame him, he's got to get along, I bear no grudges, I enjoyed writing those cheques, I thought that maybe tomorrow I'd go down and watch some of the people when they opened their mail, Stocker's Moving Company and B.C. Hydro and B.C. Telephone and the oil people, thinking surely they'd crack a smile to see that old Jake B. Carlyle had paid his debts in full, no need now to barrage him with further calls, threaten lawsuits, power cut-offs, all that crap.

So there was some mild elation, not much, nothing to shout about, and afterwards I enjoyed a hot bath.

I'm a little tired, I guess, of bathing with other people, of sharing the tub with wife or daughter. I stretched out, closed my eyes, sort of dreamed for a while.

The phone was ringing, it was some guy named Mr. Zoober, something like that.

These people who announce themselves as Mr. Such and Such, I can remember the times I'd strangle the phone and sometimes tell them to go to hell because people who say Hello, this is Mr. Such and Such from Such and Such give me a pain, they're rotten people obviously, they either want to sell you something or tell you they're cutting off your water, in the past such people have really got to me, but this time I was civil, I said, why yes, good of you to call, how can I help you, Mr. Zoober?

He told me he'd like to sell me some insurance, was I interested, and I thought about it for a second or two and then told him well I might be, tell me what he had in mind.

Which he did, and made an appointment to come over that very evening.

I put a few carrots in the pot roast, buttered a bit of bread, poured a glass of wine, and shortly thereafter sat down and had a very nice dinner.

It was during this that the doorbell sounded and I opened it and Jack stood there with his wife beside him.

Hello, Jack, I said, how are you, how are you, Alice, what can I do for you?

"We were thinking," said Jack, "that perhaps I was somewhat hard on you."

"Yes," said Alice, "you poor man, you see we didn't know that Rebecca June had left you."

I tried to explain to them that I valued Jack's comments, I appreciated his honesty, that as far as I could tell old Becky's leaving me had nothing to do with it.

"No," insisted Jack, "under the circumstances it was a mistake for me to come down so hard on you."

"You see," said Alice, "we didn't know you and Rebecca June were having marital difficulties, that changes everything, now we know why you've been such a drip, Jack wants to apologize."

It isn't necessary, I told them, the truth is we hadn't been having any special difficulty, no more so than other couples, that it would be a mistake for them to assume that such small differences of opinion as we had in any way accounted for my recent failures as a person.

No, I said, you're very fortunate to be rid of me.

They stared at me for five minutes or so and then went back to their car and drove away.

I thought it was nice of them to come by like that, a decent gesture, but it didn't matter to me.

I went back in and finished my meal which was cold by that time though I didn't care, if you ask me hot meals are very overrated.

I noticed about that time that I had cut my finger and figured it must have happened while I was slicing the carrots. Pretty deep gash.

I watched the CBC news on television and nothing much was happening in the world, which was fine with me. I watched a special next, highlights in the life of Doris Day, and finished off the bottle of wine without much thinking about it.

At eight Mr. Zoober called, right on time, and told me about the various plans and policies a man of my age and income and family status ought to have. He seemed a little worried that I was alone, he asked a few veiled questions about my wife, had a few suspicions about the empty wine bottle, but was obviously most disturbed by the dirty dishes still on the dining table.

On the whole he wasn't a bad fellow, I can't say I much objected to him, and we finally agreed that a policy for fifty thousand or so would do me fine.

I think he was quite surprised when I got out my chequebook and wrote out a big one for him, he seemed to think I had been stringing him along.

He made some joke or other about never losing a customer, and left right away, apologizing, saying he had a few more customers to see tonight, he was aiming for the Million Dollar Mark this year because his company was giving all the Million Dollar salesmen and their families a free trip to Honolulu.

I thought about inviting him back in to write out a bigger policy, what the hell, it didn't much matter to me.

Not much else happened that night, Rebecca June's mother called and asked what the trouble was, couldn't things be sorted out, she'd always liked me or anyway had liked me pretty much until recently, what had happened to me, was it another girl?

I said, no, it's been years since I felt much attraction for anyone other than old Becky June, that her daughter was a fine woman and I hoped she wouldn't worry too much about this, to try to go to sleep and forget it.

"But little Cherise!" she said, "What will happen to little Cherise, don't you love little Cherise!" and crying on and on like that about the kid until I got bored with it all and hung up and got myself a cup of coffee.

I've never much understood how people can go through their lives drinking that lousy stuff they call coffee in the supermarkets, Eight O'Clock, and Yuban and Chase and Sanborn and Maxwell House and Nabob, it's enough to make a person sick, whereas I drink only the dark French roast because there is no better coffee in the world and standards ought to begin with these most common of practices otherwise there is little likelihood they will exist in more important affairs. People all over the world are drinking their lousy coffee and thinking this stuff stinks and likely as not going out to murder and rob and cheat, all because of the lousy coffee they drink, though I've long since given up getting worked up over such trivia, it doesn't matter to me, I had my French roast the filter way and stretched out on the sofa and dozed a while before getting up to draft a few letters to people I had been thinking about that day, my mother whom I have always respected and admired and my boss the business man and the girl I had known back in college named Cissy Reeves though I wouldn't know where to send her letter.

Dear Mom,

I said, and told her of the insurance policy of which she was co-beneficiary and enclosed Zoober's card in the event anything unfortunate happened to me and no one got in touch with her because it has been my belief that those guys will not pay off unless a gun is held at their throats.

I doodled a bit on her letter, not knowing what to say, wondering idly about her life and about mine and about her nine other sons and daughters all of whom had turned out to be fairly average people through no fault of hers.

I sealed it up after a while and drew a few kisses on the envelope, it wasn't much of a letter but what the hell.

Next I wrote my boss, telling him not to expect me to show up for work the following few weeks, I was going to take time off, if he didn't like it he could find another guy.

Then I wrote Cissy and that took some time because I found I didn't much remember anything of value about Cissy, she was a fairly regular girl, fairly routine, not especially attractive I guess if one wanted to be objective about it, hard to tell now why I had found her exciting enough to chase all over campus and storm and rage whenever I saw her with another guy, Cissy with her ordinary body and ordinary clothes and a mind certainly that no one would notice in a crowd, married, the last I heard, to some guy who was expecting big things from Simpson-Sears or The Bay, hell, who could remember? Dear Cissy, I wrote, I just thought I would get in touch after all these years and tell you that I have been thinking of you today for the first time since our graduation dance when you cried on my shoulder and told me you had decided to marry this business administration guy because you really loved him and you knew I'd be hurt but it was probably best for all concerned and how you walked with me out to the car and got in the back seat with me and how even as we were undressing it came over me that I had not the slightest interest in having you naked under me so I said crap on this and said goodbye Cissy Reeves and drove away and have not thought again of you until this very day when mostly all I want to say is how are you Cissy, how has your life been though I can't really say I care one way or another and I know I'll never give you another thought once I seal this letter.

I sealed it and it was the goddamn truth, poor Cissy, probably a good thing I didn't know where to send it.

But it was pretty boring about that time, I wasn't sleepy, so I made another copy and sent one to the head office of Sears in Toronto and another to the Vancouver Bay because I wasn't up to searching out their master quarters, it didn't matter that much to me one way or the other.

I finished off the cheque-writing chores, writing a letter for each cheque, telling B.C. Telephone and Hydro and the like how much I valued their services and hoped we could continue now with a good relationship, that I wasn't one of those who believed for a minute that their profits were excessive, that they were money-grabbers and impolite and sticking it to their customers wherever they could.

I fell asleep pretty soon after that, must have, because about twelve I was awakened by the telephone, I was asleep on the sofa in my clothes when this great jangle came, and it was Rebecca June of course calling me an s.o.b. prick and a lot of other things and she hoped I was enjoying myself, who did I have with me, she wasn't surprised, naturally I had never thought one minute of her, I was a self-indulgent prig without any feelings for anyone else and she had always known it would come to this—and I let her talk on, it didn't seem worth it to interrupt, I was even enjoying it in a mild way and appreciating her lip because normally she is such a steady person, level-headed, routine, somewhat ordinary, I guess, never saying much, taking life easy, you wouldn't think she was the type to have a thought in her head nor much emotion either.

"I'll kill you, kill you, kill you, you bastard!" she screamed that several times and I shrugged more or less, I asked if there was anything specific I had done to enrage her, to compel her to leave, that I'd be happy to apologize if that would make her feel better, that I'd promise to change, do better, try harder, if that would help her cope any easier with the situation. But she of course just continued to scream, not even using words any longer, the rare one like "Pig" or "s.o.b." but mostly just scream scream scream as though someone was slicing down her back with a butcher knife and finally her mother took the phone away from her and said Jake you've got to come over here, I can't do any more with her, and I sighed around a bit, I complained and tried to find excuses, said I had a lot to do, a lot of chores, but old Becky's mother is an insistent woman and eventually I agreed I'd come over and do what I could.

That's how it happened that I came across Jack and his old glum-chum wife Alice another time. They were sitting outside my house in their car, just sitting there watching my door as if they thought it might suddenly burst into flames.

I opened the door on Alice's side and asked what they had on their minds. I don't know, it seemed to me that once I saw them there, it was as if I had expected it or should have, I wasn't very surprised.

So hello, Jack, hello, Alice, have you been here long, what's on your minds?

Alice, in the past I've felt some sorrow for Alice, she has always seemed so miserable, so glum, but always without reason, no explanation for what's troubling her, that's just the way she is, glum and miserable, as if poor Jack had never kissed her and she had never wanted him to, as if nothing had ever happened to her and why should it, the truth is that Alice hasn't any imagination or interest, I suppose if she goes through her day and finds time to wash her hair or sweep the floor then that has been a pretty good day for her, nothing to complain about, about what she expected from the day, in fact it occurred to me as I opened her door that here was the first time I had found Alice out of her houserobe and slippers and now it had happened twice today so something very strange must be going on here.

They didn't say anything right away so I told them that I hoped they hadn't been brooding about Jack's comments to me, that truthfully I didn't mind a bit and Jack was absolutely right in telling me I was developing into a first-rate cipher, that I didn't mind in the least and was only just mildly surprised that anyone had noticed any difference in me, I certainly didn't intend to go around as if I had some sign hung on me saying Nothing Bothers Me.

"Jake, Jake, Jake," Jack moaned at last. "Get in, let's drive around a while."

I thought he had in mind going down to the S&W drive-in for maybe a hamburger and Coke, because we do that together sometimes with Alice and Rebecca June and the kid along, so I had to tell them I didn't think I could make it, I'd received an urgent telephone call a moment ago and had to get across town fast.

"From Rebecca June?" asked Alice, and I admitted that was the case.

She hugged me then, quite suddenly, I didn't so much as see her arms reaching out for me, she simply pulled me to her with the strength of a wild beast and pressed my head against her neck, thumping me on the back and repeating, "Poor Jake, poor Jake, oh you poor man, oh let us help you, I'm sure you will feel better if you'll only talk about it."

It was Jack who had to make her let me go, who pried her arms from around me. "For God's sake, Alice," he said, "how can he talk with you strangling him?" and she sat back quietly after that, sulking, biting her lips like a retarded child because she doesn't like him speaking to her in those tones, I guess.

"Now the reason we are parked in front of your house like this," he explained, "is because Becky called us, she was worried."

Worried? I said, and he said, "Yes, she was afraid you might do something to yourself."

Like what? I asked.

"Something criminal," said Jack, "and she said she would never forgive herself for it."

"She figured she'd be to blame," said Alice, "that she wouldn't be able to look at herself in the mirror ever again if you went and did something stupid to yourself like slicing your wrist, oh Jake you know she worships the ground you walk on, if only you weren't so peculiar!"

They continued to talk in that vein for some time, I couldn't say anything to calm them down. Finally I said, "Look, I thought you understood me. Suicide is the last thought from my mind, who can bother, no, you don't need to worry about me."

Alice gave me a consoling look, she kept reaching for my hand or my face or my leg and I kept trying to move out of her reach, lately I have just not liked at all people wanting to touch me. "So look," I said and it seemed to me my calm ought to have been blissfully penetrating—"Look, why don't the two of you toot along and look after your own lives, I'm fine, and I'm confident us Carlyles can handle this without your help."

But they wouldn't accept it, they were offended, they insisted I get in the car and they'd drive me over to Rebecca June's mother's house, the poor woman needed their help now even if I refused it and they wouldn't dream of walking out on a friend.

I got in the car, what the hell.

During the ride I tried to relax, not lose sight of this new life I'd found for myself. The truth is I couldn't help feeling some resentment, a guy comes along who isn't bothered by anything and right away everyone starts losing their wigs.

"Who was that man who came by your house earlier?" asked Alice, and I told her it was Mr. Zoober from the insurance company, and I saw them exchange glances and a moment later Alice broke into tears, she was quite nasty, how stupid, she said, and how mindless and vindictive and self-centred suicides were, they never thought of other people, of wives and children left behind, what would happen for instance to poor little Cherise who had never done anything to anybody? She'd hate me forever, she said, if I killed myself, that would really show me up for the kind of jerk I was, and I could tell Jack pretty much shared her feelings, he looked like he wanted to punch me, he kept staring at me in the rear-view mirror as if I might do it right there in the back seat of his station wagon with its smell of dog.

All the lights were on at the house, I saw that as we turned the corner. All the doors were wide open and even as Jack made his slow approach I could see someone running out into the yard and back in again every third second, run out and pull her hair and yell and then run in again. Naturally it was dear old Becky June, in her housecoat, in her stocking feet, her hair stringy, a thousand lines in her face that I had never seen before. She looked a mess but the truth is I hardly noticed. Before the car came to a stop she was already coming at me with her fingernails, spitting and clawing and screaming, punching me around until everyone except her was satisfied. Her mother is a genteel lady, she hates scenes, she appeared at last and pulled sweet Becky off me and led her back inside.

"Don't think you don't deserve it," Alice told me, and Jack added that I'd better not try anything, he was watching me. They all went into the living room to look after the trauma case and Rebecca June's mother came out to pat my arm and lead me upstairs to where the kid was.

"She couldn't sleep, poor child," she said, "she was calling you and finally Becky got angry and locked her in the closet but I managed to find a spare key and get her out, be kind to her, Jake, she doesn't understand."

I smiled and told her I would do the best I could and she patted me again and returned downstairs.

I entered the room, usually a guest room but hardly ever used now because Rebecca June's mother says she's tired of people, and the kid was seated in a child's rocker that was much too little for her—rocking in the dark, not saying anything. She was cute, I was touched in a distant way, I really didn't feel much of anything, no more than the simple aesthetic response to a child's silhouette in a tiny tot's chair.

"Is that you, daddy?" she asked, and I replied it was, and she said, "Don't turn on the light, please."

I asked why, had her mother been pinching her again.

"Not much," she said. "On my legs and on my stomach some but it doesn't hurt very much."

I turned on the lights. She had a few welts on her skin, a zigzag of purple wounds down her legs, nothing to get upset about.

"Everything was fine," she said, "once I was locked in the closet, I hope you haven't been worried."

I told her I wasn't, I knew she could take care of herself. I noticed her hair was wet and asked her how that had happened. She told me her mother had made her take a bath but she hadn't wanted to and so Rebecca June had held her under the water.

I'm glad you didn't drown, I told her, and she said she was glad too but that someone still had to clean up the bathroom because mom had gone through the room pulling everything out of the cupboards and the medicine cabinet and throwing it all in the bathwater, she really had made a wreck of the place.

I told her not to mind, someone would see to it, that her mom probably had got confused and thought she was at home because normally she was spick and span and especially in her mother's house.

The kid said she didn't mind, she'd tried to clean it up herself. "But are we really leaving you, daddy?" she asked, "Mom says we are and that you don't mind, that you are itching to be alone."

I asked her how she felt about it.

"I don't ever want to be alone," she said, "but I can manage if I have to."

She had a blanket around her shoulders and was shivering, it seemed somewhere between the bath and the closet she'd lost her clothes.

I stepped out of the room to look for them and found the lovely spouse snarling at the foot of the stairs, restrained by Jack and Alice and her mother, furious to get upstairs and sink her teeth into me.

Let her go, I told them, and after a moment or two they released her. She charged forward, taking about five or six steps before her breath gave out and she gasped down on the carpet, sobbing. I sat down beside her on the stairs a minute or two, watching her gnaw her nails and crunch up her toes and giving her a squeeze or two and finally getting a faint squeeze back, the two of us there like scrawny birds fallen from a nest.

Now take her back to the sitting room, I told the gang, and Jack came up and got her and led her back down.

There comes a time in your life, you start giving orders and no one in the world will stop to question them.

I found the kid's clothes in the bathwater and wrung them out. I drained the tub and put to one side those things that hadn't been ruined.

I could hear Jack and Alice talking downstairs, though Rebecca June and her mother were silent and there seemed to be some sort of fight developing between Jack and Alice. No one had thought to close the doors and the house was under a distinct chill.

No go, I told the kid, you're going to have to make do with the blanket.

She turned her face away, hoping I wouldn't notice that her cheeks were swollen.

I crossed the room and slid up the window. It looked clean outside, brisk, an open sky, a hatful of stars—a fairly regular scene for this time of year.

"I'm going to cut out now, kid," I told her.

She sniffed a bit and hugged the blanket tight around her.

I climbed over the sill and felt for the fire escape rung and started down.

The kid came down behind me. I looked up and she was all naked above me, distorted like a dummy.

"My shoes," she said, when we were on the ground.

The ground was cold, even icy. I stooped and she climbed on my back. We ran across the yard, jogged under the trees. Her legs wrapped tight around my waist, one hand gripped my shoulder —she rode light and handsome as an apple.

How far can you go with a kid on your back? I don't know. After a while she began giggling, I giggled too. After a time, you don't feel anything, a slow giggle is good for you, the giggles give you wings.

"How far do we go, daddy?"

Not far. We spent the night here: a fairly routine, a fairly ordinary place. Not much happens here. We can get along. Tomorrow—maybe the next day—we'll go out, ring up her mother, run a quick check on our affairs. But there's no hurry. There never is. Our lives are routine, normal: you won't find much that bothers us.

Sing Me No Love Songs I'll Say You No Prayers

Bingo Duncan and the Clothes-line

NOW BINGO DUNCAN started out in the logging business first as a choker-setter working the dog chains behind a five-ton Cat and graduated from this to second-loading, which is easier on the lungs and limbs as it is more stationary, but all of this was in his carefree youth, those good wild days before he ever set eyes or anything else on little Judy (116 sweet pounds and every inch sugar to his tongue, when eventually the wild days came to that). By the time he got to Northern Cal and the Sundown Company job he was a full-fledged sawman who could trolley the big blade with the best of them, and Judy, bless her heart, weighed a good deal more than the 116 sweet pounds he had bargained for. But as she liked to say, he was not much of a bargain himself. Only kidding, you know.

On arriving in Cal he got a job sawing for Arcadia Lumber at their plant up in the Wichapec range, and kept it until one day the floodwater carried their plant out to sea. (And would have carried me with it, Bingo was fond of telling, had I not been hanging on to Judy at the time.) Those flash floods rooted up redwoods and hauled bears out of the treetops but Bingo's Judy never budged a mite. He was glad he had been feeding her so good.

Month after month after this Bingo haunted the Eureka employment office and watched some drab spit of a man write in whitewash on the window the jobs available thereabouts. Nothing decent, nothing permanent, nothing that might bring solace or sunshine to his pounding, urgent heart.

"Just *toe* work," Bingo told Judy. "Bottle-washers and gas pumpers, clerks and manure-stompers, seems that's all the world has need of nowadays. How I wish—"

"Wish, wash this dish!" Judy would say. "Wish, take this garbage out, and while you're at it bring in my clothes off the clothesline."

Bingo and Judy and How Pride Precedes the Fall

"If you weren't so high and mighty, Bingo Duncan, you'd go south and pick the fields. The wetbacks do it, why can't you?"

"I am your logger lover, not no wetback who roots for two bucks a day."

"You and monkeys, scratching's all some monkeys know."

"Rub it in, Judy. Hit a man while he's down."

"He's down, but is he prone? Then here I come with my spreaded knees."

Big Judy, Past, Present, and Future

She was born, she said it herself, to take what a man had to give and to give it back to him in the way nature liked best, in the form of a darling child. One or two to start with, then four or five, five or ten. More's less the worry, or so I've heard. I was made to bear offspring the way a hen's good for laying eggs. And I am plumb fed up with them ramrod women who hate the sight of a friendly child's face, with them who think the sunshine stops after birth of the first. Me, I'd as soon have a whole houseful.

Periodically over the years she stopped strangers in the supermarket aisles, touched their shoulders on the street, saying, "I swear all that man of mine has to do is look at me and I'm pregnant again. It takes a big, solid woman to stand up to a gift like that."

Blows a Melody from the Past,
Some Discord in the Wings

Out here, west to the sea, falcon and cormorant riding the breeze —out here Bingo said a man could breathe. He could fill up his chest, fill up his eyes and ears, and feel something of the sky's sway—something of God's power—in his own mean little mind and soul.

"I swear it," he'd say. "I been a different person since I come out here."

Out here a man could roll back his sleeves and work up an honest sweat. He could rely on his biceps and his brains. Work was easy on the troubled mind, fine medicine for the tumbledown heart.

"Look at Judy," he'd say. "She ain't stopped smiling since we came."

But what now? Where's work now, now that Arcadia got washed out to sea? I'll tell you, there's a cruel wind blowing nobody no good. And what's my Judy gone and done? What has that woman let happen to herself? A year ago I could lift her off the floor with one hand. Now look. It grieves me to see all my wild oats come to this. Lord help me, yes.

For in the meantime she had given birth to the first bleeding young'un and the second was pressing at the gates.

"He's pressing, Bingo. I can hear his little nose going rat-a-tat-tat."

All as Bingo cursed the employment man for his Help Wanteds and the Wichapec range for its floods and the earth for not bowing when a good sawman stood. Meanwhile, Judy took a job at the All-Nite Highway Café down on 101. "What's it matter," she'd say, "if a mother-to-be has to plod and plod."

My pride, Bingo would think, watching her go, ain't what it was.

The Sundown Company: Bringing You Up to Date

"I could have told you," Judy told Bingo. "I could have told you from the start."

"Where's the start?" asked Bingo. "Where's the end? I been told and told, since the day I first stepped from the womb."

"Well, you stopped listening somewhere. You got your ear to your own hurts and that's all you hear now."

Sundown, a wildcat gypo outfit, was on its last leg the first day it opened for work. Hit and run. That's the kind of seedy outfit it was and what Judy would have told him. Sundown had taken over and whipped into almost working shape a deserted mill far up Wichapec road, fifty-seven miles from the nearest town. And that barely what you would call a town. Bingo heard about the job opening at six o'clock one morning, standing outside the employment office window blowing on his hands, stomping his boots to keep warm. Fit to be tied. Wondering why he bothered.

"*Pzzzzt.*"

"Yeah?"

A driver who hauled timber on his own truck, patron of the All-Nite Highway Café, sidled up to him, saying, "It's a lot of much, ain't it, we ought to gone into politics."

"So?"

Bingo didn't like him. He didn't like drivers in general, and especially those who owned their own trucks. It made him sick, just the way they got in and out of their cabs.

"Listen," the man said. "I had a talk with the little lady."

"Who?"

"Your old woman. Sweetest face I ever saw. When *that* woman blows in your ear I bet you listen. I know *I* would."

"Yeah?"

"Things rough, huh? Having a rough patch? That's what the little woman said."

"It's rough all right. Not a pot to piss in and it's been that way since the flood. Manure-stompers, that's all the world has need of nowadays."

"I got news," said the driver. "You interested in news? You bring your lunch-pail?"

"I got it right here."

He lifted up his lunch-box and they looked inside. A roast

beef sandwich, an apple, and three cookies wrapped in the tinfoil of a Camel package.

"Up on the Wichapec," the driver said, "this here sawman fell off his sawman's seat into the belt run. Carried him all the way up to the waste chute to the scrap pit. Nearly fried his ass. They was still working on him when I come down with my load."

"There's a job? You saying they need a new man?"

"They find wine, nothing but wine, in his Thermos jug. One drunk skunk. They give him the boot while I'm standing there."

"What is the company?"

"It ain't much, let me tell you. A gypo outfit, they call themselves the Sundown Company. Bunch of scabs. Union wouldn't touch it. But they say they paying ten-twelve bucks the hour for a steady man."

"That's it. I'm their man. Hell, I'd work for nothing."

But when Bingo arrived up Wichapec he found the Sundown was only working part-time, hardly enough to keep the machinery from rusting any more than it already had. They could not get enough logs to work full-time, he was told, and the equipment kept breaking down, too—mysteriously.

"Mysteriously? How you mean?"

"We don't know. There ain't nobody can figure it out. It's like the whole damn operation is jinxed."

They did not pay good wages either. The sawman's pay was eight dollars the hour, take it or leave it. Nor had the former sawman simply fallen off his work seat from too much drink. The boss-man and four or five others had given the matter a close look-see. And they didn't like what they had found.

"What you mean?"

"Well, the bolts holding up the seat was right rusty. Could'a been the bolts just gave way. It happens. I mean, the machinery is old and tired. But I don't know. Sorta looks like somebody mighta taken a hacksaw to them."

"Christ!"

"Anyway, the seat give way and the sawman tumbled down onto the pulley. Poor bastard was lucky, he mighta been sawed up into a two-by-four. But he only broke his leg."

"His leg?"

"That's right. The belt carried him to the scrap pit, then the chains caught him and carried him up the waste chute. Poor bastard was about to drop off into the cone burner. He decided to jump instead."

"You don't say."

"I ain't saying nothing. Nothing about no hacksaw, anyway. But that's what I hear."

"I'll be damned."

"You're one of us, then. Glad to have you aboard."

Late that evening Bingo slung a jacket over the baby and drove in his pick-up to the café where Judy stood, she'd told him, ten hours a day on her feet, with no rest for the weary. He found her sitting in the corner booth, lapping up a hamburger steak and a big pile of mashed potatoes. First thing she did was reach over and wipe the child's nose.

"He's awfully runny," she said. "I hope he ain't coming down with nothing."

Then she fed him a spoonful of potatoes.

"Did you get the job?"

"Bet your sweet ass," Bingo said. "Although take my word for it, it ain't much."

"What's it like up there?"

So Bingo borrowed her pencil and drew Judy Duncan a map of what had happened and how it looked from a bird's eye.

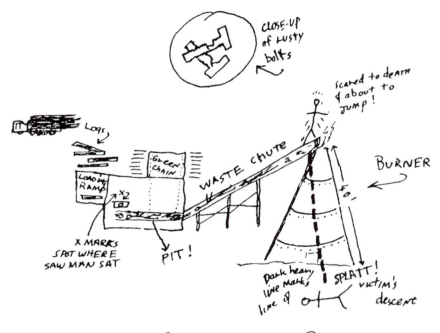

CLOSE-UP
of RUSTY
bolts

scared to death
& about to
JUMP!

Logs,

WASTE chute

GREEN
CHAIN

LOADING
RAMP

X2

BURNER

X MARKS
SPOT WHERE
SAW MAN SAT

PIT!

Dark heavy
line marks
line of

SPLATT!

victim's
descent

The Sundown Co.

"What's mysterious about rust?" said Judy. "That child's sleepy. You best take the little honey on home."

"Me with it, I guess," said Bingo. "I got to git up before the cock crows if I am to hold this job."

Bingo and How Hard Times Hardly Got Better

On good days, with no breakdowns, Sundown might cut 50,000 feet of lumber, which was good enough, God knows, Bingo said, but those days together with the bad did not hardly pay enough to pay the rent or the grocery bills for Judy back in the Eureka outskirts where each morning he left her. The days got leaner and

leaner, but not Judy still at her job, and each time as Bingo dipped
the big blade into a log and sliced it along easy as cucumbers he
thought with some distaste how it took a lot of money to upkeep
a big woman like her, who wouldn't slice at all.

Worse luck yet, he found he missed her.

What my wild oats have come down to, he would say to himself, is nostalgia. What I have got a bad case of is sexual longing.

On one of the leanest days of all he met Crow Kay G.

Crow Kay G.

At the time Bingo met Crow Kay G. both were working the Sundown job but Crow Kay G. didn't have any Judy. He had nobody.
All he had was himself and he meant to hold on to that.

"So buzz off," he told Bingo. "I already met all the people on
this earth I ever want to meet."

The Working Day and Crow Kay G.

It took a lot of money and horsepower to upkeep a big woman
like Judy but there was one thing saving his hide, Bingo figured,
and that was that on the good days no less than the bad the equipment broke down and when this happened it always happened
right after they'd started up for the day or when they were about
to close down for the night—or in the afternoon just when things
were humming—and as the breakdown hardly ever lasted for
more than twenty minutes or half an hour the company had no
choice but to pay the men simply for standing around. There was
a lot of talk about how the equipment managed to break down so

conveniently for the men and it was more and more that Bingo Duncan began paying attention to Crow Kay G., a nondescript little bastard with red hair whose personality took on the weirdest change when something in the mill broke down, like some ratty little thing that had come up out of a mud puddle, smiling. He had the wickedest secret smile about his lips, with his eyebrows shrugged down over his nose, and all but about to wet his pants from excitement—so much so that Bingo eventually concluded that maybe Crow Kay G. was going out of his way to bring about these breakdowns.

There was more to this redhead than met the eye.

The little snot was a saboteur.

Maybe. You wouldn't want to say a thing like that out loud. And if he was, then Bingo and every other man on the place was indebted to the squirt for much of their earnings.

Commuting

Bingo daily had been driving up and down the twisty curves of the Wichapec in order to be with Judy and the kid and to see when and if the baby would come.

"This here drive is breaking my back," he told Judy one night. "I can hardly live on the three or four hours' sleep I'm getting."

"Well, shoot," said Judy, "why don't you see if there's a place up there we can live? I've worn out my shoe-leather and need to slow down some myself."

SING ME NO LOVE SONGS . . .

195

The One-room Shack

This morning as usual Bingo got up at four o'clock, with the whole world dark as a witch's bottom, and he drove up the high Wichapec to be there at seven, but this morning he had Judy and the young'un with him and because of that and Judy wanting to brush her teeth and wrap the child up tight and because the pick-up was groaning from so much extra weight, this morning he arrived late. And every man waiting, for what could a mill do with no one in the sawyer's chair? So he hopped right out of the cab and went running.

"But what about me?" cried Judy.

Bingo flung out both arms, shouting, "The shack! The shack! Go to the shack."

More On That

Earlier in the week Bingo had come to the boss-man with his problems.

"I got me a woman due," he'd said.

"Do what?" the boss man replied. And when this matter had been cleared up the boss-man had looked Bingo over, sceptically observing that he had not taken him to be a family man.

"Why not?"

"Well, you seemed to me to be just another guy sowing his wild oats, footloose and fancy-free. Now I see better. I see you got those scowl lines down your jaws and the worried eyes of a man looking at a lot of responsibility. Still, I don't see what Sundown can do for you."

"I heard something about some cabins."

"Cabins? Those old shacks, you mean? Why, they don't have no heat. They don't have no water. No furnishings. All they've got is rats and vermin and God-all. They're not fit to live in."

"I heard tell that redhead was living in one."

"You heard wrong. Where that redhead is living is in a big house off in the woods that some crazy Indians built. Anyway, he don't care where he lives. For all I know he is part Indian himself."

"I reckon me and Judy are out of the same boot. We'd like one of them shacks."

"Suit yourself. They're free for the taking."

The Upshot of it All

"What do you think?" Bingo asked Judy some time later.

"That thing! The roof's broke. The windows are all cracked. There ain't no front door. It's *small!* Where will I put my washing machine?"

"It's roomy—for one room. It's got walls. It's got a floor. I could rig up a stove out of one of them big drums out in the woods."

Bingo asked the young'un what he thought. But the child had broken out in an ugly rash all over his body and could think of nothing but scratching himself.

"I guess it will do until something better comes along," sighed Judy.

"It's free," said Bingo. "It will be different with a woman's touch. Let's see what we can do."

So Judy got busy with her woman's touch.

An Uplifting Encounter

That day while Judy had been waiting in the truck, feeling mortified on account of how Bingo had left her, the boss-man stuck his head in at her window.

"Hear you're about due, ma'am," he said pleasantly to her.

Judy's face lit up. "Yes, it's like all Bingo Duncan has to do is look at me and I'm that way again. I never saw a man with such a natural gift."

"And what's that there little towhead's name?"

"That there is Bingo Two. He's my pride and joy."

"He's a humdinger, that I can see."

"Say hello to the nice man," Judy told the child.

But Bingo Two only buried his face in his mama's bosom and would not come up for air or say hello no matter how hard Judy yanked at him.

"He sure is a humdinger," said the boss-man. "Well, best of the day to you, ma'am."

And the boss-man trundled back to his chores.

This exchange uplifted Judy considerably.

What Bingo and Judy Could Do

What they could do was not much. Bingo built the stove out of the drum and put in window panes and slapped together a door out of scrap lumber and burned a great heap of rubbish in a cleared space out back. He got the snakes out and most of the rats and he knocked in a new beam to prop up the roof.

Judy put up curtains of a kind and hung a few calendars on the walls and wore out several brooms. She put a flowering bush out in a coffee can on the log step.

"Looks real neat," said Bingo. "A proper little home."

"I best sit down," said Judy. "I am all worn out."

Time Floats On

Time floated on and Judy had her baby without mishap and the mill kept breaking down mysteriously. Bingo got his proof that Crow Kay G. was sabotaging the works one day when the green chain developed a busted cog in its fly-wheel just, as it turned out, in that vicinity where the redhead had been working the previous day. The mill shut down for one hour and no one could figure where the damage was, until the redhead came up from beneath the green chain table, saying, "Aha. The trouble is down here in this gash in the cog wheel." The boss-man slapped him on the back, saying, "Good work, Crow," and brought the millwright over to put another one on quickly, but it was clear to Bingo, from the crafty satisfaction on the redhead's face, that the bugger was the culprit.

Bingo said nothing to Judy or anyone else of his thoughts on the subject but it began to bother him some, this question of right and wrong. What Crow was doing was cheating the mill owners, that was clear; but he was putting money in the workers' pockets and no one could deny that was a true blessing, especially for a family man.

Bingo did bring the issue before Judy, in its general terms.

If a man does wrong, he said to Judy—that is, if he commits *criminal acts*—but those acts serve to put money in deserving pockets—that is, it puts food on table of the poor—then is that act wrong? Is what that man's doing morally reprehensible, is what I mean, and is it morally reprehensible for that otherwise innocent party to take it?

"Good God," said Judy, "you are talking with a mouth full of mush. I am worried about your condition, Bingo. I can't make out a word you are saying."

It is a difficult issue, thought Bingo, who tried to think about it no longer, because it was giving him a headache, with Judy's attitude only making matters worse.

"I wish you would make that baby stop squalling," he told Judy. "There is never a minute's peace around here."

She told him he could go take a walk in the woods. He could go take a flying leap, she told him.

The Seven-room House

A couple of Indians had built it. One morning, out hunting deer, they had followed a creek trail down to the lower Wichapec.

"Quiet," one told the other. "I hear something."

They crept up to a knoll and peered through the brush.

"Not deer," the other said. "What is it?"

A white man was down by the creek bed, very busy.

"What is he doing?" the first Indian asked.

"He is digging a hole," the second replied.

"It is a very big hole. It is too big to be an animal trap. Shall we tell him?"

"Sure. Let's tell him."

But the Indians were smarter than that, and remained hidden.

"He is taking earth from one place and putting it in another," the first Indian observed.

"Yes. As you say, he is digging a hole."

The Indians returned to their own area on the high Wichapec, and dug themselves a similar hole. A few weeks later they again found themselves watching from the same thicket.

"He has finished the hole," one said.

"Yes, and the hole has filled with water. Perhaps he intends to go swimming."

"Then why does he not swim in the creek?"

The Indians did not care to dwell further on this.

"Why is he notching those logs and stacking them one upon the other?"

"I believe he is building a wall."

"He appears to be building several."

"Yes. He intends to erect a square box in which to catch the animals."

"It will not work."

"Who knows? I have seen stranger things."

The Indians were impressed by what they had seen and went back to their own area on the Wichapec, and duplicated the man's labour. Some time afterwards, they again came down to the creek floor.

"Very impressive," the first Indian conceded.

"Yes," said the second. "He has divided the box into seven different spaces. He has slapped mud between the log walls, and now seems to be putting a cover over it."

"It seems very snug," said the first.

"Yes," replied the second. "It is too bad, isn't it? Someone should have told him."

"Yes. Shall we?"

But the Indians were too smart for this and went away again and completed their own house, exactly as the man had made his.

Then the winter rains came and the creek swelled and rushed about mightily, and the next time they came down the Wichapec no sign remained of the white man's house, not even the hole.

But the Indians were content with their own great structure high on the Wichapec, and lived in it for many years, with their wives and children and others who thought being so enclosed was not out of keeping.

This was the seven-room house inherited by Crow Kay G.

A Bellyacheful

Things got worse and worse and no one knew which way to turn in the one-room shack where Judy and Bingo lived, with the new little baby squalling twenty-four hours a day and the other young'un acting like a juvenile delinquent, though not yet two years old, and Bingo knew that at worst he was going to kill Judy or she him, or that at best they'd leave each other or blow out their own brains or go hog-crazy if something wasn't done soon, for they hardly had room enough to breathe and they were plain sick of each other.

"I've had it up to here!" Bingo would shout, and Judy, she'd shout the same.

More and more Bingo brooded on the green-chain man with the red hair and the big seven-room house all to his lonesome. He got to thinking, too, and reminding Judy, of how when he married her she'd weighed in at a sweet 116 pounds—"And look at you now!" he'd say. "God, you're big as a moose and about as pretty!" Until these days came along Bingo had never really noticed or paid any attention or much minded her size. If anything, he'd liked it, and if he'd ever heard anyone joking about Judy's size he would have been inclined to say, "That's right, she's a good handful, but that's how I like it." But now that attitude and loving was ancient history. Now he'd say, "You're big as the moon! God knows what it's taking out of my paycheque to feed you!"

And Judy would mope or she'd yank up a child under each arm and stride off into the woods, or she'd go at him with her broom or her pots and pans.

"I am not a dog," she would say, "that you can talk to me of how much it costs to feed me." And she would feel helpless and sick with fury, hatred would spin before her eyes like a ragged ball, and weight that had always felt good and smooth and prideful on her bones now felt like a leaded sinker, felt like something with claws was raking inside her, and the mere sight of Bingo would set her to shaking.

"Eat-eat-eat!" he'd say, and she would think, Surely I will kill him. I am going to stomp on him and smush him like the rat he is.

One night Bingo went to the seven-room house and stood outside in the dark staring at it, hating and cursing the redhead, Crow Kay G., till the bones in his throat ached.

I have got a real bellyacheful, he said.

Next morning he took the boss aside and asked him how come that nasty green-chain puller had this big roomy house up the Wichapec when all he and his had was that one-room shack full of squalling young'uns.

"Work it out with him," the boss said. "Some Indians built that house and it don't belong to Sundown. But I wouldn't reckon on much. When heart was passed out that Crow kid was off chopping wood."

An Overture

"How's about it, kid?" asked Bingo.

"Buzz off," said the redhead. "Your old brain's gone goat-hair."

Time Off Without Pay

After being told to buzz off, Bingo got so mad at the redhead and at himself and the world in general that he ripped through every log in the yard and through the next truckful that was brought in and in no time at all there wasn't a stump left to be sawed. And it only two o'clock.

"That's it for the day," said the boss, "everybody gets the afternoon off without pay." Then he came up to Bingo and slapped his shoulder, saying, "That was some sawing. *Jee*-sus!"

The men grumbled at their lost wages and cast malevolent looks at Bingo, and when he passed Crow Kay G. the redhead whispered, "You're asking for it, sawdog."

Bingo said to hell with it and he went home and was sweet to Judy and they hauled up the brats and went flying down the Wichapec to the Lumberjack Bar.

"Keep'm coming," he told the barkeep.

And for all that they had a roaring good time.

Judy's Perceptive Nature

"All I could see," Bingo told Judy, "while I was sawing them logs was his red eyebrows. I kept thinking of the right and wrong of it and how I had been wronged—how *we* had been wronged—and each time I went zipping through another log I thought, 'Well, Crow, you s.o.b., here's another buck out of your pocket.'"

"What's his house like?" asked Judy. She was feeding beer to her babies to keep them quiet.

"It's just what you'd expect a couple of Indians to build. But it's been standing for over a hundred years, so I reckon it's solid. But Crow don't need it. He lives in one corner off in the kitchen. He don't have a stick of furniture in the place."

The juke-box had been going, Mervis Pearl singing "Wreck on the Highway." The baby had crawled out on the dance floor. Judy told the other child to go dance with her. The boy protested, "She can't dance. She can't hardly crawl. She barely can sit up."

"Do what I tell you," Judy said, and gave him a smack on the bottom. The boy went out, took the baby's hand, and started circling around her.

"Look at that pair," said Judy. "Cotton candy wouldn't melt in their mouths."

Bingo, too, was all smiles. "They are a pretty sight," he concurred. "I can't hardly remember the time I was ever innocent and pretty as them."

Judy slapped playfully at his arm. "Shoot," she laughed, "you still are."

Mervis went on singing,

I saw the wreck on the highway,
but I didn't hear nobody pray. . . .

Two or three of the lumberjacks were up kicking their heels. Lots of others were yelling encouragement. Everyone was getting high.

"Maybe we should invite that Crow fellow over for a meal," said Judy. "Maybe he's lonesome. Maybe when you get to know him he's just as nice as the next guy."

"Over my grave," said Bingo.

Judy wriggled out of the booth and coaxed Bingo to dance with her. Bingo put his head on her shoulder. They rocked slowly, off in a corner by themselves, with the young'un tugging at her skirt.

"You are still my sweet one-sixteen," murmured Bingo at one point. "You got my number."

Judy liked that. She let her head sink down, too.

A woman with blond hair swept high on her head came out of the ladies' and put her arms around them. They embraced her in return and together made several graceless circles of the floor, laughing, for the woman kept losing her balance and toppling against them. She had a tiny red mouth and a green bow up over one ear.

"You two give me hope," the woman said at the end. "I got hope in my heart so long as I know there's one loving couple left in the world." Then she smiled sadly and fluttered her fingers, ta-taing along.

On the drive back up the Wichapec, with the children asleep in her lap, it was determined that (1) Judy would have to do the inviting, (2) it must be a regular dinner, nothing special, (3) they must on no account beg or plead with the redhead to swap houses or offer to pay him a lot of money and (4) she would have to do all of the talking.

"I ought to get a new dress," mused Judy. "If I had hair like that blond woman's I'd be sitting pretty." She punched Bingo softly in the ribs. "Now don't deny it. I could see you liked her."

Big Judy and Crow Kay G.

Early the next morning soon after sunrise Judy crossed through the woods to Crow's big house and knocked on the door. He was a long time answering and when the door was finally opened all he did was look at her. He looked a good long time, until Judy began to get fidgety, and she recognized that he did not know how to talk to strangers.

He did not know how to talk to a woman.

She saw that.

He looked at her with a bottomless, fathomless look that made Judy not know where to look herself. His look set loose all sorts of fast and loose parts inside herself and she did not know what to think. She felt like maybe she was down to 116 pounds again and she scrunched up her toes inside her shoes and swayed a time or two, trying to get hold of herself.

She looked up at the treetops and over to the side of the house where there was a big rock, and when she looked back again at him he was still looking.

My, my, she thought—and had the feeling that with wings she could fly right up to the roof or the treetops or clean out of the world.

"Bingo and I was thinking," she said in a light voice, "we were thinking how you must get terrible lonesome in this big house all alone, and we were wondering if you'd like to come over to our place tonight for potluck supper."

The redhead didn't reply to this. He had the reddest hair Judy had ever seen and she must have caught him shaving because one side of his face still had the lather.

He had only one boot on, and that half-laced.

"Supper tonight," she said. "You coming?"

She saw he did not know how to say no either, or any other word; he seemed straight-out entranced.

"Judy," she said, extending her hand. "Judy and Bingo . . . the sawman . . . I'm his other half."

He blinked at that. But he took her hand and for a minute she thought he was going to kiss it.

She backed down the steps.

"About six," she said. "After I've had time to get the shack tidy."

The redhead kept on looking.

Heading back through the woods, Judy thought: *My, my, he sure can LOOK!* She thought, If I die tomorrow I know I can go to my grave knowing I have been *looked at* once in my life. He has stripped my dress clean off me and seen everything I have.

Thrilled, is how Judy felt. Good Lord, she thought, and me a married woman. And me with my hair hardly even combed.

Supper at the Shack

Waiting for the meal to get to the table, Bingo saw how Crow Kay G. and Judy kept looking at each other. He saw how Judy was acting flighty and tipsy and how she kept blushing. He saw how the redhead kept staring at her ankles.

But he didn't mind Crow's looking. How he felt about it was that it was a free country. Despite her size, Judy was a good-looking woman. She was a real eyeful.

It was high time she got a little attention.

He just hoped the spaghetti didn't boil over.

Supper at the Shack—Another Angle

Crow Kay G., waiting for the meal, saw how, moving about, the sawman and Judy kept bumping into one another and even into him; he saw how the little boy was always at your elbow as he

played, and how the baby's squalls were right in your ear, and how
the only space she could crawl was down under the table and
between your feet and around the chairs; he saw how the bed had
been jammed in and how pallets had to be made for the kids, and
how, once the spaghetti was cooked and then lobbed out into
plates, there was no room on the table for your elbows or for dish
or glass, and no way you could scrape your chair back and how
you couldn't move without thinking you'd step on the baby, and
how when Judy had to change a diaper she had to do it right there
in plain sight, and how you had to hold your nose; and how,
although it was plenty cold outside, the heat from the cooking
on the open barrel made the room so stifling hot you had to take
off your jacket, and then no place to put it, and how, even so, a
draft came up through the floorboards and froze your ankles, and
how pots and pans and all their belongings were stacked all over
the room—and how, despite all this, Judy kept the sparkle in her
eyes and lit up the place with her sunshine, without one word of
complaint.

He frankly couldn't see how human beings could live like this.

I'd die, he thought. I'd sure-as-shooting kill myself.

Midway through the meal the oldest young'un cut his knee
from a nail protruding from the wall, and there was much squalling about that.

Then the baby squalled because it wanted to nurse, and the
next course never did come. But Crow didn't mind, for the sawman had out his jug.

Crow, from time to time, kept trying to get a bead on the sawdog—on how a woman like Judy could be hooked up with a
snake like that—but he couldn't get anywhere. He couldn't figure
it out. This Bingo character, it seemed to him, was a born Nothing. Real Low-life.

"I hear tell," said Bingo of a sudden, "that big house of yours was built by Indians."

Crow cautiously nodded.

"Must be hard for you," said Bingo, "keeping up a big house like that. The heat bill alone must keep your pocketbook empty."

"I manage," said the redhead. He thought it best not to tell the sawdog that he had shut off the rooms and now lived entirely in the kitchen.

"Now if you'd want to trade abodes," Bingo trailed on, "I wouldn't mind—Judy and me wouldn't—sweetening the pot. To make it worth your while."

Crow remained silent. He was watching Judy burp the baby. Then he watched her button up her blouse. He watched her laugh and spin her hands as if she were chasing away flies.

"I declare," she said, "all Bingo Duncan has to do is look at me and I'm pregnant again."

Bingo let out a sound, half groan and half surprise. He gazed searchingly at Judy. He clearly was wondering whether she was telling him a third child was in the oven.

Shortly after this, Crow Kay G. departed. He left with mixed feelings, not quite wanting to go but thinking he'd best move fast, for in truth he found the evening confusing. He couldn't figure out what to make of all those signals he had been getting—nor even from where they had been coming from.

"That Judy," he exclaimed to the air, "now *that's* a woman."

The night wind was invigorating, however, and by the time he arrived at the house the Indians had built, he felt again half normal. He entered the back door with grand satisfaction, and before going to bed strolled through each of the seven rooms, delighted they were all of them his.

Cleaning Up from Dinner

"Well, we blew that," said Bingo. "We can say goodbye to that idea."

"Like I said," said Judy, "it's too early to count chickens."

In Bed That Night

"I feel *this* light-headed!" said Judy. "I feel a small breeze could blow me straight up to the treetops."

"What was that about an oven?" said Bingo.

"Stop talking," said the young'un. "How can I sleep with your yakking going on?"

"Put your arms around me, Bingo. Hold me tight. Or I'll float on out of here."

"Where would we put another one?" asked Bingo. "How we going to feed another one? What's the percentage?"

"One little gust and I'm gone," said Judy, trembling.

Bingo put his arms, and one leg, around her. She held on tight.

The boy stayed quiet. He had the feeling something strange was going on. He didn't move a muscle.

The baby was sleeping.

"When tomorrow comes," said Judy, "I hope I'm back down to earth."

"I'm getting woozy up here."

The Cup of Coffee

Lunchtime the next day when the mill shut down there were only a few logs in the yard and they all knew no more trucks were bringing in logs that day and they were uneasy; talk was circulating to the effect that the mill was going to close down for good now, Sundown was going to call it quits, and some were passing along the rumour that the company wouldn't even be able to pay them for the week already put in.

Crow Kay G. sat over on the two-by-eight stack by the green chain, eating a tomato sandwich. The bread had gone soggy and he didn't much like it.

Bingo came over and sat down beside him. He had two or three roast beef sandwiches in his lunch-pail, together with a wedge of cake, a carrot, and a red apple. He had a large thermosful of hot coffee as well.

"You think they gonna shut down?" Bingo asked.

Crow shook his head, not yes, not no.

"*C'est la vie*," he said.

Bingo ate his lunch and drank his coffee. The day was a cold one and he held his hands over the steaming cup, for warmth.

"I see she looks after you real good," said Crow. "I see she packs a man's lunch."

"Who?" asked Bingo.

"Your wife. That Judith."

Reflecting on That

Just as they had figured, the mill did not start back up after lunch, though there was word more logs would be coming in in the morning. Walking back to his shack, swinging the empty lunch-pail, Bingo had mind to reflect back on those minutes by the green chain. Judith, he thought. Well, I'll be damned. That *is* her name. I'd plumb forgot about it. Little Judith, that is exactly what I used to call her.

History Repeated

As Bingo walked through the door, Judy asked, "Did you?"

"Did I what?"

"Bingo Duncan, don't tell me you forgot!"

Bingo hemmed and hawed. Finally, he said, "We had a lot of other stuff to talk about. I guess it slipped my mind. Anyway, it is his turn to ask us."

But Judy would have none of that. Fast as she could she went running over to ask Crow Kay G. if he wanted to come over tonight for meat and mashed potatoes.

She shortly returned, looking downcast, explaining: He could not come. He was on his way down to the beach to cut grape stakes. He says he sells them for thirty, thirty-five cents to the grape and berry people down south. It is clear he is an Up-and-Go-Getter. Why did you not ever think of that for making extra money?

Bingo sighed. He said he was tired. He said the one thing in the world he wanted right now was a nice easy chair to sit down in.

"If you'd thought of cutting stakes like that redhead," Judy said, "maybe we'd have one. Maybe we'd have us a seven-room house, too."

Bingo went out and sat on a stump in the cleared space out back. He was in no mood to hear any more about the world's Go-Getters.

"He said he'd stop by on his way home," called Judy, "if our light was on."

The Light, and Crow and the Young'Un, and Judy Alone with her Thoughts

Each time Bingo turned off the light Judy came by and turned it back on.

"One would think you were taken with this fella," said Bingo.

"Don't be silly," she said. "You may not have noticed, but your oldest child is not home."

"Good God! Where is he?"

"He is out grape-staking with Crow. He asked if he could, and I let'm."

About midnight the child came in, very excited, with his pant legs wet.

"We cut seventy-eight stakes!" the young'un exclaimed. "That's over thirty dollars!"

"Why didn't Mr. Crow come in?" asked Judy.

"He said his ass was slinged, he had to get home to bed."

Judy asked the young'un if he was hungry. She said, "Child, you must be starved."

But the boy was already dropping down on his pallet. "Not me," he said. "We had us three cans of potted meat, down on the beach."

"I didn't think you liked potted meat."

"I do now. Crow has got a whole room full. He says it's about all he eats. Do you know what else he has? He has one of those old oil drums cut open with a velvet seat half-way up, and a red canopy over the top. He says he sits in it when he wants to think about his kingdom."

Judy shook her head, marvelling.

Soon the child fell asleep, and Bingo with him. For a long time after the shack had settled Judy stood at her dark window, looking up at the stars. Alone with her thoughts.

The Jeep

For three days running, four if one counts Sunday, the Sundown mill stayed shut down, and each day the young'un went out with Crow to cut stakes.

I hope he pays you, said Bingo. Then we all can retire.

The fourth day Judy went herself to bring the boy home, for he had been sleeping over, and while at the big house she told Crow Kay G. how she had heard Bingo say that the way to cut stakes was to buy or borrow a chainsaw so you could go at the really big logs and how if you did that you could cut tons more stakes than you could with an axe and chisel.

"What we need is a jeep," said Crow. "With a jeep we could zip up and down the beach without getting stuck in the sand. We could hunt out the really big logs."

"I will ask him where we can get a jeep," said Judy.

He was not coming over to dinner that night, but then he said he would.

Judy perked up.

Wonder what changed his mind? thought Judy. Wonder has he been missing me? Maybe it was my saying all Bingo had to do was look at me and I'd be pregnant again.

Maybe he's jealous.

She jumped her way home, happy as a kid, uplifted by that.

Cutting Stakes on the Beach

The next weekend Bingo had the power-saw and the jeep and they drove down to the beach and looked about for a huge, washed-up redwood and when they found one they got out and sawed it into sections eight feet long like the growers wanted, and with the axes and chisels they split these into two- to three-inch stakes and chopped the point on their tips so the growers could drive them into the ground. While the men worked Judy and the kids zoomed up and down the beach in the jeep and sometimes Judy drove the jeep into the water where the water and sand were swirling together, and the tires kicked up a splash and spun deep into the sand and she drove the jeep very fast and snake-zithered against the waves which shot up a fine spray over the jeep and made the baby and all of them cackle with laughter.

End of the first few weeks they had collected themselves over three hundred dollars.

Popcorn

One night after splitting stakes and roasting wieners on the beach they were driving through Orick when they saw on the movie marquee that what was playing was a movie called

Lady Godiva and the Lone Ranger,

and when Judy saw this she said, "Whoops, just what I want, a big bag of popcorn!"

The Lumberjack Bar

Where they were going was the Lumberjack Bar, and Judy brought
her popcorn with her, and they took a booth in the back near the
juke-box.

I want to dance-dance-dance, said Judy, and she danced first
with Bingo, then with Crow, and then she danced with the baby
wiggling in her arms and the other young'un swinging on her
skirt. One of her old friends from the All Nite Highway Café,
sauntering by, said, Well, darling, I see you're still dancing, and
Judy said, Yes I thought I'd best get it out of my system while I
can, for I've up and got pregnant again.

Meantime, Bingo and Crow were back in the booth drinking
their beers, paying no attention to the conversation of two log-
gers, a skinner and a faller, seated near to them.

The Skinner: "Now here, now there. Not anywhere."

The Faller: "I ain't telling, but the bastard stole my shirt."

The Skinner: "Flipped right over the canyon, bottom-side up,
and when I got down to him the sonofabitch was sitting up on
the frame, grinning his head off."

The Faller: "Speaking of fire, that was her to a tee. So hot she
burned holes in my blankets."

Bingo wiped wet circles on the Formica. "What the hell are
those two bull-shooters talking about?" he asked Crow.

But the redhead was not feeling talkative. Sure, he could split
stakes alongside this character, and drive up and down the Wichapec with him. Sure, they were partners, but still there was something about this sawdog that rubbed him wrong, and he didn't see
why he had to sit here shooting the breeze with him.

What he wanted to do was go dance with Judy.

But it looked to him like the children had her all tied up.

"Let's have another beer," he said. "Let's tie one on."

A blond woman with piled-up hair approached and stood grinning beside their booth. Then she slipped in beside Bingo, and slung an arm around him, saying, "Hi, honey. Long time no see."

The redhead watched this with an open mouth. Son-of-a-gun, he thought, this character has been running around on Judy. And me staying pure as the snow.

He got up and went outside and sat in the jeep, banging his fist on the steering wheel.

The Eternal Question

Was he or wasn't he, that was the eternal question plaguing Judy, once Crow Kay G. first hinted at it and then said his suspicions straight out. She took to searching his pockets for phone numbers and looking over his shirts for lipstick stains and his drawers for you-know-what.

"What's the matter with you?" Bingo would say.

For Judy had stopped eating, too, and anytime he was out of her sight for a second she would be calling his name, and some days she would walk up to the mill just to make sure he was seated in his sawyer's chair.

"I believe he's innocent," she told Crow one day.

Another day she did find a telephone number scrawled on a sheet in his pocket, but when she asked him about it he said it was some fella he'd heard of who had a dog for sale and he was thinking of buying a dog.

"Don't lie to me, Bingo. I bet it's that blond woman's number."

But when she called an old rasping voice said, "Hell's fire, lady, you're the second caller I've had this week. I sold that dog more than a month ago."

Not that Judy was convinced.

Family Changes

One morning Judy went up to the seven-room house and opened all the doors, aired the rooms, swept up the dust and cobwebs, washed the windows, and that night told Bingo it was as pretty a place as she'd ever seen. It was like heaven.

"Them Indians really knew what they were doing," she said. A few days later they rushed her down the mountain and Judy gave birth to their newest baby.

"That tears it," said Bingo. "We can't all live in that shack now."

While Bingo was down overseeing Judy's condition in the hospital the oldest young'un had taken to staying over nights at the redhead's house. For several days Bingo hardly even saw him.

"I guess I could build another room on to the shack," Bingo told Judy. "Maybe that's one solution."

Judy objected. "You think I'm going to come home to your sawing and pounding? You think I would make our baby live like that?"

"It's all I can think of. One thing for sure, we can't all put up in that one little room."

Crow, standing out in the hospital corridor, ventured in. "She could put up with me," he said. "While you're building. Judy and the baby. I wouldn't mind having them."

The Dream

That night Bingo had one of his worst dreams. He waked up sweating. What had happened was that the saw seat had warped under him and dropped him off backwards into the log chute and he'd been carried right along the belt, tumbling over midst the bark and slivers and chunks of wood, and try as he could he couldn't get upright again. Then he'd got scrambled around between the green chain hooks, the chains carrying scrap up the waste chute to drop it off in the cone burner, and first thing he knew that was what had him. He was on his way to being burned alive. Up ahead were flames licking from the burner, and the chains kept tumbling him over, wood chunks knocking him one way and the other and his arms and legs gone all twisty. And knowing he was finished, he had done a strange thing: he had started calling for his mama. *Mama, help me!*—that's what he'd screeched out. But what part of the dream his mama might have occupied was all dark and mystery and he knew there was no help there. He could feel the heat of the burner. Could see the red flames. And he made one last effort to stand—one last claim that his life was not yet over. Up that high, his clothes already catching afire, he had a clear view of the Wichapec before him. Down there was the one-room shack with nobody in it, and up there was the redhead's place, glaring bright as a mansion, and, yes, there stood Judy waving her arms from the front door, screaming in a silent way, *"Jump! Jump! Jump!"* And the funny thing about it to his mind was how Judy had skinned down to her old weight of 116, how she looked pretty as a picture, even as—when he looked twice—his kids were climbing all over her. Kids running through her like a fast-growth vine. Funny thing to him was how beautiful she looked. How clean and simple and next to ravishing. Just the way she would look—would stay looking—if she'd never hooked up with him. The other funny thing was how Crow Kay G. was absent. How he wasn't where you'd think to find him. Not up at the house with his arms around Judy, nor down there by the sawyer's seat waving a wrench, saying, "Look what I done. Look how I fixed your goose." No, Crow was nowhere to be seen. Then he came back to Judy's voice calling "Jump! Jump!" though now she had disappeared too . . . and the shack had, and the seven-room mansion, and his three little kids . . . because all that was around him were the roaring hot flames and the clear knowledge that he was falling.

What the Dream Looked Like When He Tried Recalling It Later

Sea Lions

One night a few weeks after this the whole gang was down on the beach having a wiener roast after cutting up stakes. They built a fire out of driftwood and the five of them stretched out in the sand.

Bingo had the new baby wrapped in a blanket under one arm.

"How are things for you up at the big house?" he asked Judy.

Judy gave him a meek smile.

A bit later she said to him, "I see the shack addition is coming along."

Bingo nodded yes it was.

Crow Kay G. got the kids assembled for a ride in the jeep. He asked Judy if she'd care to come along.

"I reckon so," she said, "as no one around here will talk to me."

Bingo threw more driftwood on. He sat poking the fire, talking this and that to the baby, as the others roared in the jeep down the beach, swerving into and out of the waves.

Tonight Crow had brought his pistol along and as he burst across the dunes he would rest his pistol wrist over his driving arm and take pot-shots at dark shapes as they surfaced far out in the water.

"What are you shooting at?" asked Judy.

"Sea lions," said Crow. "The ocean is packed full with them."

They drove as far as they could down the stretch of sand and when they came back, more slowly now because it seemed something had gone out of each of them, they saw dead black shapes washing up on the tide.

"What's those?" asked Judy.

"Sea lions," Crow said.

Horseman, Pass By

First the young'un came in.

Then the toddler.

Bingo, stretched out on the bed with the year-old copy of a book found between the floorboards—*Eccentric Millionaires*—watched the black entrance to see who next would come.

Judy's voice, outside in the dark, summoned him forth.

"I'm home," she said, "for anyone who can carry me over the threshold!"

Thirty Years Later

"Well, tell me, Bingo," Judy would say, "was it worth it?"

"Sit down," Bingo would say. "I am going to sing you a love song."

"But will it be pretty?"

"It will be a honey."

And she would sit down, patting her feet, and he would do it.

Nine children and nineteen grandchildren, she'd think, and I don't feel a day over forty.

Then they'd go to bed where, to her mind and his, every time it was like starting over.

The Woman Who Talked to Horses

"THAT'S RIGHT," SHE SAID, "I talk to them. They will talk to me when they will talk to no one else."

"But they *can* talk," I said.

"Oh, sure."

"To each other?"

"All the time."

I looked over at the horses. They were in their stalls, eating hay, their rumps and hind legs about all I could see of them. They looked the same as they always had. I didn't believe they talked. I certainly didn't believe they would talk to her.

"What's your fee?" I asked.

She looked off at the horses, too, then glanced at me, then worked one toe into the ground and looked at that. She was wearing blue cloth shoes with thick white shoelaces—all very clean.

Too clean. She looked clean all over. I didn't think she knew snot about horseflesh or about anything else. I figured she was a straight-out phony.

"Your fee," I said.

She had a little itch behind one ear. She scratched there.

"Before we go into my fee structure," she said, "we need to have a quiet discussion."

Fee structure? Holy Christ.

I had a good mind to turn and walk away.

"You won't tell me your fee?"

She pawed the ground again and the hand again went up to get at that itch. I stared at that hand. She had long, slender fingers and white immaculate skin with hardly any fuzz on it, and wrists no thicker than my thumb. All very feminine. She wasn't wearing a ring; I noticed that. I had her figured by this time. She was another one of those frail, inhibited, emaciated females who knew nothing about the real world but like to think they could tell you about horses. One of those grim, pitiful creatures who were forever saying to themselves and to each other, *I can relate to horses.*

I'd had my share of that lot back when I had been boarding.

"I can't tell you my fee," she said, "until I know what you want of me and why you want it."

I nearly laughed in her face. The whole business was stupid. I didn't know why I'd let myself get talked into calling her. I wished now that she'd just get in her car and go away, so I could go into the house and tell Sarah, "Well, Sarah, you got any more of your dumb ideas? Let's hear them, Sarah." Something like that. And watch her shrivel up. Watch her mew and sob and burn and hide away.

Christ, the time I was wasting. *All* the time I had wasted, listening to Sarah. Trying to take her seriously. Giving in when I knew it would prove a waste of time, all to keep a little peace in the house. To keep poor Sarah upright and not shrivelling.

I stared up at the house. Wondering if Sarah was watching. If she wasn't up there gritting her teeth, gnawing the woodwork, the broom in one hand, shoving hair out of her eyes with another, as she pressed her scared little face against a secret window. That was Sarah. Ever spying. The one way she had—so she'd tell it—of keeping her guard up.

"Mr. Gaddis?" the woman said.

"Yes, what is it?"

"All I need to know is what trouble it is you are having. With your horses. Then we can talk price."

"How about we talk *method*," I said. "*Then* price. You going to go up and whisper sweet nothings in these horses' ears? Is that what I'm paying you for?"

The woman eyed me peculiarly. Her head tilted, her mouth a shade open. It wasn't dislike so much—though I knew she didn't like me. Nor was she making judgements. I didn't know what it was. A quiet distance. A watching.

Disapproval, too; that was there.

"I don't know what the trouble is," I said. "That's why I called you. I want to know what's going on. All I know is they've been acting funny lately."

"Funny how?"

"It's hard to say. Standoffish, maybe."

"Horses are like that. Can't horses have moods, Mr. Gaddis?"

"Not on my time," I said. "They're not producing. You'd think the bastards had gone on vacation. Zombies, the lot of them."

"I see," the woman said.

Bull. She saw nothing.

I stared at her open throat. She had on this soft cottony blouse, tinted like old rose, with a wide, folded collar, and at her throat a gold necklace no thicker than a fish line.

She had on these black britches.

Up at the house Sarah had all the doors and windows shut up tight and outside not a hint of wind was stirring. Even the grass wasn't growing. It seemed to me all the life had gone out of that house. It looked dumb and impenetrable and cold.

"Sure they can have moods," I said. "And they do. All the time. But this time it's different. This time it's affecting me."

She closed the blouse and held the hand at her throat.

"How do you mean?"

"I'm losing. I haven't had a horse in the running all year."

"That could be bad luck. It could be that the other horses are better."

"Could be, but it isn't," I said. "These are good horses."

She glanced up at the house. Then she looked on up to the roof line and from there to the hills behind it. She wanted me to know she'd heard that story a thousand times before. Every owner thought he had good horses.

I thought to tell her I had a fortune tied up in these horses. That they were top dollar. Then I thought I had better not. You didn't talk fortune and top dollar when some nut was trying to get it from you. Especially a nut who imagined she could talk to horses.

"About fees," she said. "Naturally, if your horses that now are losing begin winning after I've had my chat with them, then my fee will be higher."

"A chat!" I said. "You're going to have a chat with them?"

"A serious discussion. Do you like that better?"

"I don't like any of it," I said. "You wouldn't be here if—" I stopped. I didn't see any point in raking up the family history.

"I didn't invite myself, Mr. Gaddis. You invited me."

She didn't say that with any anger. She was playing it very cool.

We both heard a door slam, and turned. Over at the back door of the house my wife stood, splashing out water from a white enamel pot. Then she swayed a little, standing there with her head bowed. Something must have told her we were looking. She glared our way, then flung her pot into the yard, and strutted back inside.

The woman beside me laughed.

I was pretty surprised myself. Sarah is prone to the odd explosion now and then—for reasons totally incomprehensible—but she'd never done anything like this before, not when someone else was around. Meek and long-suffering: that was the word for Sarah.

"I gather your wife dislikes that pot," the woman said. She laughed again, a velvety, softly arching laugh. I wanted to tell her it was none of her business.

"Forget Sarah," I said. "A minute ago you were saying something about your fee structure and my hypothetical winnings."

"Was I?"

For no reason at all this woman suddenly squatted down on her legs and began rooting through the thin grass with her long fingers. I couldn't make it out. I couldn't tell whether she was searching for rock or flower or clover, or for nothing at all. Maybe she had dropped a nickel. I had no idea what the hell she was doing. I moved a little closer. I was tempted to step on her hand. Her blouse ballooned out and I could see down her neckline to her breasts. She wasn't wearing any brassiere.

Maybe that's why she was kneeling there.

She began speaking without lifting her head. "Yes," she said, "I think that's fair. Obviously much more is involved, more work for me, if I am to talk to your horses, root out their troubles, and get them winning. On the other hand, if you simply want me to walk over to the stalls and ask how they're doing today—'How you making it, kid,' that sort of thing—and then come back here and simply repeat to you what they said, well in that case my fee would be minimum. Thirty dollars, let's say. Is that what you want?"

My wife was standing at the back door again. She had this fixed, zombie-like expression, which altered even as I watched. The skin reddened, her lips twitched, and in a moment she was twitching all over.

Then she pitched a pillow out into the yard. One of our big bed-pillows with the green slipcover still on it. Then she retreated.

The horse lady, down on the grass, hadn't noticed.

I had got around so that my back was to the door. "I was looking for something more solid," I told her. "Something tangible that I could act on. *Useful*, you know. Useful information. I *have heard* that you get good results."

She stood up. She turned and silently regarded the pillow in the yard.

"But you want my services for free, is that it, Mr. Gaddis?"

This made me mad. It was clear to me that this woman carried some sort of chip around on her shoulder. That she had no use for men. One of *those*, I thought.

"Now, listen," I said. "George Gaddis pays for goods and services properly rendered, and he always has. He pays top dollar. But it's crazy for me to fork over hundreds of dollars just to watch you go over there for an hour or two and whisper into the ears of my horses."

She stopped studying the pillow and looked across at the door. No one was at the door. Sarah had closed the screen door, then she'd closed the cedar door behind it. It was quiet as a tomb in there.

"I don't often whisper, Mr. Gaddis," she said. "I speak distinctly and usually with some force, and if you'll allow me, most horses do the same."

Haughty and reproving. She seemed to think I deserved this.

"Their powers of articulation are quite well developed, Mr. Gaddis. Perhaps more so than our own."

"They *do* talk?"

She bristled. *"Yes, they talk!"*

She struck off, moving down towards the fence at a determined pace. She truly disliked me. There, she stood leaning up against the fence with her hands in her pockets. She had narrow shoulders and narrow bony hips that would fit in a cigar box. She was a woman all right, but she was too mean and skimpy for me.

"That filly I got from Quebec," I said, "she'd be speaking French, I suppose? *J'ai la mort dans mon â, J'ai la mort dans mon â, mon coeur se tend comme un lourd fardeau.*"

She spun and stared directly at me, her face burning. Mercy, one of the horses, plodded up to the fence and nuzzled her neck and shoulders. I wasn't impressed. Mercy was a dreamer. She liked people.

The woman strolled back, calm once more.

"We are getting nowhere," she said, "and my time is valuable. I did not drive out here to give you a free estimate, or to illustrate my capabilities, or to listen to your troubles. No, Mr. Gaddis, the horses do not *talk* as such, not as we are talking, but they do think and develop their thoughts logically, except in dire cases. I am able, in a word, to read their minds."

"ESP, you mean?"

"Something like that." She fluttered a vague hand.

"You can guarantee this?"

"I do not give guarantees. I can swear to you that I will talk to your horses, but the effectiveness with which you utilize the information I glean is clearly out of my hands."

"All right," I said. "Suppose I employ you and make good use of your information, and my horses begin winning. What's your standard contract? How much do you get?"

"Normally, ten percent."

"Good God! As much as that?"

"Yes. But in this instance I shall demand twenty-five."

She shot that out. She wasn't negotiating any more.

"You're out of your mind," I told her. "You got a screw loose."

"You are a difficult person to talk to," she said. "You are a distrusting person, a bullying one, and I should imagine your horses have picked up these traits or are responding to them. It will make my job that much more difficult."

"Twenty-five *percent*!" I laughed. I still couldn't believe it. "Hell, lady, you'd be costing me more than my trainer does!"

"Then let your trainer talk to your horses."

It was my turn to walk down to the fence. Mercy saw me coming, and plodded away.

"I'll have to think about this," I said. "I don't know if any of it makes any sense."

"You have my literature, sir," she said. "You have my testimonials. Call or don't call, as you wish."

She started over to her car, a low convertible, red and shining and new, which stood in my driveway with the top down. Very expensive. Just as she was.

"I'd much prefer you *didn't* call," she said, stopping. "I don't believe I like you. Your situation does not attract my interest."

I waited until she got in the car.

"I don't suppose you like my horses *either*," I said. "I suppose you find *them* dull, too. I suppose you're one of those sanctified, scrubbed-out bitches who puts the dollar sign first. I don't suppose you care one crap about my horses' well-being."

Go for the throat, I thought. Get them in the old jugular.

She wasn't offended. Her expression was placid, composed, even a little amused. I knew that look. It was the look Sarah had when she found me in something foolish. The look would last about two minutes, then she'd begin slamming doors.

She started the engine.

I stayed by the fence, close to laughter, waiting to see if this was a woman who knew how to drive a car.

She cut the engine. She stared a long time over at my house, her hands still up on the wheel, that same benign, watchful, untroubled look in her face. Then she turned in her seat and looked down at my fences and barn. All four horses had come out. Mercy had her nose between the lowest boards, trying to get at grass, but the other three had their necks out over the fence, looking at the woman in the car.

Something funny happened in the woman's eyes and in her whole face. She went soft. You could see it soaking through her, warming her flesh.

"Go on," I said. "Get out of here."

She wasn't listening to me. She seemed, for the moment, unaware of my presence. She was attuned to something else. Her jaw dropped open, not prettily—she *was* a pretty woman—her brows went up, she grinned, and a second later her face broke out into a full-fledged smile. Then a good solid laugh.

She had a nice laugh. It was the only time since her arrival that I had liked her.

"What is it?" I asked.

"Your stallion," she said. "Egorinski, is that his name? He was telling me a joke. Not very flattering to you."

Her eyes sparkled. She was genuinely enjoying herself. I looked over at Egor. The damned beast had his rear end turned to me. His head, too. He seemed to be laughing.

She got her car started again and slapped it up into first gear. "I shall send you a bill for my time," she said. "Goodbye, Mr. Gaddis."

As she drove out, down the narrow, circling lane, throwing up dust behind her and over the white fence, I could still hear her laughing. I imagined I heard her—sportive now, cackling, giving full rein to her pleasure—even as she turned her spiffy car out onto the highway.

Sarah was at the yard pump. She'd picked up the enamel pot and was filling it with water. She was wearing her print work-dress, but for some reason she'd put back on the high heels she'd been wearing last night. She'd put on her lipstick. The little scratch on her forehead was still there. It had swollen some.

She'd brought out a blanket and dumped that out in the yard beside the pillow.

As I approached, she glanced up, severe and meaning business.

"Stay away," she said. "Don't touch me. Go on with whatever you were doing."

I could see now wasn't the time. That the time hadn't come. That maybe it would be a long time before it did.

I went on down to the barn, scooted up the ladder, and sat on a bale of hay at the loft door. I looked out over the stables, over the fields, over the workout track and the further pasture and out over all of the long valley. I looked at the grey ring of hills. I wondered what had gone wrong with my life. How I had become this bad person.

Dust

dus

Dust. I am thinking that.

I am thinking street-pavers.

I am thinking big orange machines, giant rolling pins that weigh twenty tons and can mash you flat.

I leave my room that last time, I see these thundering buggers, I am thinking, Yeah, just throw yourself down.

Down on your belly, go head first. Let fate handle the rest.

I am thinking that.

I am thinking Expo.

Clean-up, I am thinking that.

Mostly I am thinking Princess Di. On the face of it, yeah, no kidding, I am thinking Di.

Street-pavers, they come and go.

But Di?

Her picture in all the papers.

That *wan* face.

So forget street pavers, forget my eviction from flop-house hotel. Forget those Spruce-up/Renovate-me times.

Forget I left the room that day, saw the paver, said to myself: Just throw yourself down. You're gone. Let fate monkey with you.

It's allowed.

Dust, I was thinking that.

Okay, I didn't have a clear head that day, nothing to live for, let's say that.

The feeling, you know, it comes and goes. It wasn't the first time. It's a feeling will make you faint. Ask Di, she knows.

But I put this to you: When Di fainted whose arms did she fall into? Whose? Not yours, not theirs, not the Prince fellow's. But mine. Mine only.

That proved something.

It may mean nothing to you, you can call it accident, the way the wind was blowing, call it what you want, and that Prince fellow can put forward excuses until his ears grow mud flaps, but *I* know. I *know* what it means. And I savour the news. I lick at it the way you would your Häagen-Dazs.

Here's how it happened.

I saw her wilting, saw her leaning, saw her pale countenance, and moved to where I wasn't supposed to be: *between* them. Between all those dignitaries with their beaming grins. "Out of my way, Prince. Move over, please." That's what I said. And I caught her.

Me.

That proves something. It proves something I'm not going to put into print, not wanting to embarrass the Prince, the premier, all those VIPs. But what I say is *read between the lines*. You can hold Perrier in your hands, you can toast ships, cut the Coquihalla highway, take down a million trees, tout this and that new enterprise, then by God you can *read between the lines*.

The eyelids fluttered, the knees buckled, and I was there to catch her.

That illustrates some big difference between the VIPs and me, but I am not one to rub it in.

Okay, the Prince fellow sleeps with her, he guides her to right or left, he has seen her in the string bikini, has seen the lady-in-

waiting towel her dry between the toes, but that is not the end of
the world.

For me, that is not the end of the world.

I give him credit, that Prince fellow: *he* found her. We didn't
know she existed until he came up with her, that's basic, that's pri-
meval, and I am not one to deny another party his proper credit.

Even so, I cast a stone. I cast it. Because listen to this. Who has
been *losing weight* since practically the minute they hooked up?
Who has gone *toothpick thin?* You guessed it, Di. So that's one
drawback to him.

And who has got that *wan* look?

You guessed it, poor Di. That wan, downtrodden, I-want-to-
throw-up-my-hands look? Yes, *Di.*

You'd think she'd just been told to mop the floor again, that's
the look she's got.

Why don't you walk all over me? That look.

Dust. She's seen the dust too, I know she has.

And he's responsible, that Prince fellow. So I'd have to give fail-
ing marks to him on that score, however princely he may be in
other quarters.

Not to claim I don't like them thin myself, not to claim that.
No, I like them thin myself, pretty thin, on the thin side, I never
denied I didn't.

My wife, my once-upon-a-time wife, she was thin.

And another thing I'll admit, I admit it right off, despite
the prejudices it might invite against myself: I like to see Di in all
those outfits. Those outfits, I never saw so many outfits adorning
a single human body, and I never thought I'd say it, being deprived
myself, but I suddenly, with her I suddenly saw the advantage in
a big wardrobe. I sat down with my mates each evening in the

lobby at the Albert, we'd talk about it. We'd debate the issue. And I took Di's side. Whereas before I'd of said it was a monumental, inhuman waste, that this minute-by-minute sporting of the virgin garment was a colossal forging of human sin against the eye of all humankind and a crime which would cause God to thunder and drop to his knees in screaming rage—plus being salt in the wounds to your Third World—after watching Di for weeks on end what I and my lobbymates finally concluded was, well, damnit, what the heck. Why not? Because she looked so pretty, you see.

So fetching. She looked so *forlorn* and *wan*.

So, sitting there each night with my mates, coughing and passing the bottle, and a body going off each now and then to up-chuck and maybe panhandle another buck, I took to thinking about what *I* would be wearing when I met her.

God's truth.

What virgin apparel might be mine when I finally got to meet her.

Well, *clean socks*, that was about the best I could come up with. A symbolic gesture, merest dollop of good faith and intention that she would recognize and appreciate.

And she would, because that *wan* look we shared would see us past all the polite intros and social doodling.

The guys at the Albert, they'd taunt me. "You got to look spiffy, Jack. You got to knock her dead."

But their hearts were with me. They got behind my plan. I'd come in from my street business, find little tied bundles of clean clothes outside my door.

Little dregs of drink.

"You got to offer her *something*, Chief. Classy lady like that."

On this *clothes* issue what I essentially feel now is pity for the poor Pope. The poor Pope can't go anywhere, be seen any place, without his—what are they called?—his *vestments*. That *hat*.

Now that hat's a mockery.

You can't tell me that hat's good taste.

And that white robe of his, you can't tell me it isn't tatty now from all the times he's had to wear it.

Just consider: all that wealth in the chambers, the Vatican catacombs, gold that has been in the vault since the Middle Ages, but still he *elects to be seen* in public in that same, eternally the same, white chemise!

Your unisex attire.

What kind of role model is that?

But okay, each to his own.

But where's the guy's sense of adventure?

So I give the nod to Di on the "outfits" question.

Never mind that she was seen in this same dress she showed up in at Expo, seen in that same dress in Washington, D.C., six months before.

Never mind that.

Never mind she wore the same Expo shoes two days running.

Never mind that.

Let's just say she liked, she was fond of, her feet felt *right* in those shoes.

Or let's say her lady-in-waiting made a mistake.

Let's say Di slept late, wanted a minute's extra snooze, she got up and there was a rush on, the Prince fellow bellowing, so she picks up whatever footwear is nearest to hand.

Let's just admit matters are not as *sure-footed* in that household as we'd like to think they are.

People of my estate, we pay a good deal of attention to the footgear.

That fellow up in the cab of the street-paver machine, you want to know what footware he had on? *Running shoes.* The truth, so help me. These white Nikes. Spanking new.

Which is why I chose him, because a fellow in your new Nikes wasn't likely to get cracked up. He rolls over a fellow human being, it isn't likely to ruin his life.

Run of bad dreams, maybe, then it's gone.

Not that I could worry about him. No, my head was full of Expo and Di, full of my being kicked out of my room because of the spruce-up.

I'm thinking dust.

I'm thinking aeons of dust on my big rubber plant, dust all over.

I'd always felt at home in the Albert.

But there came days I'd be sitting in the lobby, passing the bottle, watching the TV for sight of Di, and to my mind dust was falling thick as our famous rains.

I'd run a finger over the window sills, over the lamps, over the lobby chairs, and you could fill pillow cases with what I rolled up.

The guys shuffling about, they're covered with dust too.

It's over everything.

And I'm thinking, I can't bring Di to this place! Expo's right, we got to spruce up!

I was a confidence-loser, that's what I mean.

Okay, use the media's word, my hotel was a dive. Transients' transigent abode. Skid-row flea bags, that's what they called places like mine. But on that issue I've got ideas of my own. Okay, dust, but I was proud of my place. Most of us, we'd been domiciled there five to fifteen years. We thought of the Albert as home. And on the spruce front, I spruced up where I could. I used the Pine-

Sol. I pulled in my rubber plant off the street, ten feet high, one some restaurant had dumped. The waste! But I was glad. Finding that rubber plant, that was fate looking after me.

Di will like this: that's what I told myself.

She sees this rubber tree, she'll feel right at home.

On the Di question I went up and down.

I had this tulip glass on my dresser drawers, I'd wipe it three or four times a day and return it to its plastic sack. Because that was Di's glass, I was saving it for her. Such a shine, one speck of dust on it and I'd fly into a rage.

Up and down. She was coming, she wasn't coming: up and down.

You had to step over this and that drunk, getting in and out. Would she be able to go with that?

The dust on that plant! You wouldn't credit the aeons of dust I wiped off.

Dust everywhere, I'm continually wiping.

But you want to know the secret? My full plan?

I figured, all along I figured, I'd bring her back to my room, pour a little something in her glass, explain my regrets at the dinginess, let her know how sorry I was she had to sit on the bed. Ease her worries with a little joke, tell her my chairs were out getting restuffed.

Yeah, upholstered, you know. Sorry, Di.

She's settled, then I'd tell her the story of my life: the flyaway parents, the jails, my own abandoned wife and kids, my itchy palm for the bottle. All my little exploits. How I never could quite get myself settled, hold the job. One thing and another, things slide, then suddenly one day you look up and it's too late.

"I've told you my story, Di. Now you tell me yours."

A fair trade, that's how I saw it.

She'd come, too. She'd listen. She'd sit on the bed. She'd get her own tale told. Because didn't we share that *wan* look? Because weren't we on the same planet and somehow in the same boat?

So I'd want that room looking pretty as could be, when she came.

Dust-free.

Okay, my secret's out. In the beginning I was in this for myself. For what *I* could get out of it. I'd be able to keep my room. Because what I truly figured was that if word got out Di was coming to the Albert, to my room, that she was making plans, then the people razing, sprucing up our old buildings, knocking down our homes, would change their plans. They'd scuttle that idea of kicking out the bums.

Because it *was* a bum Di was coming to see. I never deluded myself on that score.

Dust, okay, but otherwise I was seeing fine.

Him, the Prince fellow, I never entertained the thought he'd come. The Prince fellow, I just decided a person of my walk in life couldn't talk to him.

But then I see in the newspaper my place is not on her itinerary. I see I've been left out.

I see she's got every minute packed.

No mention of the Albert.

The minute I read that, that street-paver machine machine pops into my mind. "Throw yourself under it. Just dive head first." That's what I told myself.

Because a fellow only has room for so many betrayals in his life. Comes one more, it brims everything over, and your whole system collapses.

You give up.

It's down the drain.

Why go on, that's what you say. Let fate take over.

So I see that big street-paver, those Nikes, and from then on it's out of my hands.

But here's how that fainting happened. First there was the street machine, the guy with his Nikes, me diving, then there was the next second and what I see is Di at the California Pavilion, swooning. Definitely swooning, and no one to catch her.

She's going to fall and have a big ache.

And, like that, that big twenty-ton roller wasn't there any more. Only Di is.

Di's perfume, I smelt that.

Her body heat, I felt that.

Her sweat, too, I felt that.

Because I'd already caught her, you see. I was holding her up. One of my hands actually nudging a breast. My crusty wino's hand nudging that petite, lovely breast. My face up against her neck. Her soft skin, the perfume, the sweat.

"Is that you, Jack?" she says.

Exactly! "Is that you, Jack?"

In this fainty voice she says it, and I know then my message has got through: she meant coming to my room, only they wouldn't let her. Expo wouldn't let her and that Prince fellow, well, he'd made a fuss too.

"I meant to come, Jack. That rubber plant, all the dust you wiped, your preparations. That interested me."

She gets all this out despite the wilting.

"I could have stepped over a few drunks."

She says that.

"I'm made of tougher stuff than you think."

Imagine. She's saying that.

I've got this sensation of dampness under her arms, spot of

sweat there under her arms as she's falling. One of her shoes scoots across the floor. Her little green hat teeter-totters. Her face is stone-white, not much oomph in that smile, but she's still duti-fully upholding the nation's business. Those beautifully contoured legs have gone limp. Her weight is practically nothing, but I'm woozy from her perfume, woozy with the realization that *wan* Di is actually talking to me. That I'm holding her.

There's this too and maybe I'm ashamed to say it. Letting her down, I actually snoozled my lips against her neck. I nuzzled her. She's so warm there, so scented, so sweetly sweaty, that my tongue, as though it had a brain of its own, slid along her neck, buzzed her cheek, punged about inside her ear. My hand nudged the slopes of her petite, lovely breasts. Her lips were open, waiting.

"Love me, Jack," she says.

God's truth.

And—not to embarrass anyone with this intimate report—for a mad second I experienced a powerful desire to steal her away from this Expo site, from all these gawkers, find us a cove lit with moonbeams where we might cuddle and coo and get down to love's serious business.

Because it's clear she's willing.

She's in a weakened state, but it's clear she's willing.

She's maybe not herself, but she's agreeable.

"Say you forgive me, Jack."

And what I'm thinking is that this is *better* than having her back with me in my dingy room. That she's too fine, too nice, to be stepping over drunks and having to exclaim nicely over ragged curtains and a greasy one-burner cooker and a ten-foot rubber plant a shabby restaurant wouldn't have.

And that tulip glass, it's shiny, but it's nothing special. I'd have to tell her it was a shoplifted item.

And the dust, wouldn't that make her sneeze?

No, the Prince fellow, he's more her style. He can give her the life and creature comforts she deserves.

We're *fated* only to meet like this, to kiss, and part with these gentle, loving words.

But get this. This is what she says.

"Don't leave me, Jack."

A silken moan.

Her brow beaded with sweat, her words delivered with a desperate ache. *So* wan.

Because she knows I must. The roads divide and never the fated lovers may commingle.

Plus, there's our age difference, my liver spots, my red, bloated nose, my taste for demon juices. All my little exploits that in time would turn her love to hate.

That happens, she's really finished.

Do I want to take her down that road? Through all that?

So here's how it ended.

I lay her down. I whisper in her ear. "Rest, Di," I say. "We can't muck about with fate."

Trickle of moisture from her eyes. She's weeping.

"I get so tired, Jack," she says, "of protocol."

And hold your horses, because she hasn't given up. Do you know what she's doing? She's weak, she's fainty, a person might say she was on the point of expiring, but what she's doing is tugging at me, whimpering, trying to pull me down on top of her.

Heaven's truth, she was.

"Polish my basin, Jack," she says.

And she's tugging my hands down to that basin she means.

But I'm showing good sense maybe for the first time in my life. I've abandoned wife and kids years ago, I've mooched, I've soaked in life's tub of alcohol and been a drear weight on the whole of mankind, but I've got ethics grabbing me from some-place. She could be mine, wants to be, but I know when to stop a thing. I know when a thing is getting out of hand.

"It wouldn't work, Di," that's what I say. "We just couldn't make it, how we are."

She wilts. She truly wilts when she hears that. The eyes roll up inside her head. A sweet, wounded sigh, the most *wan* of looks, and she's gone.

She's out.

She's in never-never land.

So here's how it ended.

The lady-in-waiting is in a fit to claim that flyaway shoe.

The prince, your Royal Highness fellow, that one thumb hooked over his suit pocket like he's lost the remainder of his fingers, is bent at the waist, now dropping to his knees, showing his concern.

"Hon?" he says. "Can you hear me, hon?"

Hon. I never would have imagined.

The VIPs are in shock, can't move, except for one. He's study-ing me, hand cradling his ruddy jaw, his eyes pools of limpid water. *Don't I know you from somewhere?* He's not actually saying this, but I can see the urge, the thought. That's right, I'm saying back. I'm here. You recognize me. *Read between the lines.*

Our premier. Expo's big daddy.

The lady-in-waiting squirrels through. She's in a rage, pelting everyone, swinging that shoe. "It's these twelve-hour days," she rants. "Do you think she's made of stone?"

Everyone is bent at the waist, peering at the beautiful Di.

"No, no," she cries. "No, she's not pregnant, definitely."

I drift back, wondering. In these uncanny days, who knows?

You kiss a lady's ear, nudge a breast, anything can happen.

The premier's still watching me, a red-eyed malevolent gaze.

He comes up to me, grabs my lapel, speaks in a sneering whisper, "Aren't you that old geezer got evicted? What was it, from the Albert? Threw yourself under a street-paver?"

He's got me dead centre. I am indeed that guy.

But how? How am I here?

Wasn't there something about a fellow wearing Nikes? Wasn't there a street-paver machine in my picture?

It comes to me that I'm a time traveller.

Weird, but that's the thought that comes.

I'm a space floater.

The truth. God strike me if I lie.

But hold on.

Di is getting up. She's moving. She's going. She's drooping some, leaning on the Prince fellow's arm. Now trying to shake him and everyone else away.

"I'm perky now," she says. "Just sparkly." But she's looking around for me. She's shooting signals over her shoulder.

It comes to me in that second that we are all time travellers.

But the premier is shaking me. "Yeah," he says. "You're the guy."

We are all space floaters. That's the revelation that comes to me: that lovers can meet in unclouded future, seed and refurbish and complete anew the bonds of affirmation; that the victimized, too, may stand one day in a groaning void, and accuse their oppressor.

That it comes to us all, in the space of time, a chance to spruce things up. To renovate.

But as I open my mouth to speak, to tell this guy my beef against his way of doing things, already the premier is fading. He is, they all are, and I am myself.

No pain, hardly even a vestige of regret, but I'm plain disappearing.

I'm going.

I see my old room, the sagging bed, the ragged curtains, my rubber plant on the warped floor.

Dust is falling.

Falling on my lobby-cronies.

Dust is covering us all.

I want to scream out warnings.

Run, Di! All of you, run!

It won't stop coming.

Dust.

It is all . . . over.

Lady Godiva's Horse

FROM THE BEGINNING I did not believe, could not make myself believe, Jack wanted me. "There must be some mistake here," I'd say to him, "or am I dreaming?"

"We are hitting it off beautifully," he'd reply, "don't create trouble where none exists."

The women I work with took my position, they said, "Honey, you're heading for another nosedive, prepare yourself."

Jack was livid, he straight-armed me back against the plywood wall on Hastings Street where demolition work is going on, and said, "Rebecca, if these people make such remarks they are being thoughtless and unkind, the truth is they are not good enough for you, no doubt they are jealous of our happiness. Do yourself a favour and pay absolutely no attention to them."

This exchange took place on our lunch hour and when I got back to Vancouver Brake and Wheel the women in the office stared, they said, "Look at Rebecca June Carlyle, she must have got the bad news already."

They brought me chewing gum and a package of Scotties for

me to blow my nose on and I could tell they didn't believe me when I said, "No, I didn't get the kiss-off yet, it's just that I have a headache and my stomach is upset and I know I'm going to get the kiss-off soon."

"I've got some uppers I can give you," my friend Lydia offered, "for when matters go from bad to worse, aren't men dogs?"

Jack's own friends are wonderfully supportive of him, they go out of their way to let him know that whatever happens he's their man, they want only the very best for him.

When he came over that night I said as much, I threw his flowers on the floor and turned off *Hourglass* which is what they call the Channel 2 evening news out here, which I don't watch anyway, and I said, "Jack, it's perfectly clear to me that your friends think the world of you, time and time again I've heard them remark that nothing is too good for Jack. So tell the truth, I really would like to know: don't they wonder why you're wasting your time chasing fluff like me? Don't bother answering, I'm sure they do, but I don't blame them because the fact is I'm just not in your league."

Jack went all fence-posty, we could have heard a tack drop.

"I know exactly what they must be telling you," I went on. "'Drop her, Jack, she's bad news, that Rebecca June Carlyle is a worn-out mop and not good enough to wipe your feet on.'"

He picked up the flowers and unwrapped them from their green paper and began arranging them in the silver vase he'd given me on Groundhog Day. "Don't be dopey," he said, "my friends admire you, they see you as the answer to my prayers."

This was so absurd I laughed out loud.

I laughed about it all through dinner and in bed that night I still laughed each time I thought about it.

Oh it hurts, but I can laugh easy as the next person.

About two in the morning he got up and put on his clothes. "If you're going to keep playing that tune," he said, "I'm going home."

This is it, I thought, the kiss-off, I'll never see this beautiful man again.

"This is not the kiss-off," he told me, "it is simply that I can't take any more of it tonight and I'm going home before I get angry."

I pleaded with him to stay, I begged and begged, I have no pride. But he reminded me we both had to go to work in the morning and needed our beauty sleep.

"Especially me," I said. Then I lost my temper and threw his shoes at him, I told him it was rotten of him to leave me when I was so upset, but that I wasn't surprised, not the least little bit, no, I had always expected it.

He told me to calm down, that I was waking people, that we'd have the law on our tails.

I told him he could take his law and stuff it, I called him a lot of loud bad names and said that even if I wasn't in his league he could at least show me a little human decency and I cried and apologized and begged him to come back to my bed.

"Get up," he said, "I can't stand to see a woman weeping at my feet," and he helped me up and brushed my hair back and dried my eyes and led me back to bed and got in with me.

It was lovely after that, I truly believe it was the most exquisite night I ever had.

I didn't see him the next night. He said he had to take the ferry over to Victoria to see a man about a business he was thinking of investing in. The girls at the office said, "Yeah. I'll bet," and mentioned any of a dozen things he was more likely doing, although that day they didn't have much time for me since my friend Lydia was having a breakdown, something about her despot husband, I forget the details.

At midnight Jack called me from what he said was Ye Olde English Inn. He said he always stayed at the O.E.I. when in the Flower City because he loved it and because a replica of Annie Hathaway's cottage was right on the site and he wanted to build a house just like it for me sometime.

"Who're you with?" I asked.

"I'm with my lonesome," he said, "and missing you."

I told him I was sure he had a woman with him, but I could understand it, I certainly didn't expect faithfulness to a non-person like me.

"Don't start that again," he said.

I told him about the girl in the office, my friend Lydia, who was having a breakdown brought on by her jerk husband.

He said he was sorry.

Finally I let him hang up, it must have been about one.

I couldn't sleep and tried doping myself up with a late movie. I knew he was with someone. A man like Jack can't go ten minutes without some pretty trick pulling on his arm. The fact is, as I told Walter Pidgeon, Jack is Vancouver's most eligible bachelor. He can have any woman in town. Before I came into the picture he had women dropping in on him from as far away as the Yukon. Right there on the cover of *Miss Chatelaine* I've seen a woman who chased him for years. One time at his place while he was taking a shower I had a sneak look around his bedroom and found in his closet six shoeboxes stuffed full of love letters from scores of women who promised him eternal love and anything else he wanted, not to mention those from his ex-wife, poor Alice. He can have beautiful women and smart women and women so rich I guess their feet never touch ground.

"You can see," I'd say to him, "how that makes me feel."

"Aw, dry up," he'd say. "Even if all that is true, and I doubt it, you're the girl for me."

Walter Pidgeon went to war and got shot down and June Allyson was left with his baby and with Van Johnson who had been her boyfriend before Walter moved him out.

One of the office girls said she'd stayed up to see it too and had almost puked, but most of us wondered why they didn't make movies like that any more.

Jack showed up at lunchtime right on the button and took me to a restaurant nearby, Murphy's Chinese.

He asked me why I was so grouchy, had I been losing sleep?

"You know I can't sleep by myself any more," I said.

"So what's the problem?" he asked.

"Us," I said. "We are the problem. We are mismatched."

"How so?"

"You have everything and I have nothing. Charm, brains, good looks, all that was passed out when I was off somewhere hiding. I have nothing to offer a man of your qualities."

Jack ate his noodles in silence. He gave me a brochure of dear Annie Hathaway's cottage to take my mind off matters.

"Let's set the date," he said.

"I can't do it, Jack," I said. "If you marry me they'll laugh you out of town."

He ordered me a second glass of wine, since I wasn't eating. But he was reluctant, because Jack hates to see me get high. He's right, too, because when I get high I get arch and argumentative and take offence at any harmless remark passed.

I truly am an impossible person.

"That's not true," he said. "You are more apt to get vague and dreamy and happy all around. Drink it down."

I asked him why he was stringing me along. "What's in it for you?" I asked.

"I was hoping you could get me a cut price at Vancouver Brake and Wheel," he said.

Our lunch hour was over but I just sat there vague and dreamy and not the least bit happy. "Duty calls," Jack said, and came behind me to lift my chair. I refused to leave. I told him I wasn't going back to work, not ever. Vancouver Brake and Wheel could take their chintzy mindless job and shove it, nobody there liked me, I was paid dog wages and taken advantage of in every conceivable way, and I was quitting, I had just quit, I meant to spend the rest of my life at this table in Murphy's Chinese looking at a plate of wiped-up noodles.

Jack whispered I was making a scene and if I didn't get up that very minute he was going to leave without me.

"I know," I said, "you're only looking for an excuse to kiss me off."

He sat down and bent over the table to talk to me in reasonable tones about personal responsibility and our debts to humanity at large and how Murphy needed our table because other people were waiting.

So I got up, that's just the kind of inconsistent, led-by-the-nose person I am.

"I know I'm a wipe-out," I told him out on the street, "you best walk on now and forget all about me."

We stopped to look through a peep-hole in the wall where the demolition work is going on on Hastings Street. Their big crane was up with this huge steel ball suspended on a chain and they were slamming this ball against a building that had been perfectly satisfactory for sixty-five years and now they were knocking it all down.

Jack gave me a kiss and hurried off because he had a bunch of very important people waiting to hear what he thought about some big project of theirs.

Soon after I got back to work Lydia's husband came in looking for Lydia who hadn't showed up that day and when none of us could help him he picked up her old adding machine off her desk and threw it against the wall, and then he tore apart her desk apparently looking for secrets he believed she kept in there, and he kept shouting these awful insults about Lydia and her secret life and how he would punch her in the snoot if he ever found her and how she was crazy if she thought she could walk out on him. "You *robots*," he shouted at us, "what do any of you know about life, you're just living and working here in your little garden world at Vancouver Brake and Wheel and you know *nothing*, you might as well all be *dead!*"

I tried calming him down but he told me I was shrivelled up and stupid and ought to go live my life in a cage.

Then he left before the police could come.

"Mark my words," one of the women said, "a few days from now when Lydia gets over her embarrassment and her black eyes heal she'll come in and explain that Simon was drinking or wouldn't have behaved that way, that she feels sorry for him, that they've worked all their problems out now and their marriage is a bed of roses."

Most of us disagreed, we figured this was the final straw.

The manager made a cute speech saying how regrettable this incident was, he was sorry it had upset us, the man was an animal and ought to be beheaded, but it was over now and he hoped the company could expect a good day's work out of us.

At five o'clock every afternoon I feel this insane love for Vancouver Brake and Wheel, it takes about three seconds for everyone to clear out, one would think we were running from a sex-starved maniac.

I went home and had a slow hot bath, it turned out I had tiny slivers of glass imbedded in the skin all along my arms and shoulders from when Simon threw Lydia's glass desk top against the filing cabinets.

Jack came hurrying over, he had the idea I was bleeding to death and should be rushed immediately to the Emergency.

He used his own key to get in and when he saw me in the bath with bloody water up to my neck he almost fainted.

I hadn't planned he'd take it so seriously and had to show him the empty bottle of red food dye I'd used before he would calm down.

Then we got under the sheets and that was exquisite.

"Are you hungry?" he asked later, and I said I was ravenous, I wished aloud I could just once cook him something better than bacon and eggs but in that category too I'm a washout, I was always too lazy to learn.

"Never mind," he said, "I'll cook up something nice," so he leapt out of bed and went to it.

The TV had been wheeled up to my bedside to keep me company and I threw a shoe at it and it came on. The *Hourglass* people were announcing that hikers earlier in the day had come across the nude body of a young girl murdered in Stanley Park, and naturally I thought of my daughter Cherise and shrieked for Jack. But then they said she'd been there for months under a bed of moss so I knew it couldn't be Cherise who was safe with her father, but even so Jack had to hold me until I stopped shaking.

"God," I moaned, "there are times when I think the world is coming to an end."

"Don't dwell on bad news," he told me, "people fell in love today, had birthdays, brought each other flowers, life goes on."

The mysterious firebomber had struck again, this time at First Federal Savings and Loan, and I let out another shriek because First Federal is only two doors down from Vancouver Brake and Wheel.

"No, it was another branch," Jack explained, but he turned off the TV and passed me a book to read, *The Lifetime Adventures of Mary Worth*, which he'd given me and which I have come to dearly love. It has become such a comfort to me, at every crisis I find myself asking, "What would Mary do? How would Mary cope with this?"

A few minutes later Jack brought in our dinner, bacon and eggs, all he could find in my refrigerator, and we ate off the hand-sewn patchwork quilt I've carried with me all these years.

I asked him what he thought about Lydia's situation. "Do you think she really has a secret life?"

He turned traitor, he asked me about mine. "How was it," he asked, "with you and Jake?"

I went mopish and quiet. I was married for some great horrendous while to a man who refused on principle to reveal any emotions about anything that happened anywhere in the world or at home, to him, to me, to our child, or our friends.

"Ask Jake," I told Jack.

"I have. Jake's like you, he dries up, won't say a word."

I didn't believe this and said so. Jake's the most horrible person imaginable, next to me, and he wouldn't pass up any opportunity to dish the dirt on me.

Just my luck that he was Jack's best friend.

Jack had to go out that evening, "to put out a fire," he said.

I didn't ask for explanations, I was too tired and knew I could do nothing to hold him anyway. Before going to bed I sat a long time at my dressing table, contemplating my face with the intense hatred of Medea: my complexion is too sallow, my left eyelid is droopy, my face is blotchy, my eyes are blah, my skin is so oily, my nose is too short, my jaw is too square, and I've got a neck like a lamppost.

A moustache like Hitler. I'm ugly as a rat.

No bosom to speak of.

Jack is so handsome, he's everyone's dream, when I walk into a room with him everyone goes silent, they feast on him. Often the Art Museum will hire him just to come in and walk around.

I walked in my pigeon-toed fashion to the bed and slid between the sheets with all the grace of an orange crate.

I really ought to give up.

The phone rang. It was my daughter Cherise, wanting to know if she could spend the weekend with me.

"Why," I asked, "is Jake having a party?"

"No," she said, "it's only that I thought it was time I saw you."

"I'm still dangerous, you know," I said, "I might slice off your thumbs."

She told me to stop talking that way. She said I sounded distant. She said if I wasn't in the mood or had plans we could make it another time.

"How's your father?" I asked.

She said he was fine, that he had been crawling around on the floor with her on his back.

I told her she should be asleep, that tomorrow was a school day and that it was outrageous of him to allow her to stay up so late. I heard her turn away from the phone and tell her father what I had said. I couldn't hear his reply.

"Can I come?" she asked me.

I told her it was sweet of her to want to and that certainly she could.

"How's Jack?" she asked.

I said fine.

"Is he there now?"

"No, he's out."

"Are you going to marry him?" she asked. "Daddy says you ought to but that you won't because all men scare or bore you to death."

I told her to hang up now and go to bed.

She did.

Jack didn't wake me when he came in. But he put his arm around my waist and I must have been dreaming because I thought it was Jake's arm and I started up screaming and hitting at him.

He apologized, and both of us immediately fell asleep.

In the morning Jack rolled over, asking "What is it now?"

I was at my dressing table, weeping. My skin had broken out in a rash. My stomach was upset too. I couldn't do anything with my hair.

Jack went into the shower.

I quickly went through his suit coat pockets and the trousers he'd neatly draped over a chair, but found nothing revelatory.

He's been extremely careful lately.

Even his shoeboxes have disappeared.

I wrote out a phone number and folded it to the size of a postage stamp and hid it inside his wallet. Later on I intended to "find" it and accuse him and see how he attempted to excuse or defend himself.

A bag of groceries was on the kitchen counter and he had filled the refrigerator. I made instant coffee and toast and had them on the table waiting for him.

He said, "Oh, Christ!" and dumped out the cups and began making what he considers a proper breakfast.

"Would you like pancakes?" he asked.

I said yes.

"Or an omelet?"

I said an omelet would be fine.

He asked if I wanted grapefruit.

I said yes. I told him Cherise was coming over for the weekend.

"That's good," he said, and stopped in his kitchen duties to kiss me because he thinks I like feeling like a mother. "I'll stay at my place."

"That's not necessary," I said. "She knows we sleep together."

He grinned. He said she might know we sleep together but she didn't know it was exquisite.

"That's not funny," I said.

He insisted it was. "You always say it's exquisite whether it is or isn't," he observed.

It's true. I don't mean to deceive or pretend, it's just that I was born a hypocrite and have always been one.

"But I can always tell when it is," he said, "because your toes turn green."

I didn't respond to this. I was thinking about being with Jake and how that had been exquisite too, much of the time. Jake was a good lover, in bed he was another person, all warm and delicious, and he would cry when at last he had to get up and put his pants on.

Jack put the first pancake down in front of me, buttery and thin and very like a crepe, and asked should he cut it for me, should he douse it with true maple syrup and say grace if I was so inclined.

I let him.

I *adore* being looked after. That's what finally did it with Jake, he simply got fed up with pampering me.

From the stove Jack said, "Cherise is the kind of girl who will very much enjoy having two fathers."

"Why is that?"

"Jake is wonderful," he said, "and I am wonderful, and together we make up for all your alleged shortcomings."

"Then you should marry Jake."

He said no he shouldn't.

He poured my coffee, and brought it over, along with milk and sugar. "Shall I stir it for you?"

I admitted I was capable.

Jack makes delicious pancakes, unlike Jake. I could eat them for a week and put on thirty pounds and then I would look more nearly the way I feel inside.

Jack was getting edgy, he showed me his watch and said time was moving on and we'd best shake a leg or both of us would be late to work.

"The world will not end," I told him.

Jack is one of those odd people who regards punctuality as a virtue.

"I'll have to clean the apartment," I moaned. "Cherise is like her father, it's white gloves every time."

"Hire someone," Jack suggested.

I said I hated doing that, people were not made to clean up after me.

He sighed. He put aside the pancake batter and went to get the vacuum.

He's faster and more thorough at cleaning up than Jake ever was. He's more organized. Jake liked best cleaning up those places the people never saw, like closet interiors, door mouldings, or under the bed.

I put my dishes in the sink. I could do that much. I was feeling very depressed. It was on account of Cherise, whenever she is about to visit me I go into a nosedive. She arrives and her eyes never leave me, she measures everything I say and do and then she goes back to Jake and tells him what a cripple I am, how shabby I look, she says, "Boy, were you ever wise to get rid of that loser."

It was on account of Cherise and because I hate my apartment, it's the most depressing, lonely place in the world, I loathe it with every breath I take, it is exactly like me, it has no personality and it oozes laziness and stupidity and insufferable bad taste, although it isn't the fixtures or the furniture or the decorating that explains this since the place is exactly as it was when I moved in, I haven't done a solitary thing to it, not hung a single picture or slapped on a single dab of paint, just my presence in the place makes it drab and horrible and it has been that way every place I ever lived.

"You're in a mood today," Jack said.

I said no I wasn't.

"Yes, you are." He was standing beside my plastic fern, staring at it, holding the vacuum cleaner hose in his hands, looking like a beat-up dog.

"Anything I've done?" he asked.

I told him I wished he would shut up, there was nothing worse than being told you were in a mood when you knew perfectly well that you were not.

He shrugged, and started vacuuming.

I went into the bathroom to brush my teeth. The cap had been left off the toothpaste tube and although I remembered leaving it that way myself I shouted at Jack, accusing him. The paste wouldn't come out and finally I had to stomp on it. It shot out like a thin white lasso half the length of the floor and it shocked me so that I screamed, and Jack came running.

"What is it?" he asked, and I said, "Snake," and laughed at his face, and passed him a tissue and he dropped to his knees and wiped it up.

Jake would never put up with madness like this, he'd glare at me or take a swing and then he'd storm out of the house and I wouldn't see him for a week.

"There, that's got it," Jack said, standing, and he moved to kiss me but I wouldn't let him. "God," he said, "you are being disagreeable, what has put you in this mood?"

"I don't know."

"You can tell me."

"All right," I said, "if you really want to know. The truth is that I've been thinking this morning that I'm tired of sex and think we ought to lay off it for a while, say six months or so until I'm in the mood again. I'm sorry, that's just how I feel."

He said okay, no problem with him.

"Are you sure you don't mind?"

He said he thought we ought to talk about it.

"We have talked about it," I said, "and that's my decision, like or leave it."

He looked uncertain and deeply hurt and I could feel it coming, the kiss-off, I knew this time I had gone too far.

"I mean it," I said.

He said he knew it, and tried out a smile. He said it would be a great personal loss to him to go without sex with me for six months but that he would be willing to go five years without it if that's what it took to give me peace of mind.

"You'll go elsewhere for it," I told him.

He said no, no, he wouldn't. Then he came up behind me and put his arms around me, watching my face in the mirror. "Even so," he murmured, "I see no reason to change our plans. Let's set the date."

I finished brushing my teeth and spat lather all over the sink and didn't answer him.

Jake had never said, "Let's set the date" or anything else to me in the area of romance. I had pursued him through a dozen cities and finally had worn him down until he was forced to say, "Yes, yes, I'll marry you for God's sake, if that's what it takes to get you off my back."

Of course I was carrying Cherise then and he had a vague interest in sticking around to see whether she would resemble him.

No, that's wrong, Cherise came a full two years later, I've got to stop making up these stories just to dramatize myself and retain the interest of men like Jack. Why bother, since the kiss-off is coming in any case.

Jack came back in to tell me someone was hammering on my door.

"Can't you answer it," I said, "are your hands tied, can't you do anything around here?" My tone was blistering, I was in a mood to kill anyone who got in my path.

Jake would have knocked me down.

He was right, the door was shaking and Lydia was calling my name.

I opened the door and she rushed in. She looked terrible.

"Whatever it is," I told her, "I can't be bothered."

"I've got to hide," she cried. "Simon is after me, he's trying to kill me!" Then she saw Jack and instantly perked up, she went from brutalized, trampled-upon womanhood to sexy female all in one amazing second. "Hi!" she said, and batted her eyes.

Lydia is what is known as vivacious or fun-loving. She is just over five feet tall, she's sway-backed to the extreme although she uses that to her advantage, and she has jet black hair cut even with her ear lobes and whenever she's in the vicinity of a man her body is a constant wiggle, she becomes part vixen and part pixie and she flirts outrageously and her whole performance makes me sick.

I was like that myself when I first took up with Jake, but he cured me of it by locking me in a closet every time I did.

Lydia never addresses her remarks to a woman if there is a man around. She was telling Jack she hadn't been home all night. "I spent the night in the train station," she said, "I know I must look awful, I can almost feel the vermin crawling over me. A thousand men must have come on to me, it's disgraceful that in a public place people can make such lewd proposals."

Jack pretended to be interested, he's much too civil for his own good.

"I thought you had given her the kiss-off," Lydia said, hooking a thumb over her shoulder at me.

"No," Jack told her, "I'm up to my neck, but I'm in it for good."

Lydia squealed, she seemed to think that very funny.

She turned to me. "You've got to hide me out for the day," she said. "Simon would stick an ice pick in me if he found me. Don't breathe a word of my whereabouts to anyone because he has his spies everywhere."

I told her I was willing but that I didn't like it, what if Simon got it in his head to kill me too?

"He won't. Simon likes you, he says you're a very steady and dependable person. Sometimes I even think he has a crush on you. Anyway he's too chicken to kill anyone except me."

Jack put his arms around me. He informed Lydia he was going to build an Annie Hathaway cottage for me, and protect me, and keep me smiling for the rest of my life.

I broke into tears and fled into the bedroom, unable to help myself. It seemed to me Jack was patronizing me in front of one of my friends, he knew Lydia gossiped like a pirate and now everyone would know how much I was being played for a fool, because whether Jack meant it or not and whether I wanted it or not Jack would come to his senses soon and give me the kiss-off good and fast just the way Jake did, and I would never know true happiness. I would never know a normal life. I would be bound to go from man to man and be their plaything, give them the one thing I could give, give it until they tired of me and dumped me and went out to find a decent woman.

Lydia rushed in to comfort me. "Don't go to pieces," she said. "I think he means it," and somehow that made me cry all the more, I'm such a sap, I fall into these weeping frenzies now and then, weeping is all I can do and sometimes it will go on for weeks.

The phone rang. "Excuse me, I can't answer as it might be Simon," Lydia said, "and Jack is finishing up the vacuuming."

It was Vancouver Brake and Wheel wanting to know whether my stomach was upset again, did I mean to come in today.

I told them yes, I had been fighting a small fire at my place, a three alarmer, but it was under control now and I would be in shortly.

I dried my eyes and told Lydia to make herself at home. I promised I wouldn't let on to Simon where she was. Then I went out to meet Jack, all smiles again because I know he expects it of his women.

Jack's car was parked on the street and someone had left a leaflet under the wiper informing him he could get his house Kinetexed at a surprisingly low cost, Never Paint Again and Make Back Your Kinetex Costs by What You Save on Fuel from a Properly Insulated and Kinetexed Home or Business Establishment.

"Annie Hathaway wouldn't like it," he said.

We didn't talk much on the way into town. I guess Jack thought I was too upset to speak but really I was thinking about what the women at Vancouver Brake and Wheel would say when I told them where Lydia was, and I wondered whether they'd agree with me that we should telephone Simon right away and put the bee in his ear.

He pulled in at the curb and grabbed at my hand as I was getting out. "Lunch?" he asked.

I said I'd have to see.

"I'd like to shake you," he said. "Why are you doing this to me?"

I told him I didn't know what he was talking about, that I had to go.

He banged his fist on the wheel and spun his tires getting away, and I knew I had had it then, the kiss-off but good.

The women were in a fever, listening to me tell of Lydia's adventures, and they began exchanging stories of what had happened to them when they had been caught for the night in a train station.

Simon said he'd roar right over to my place, this time he'd teach her a lesson she wouldn't forget.

Jack didn't show up for lunch and didn't call and when I called his office his secretary told me he'd been sent spur-of-the-moment to Calgary for an important business meeting having to do with Gulf Oil's attempted takeover of Canadian nursing homes.

She obviously believed I'd swallow any lie.

But that evening I returned from work to find twenty-one boxed Canadian Beauty roses outside my door, together with a hastily scribbled note from him.

Lydia and Simon had had it out in my bedroom, I could tell by how tidy everything was.

Jack's note said I should keep the home fires burning.

I am so tired of eggs and bacon, I think the Egg Marketing Board ought to be hung, but that's what I had for dinner. I missed Jack and I wept for him, I was lonely and went through the apartment talking aloud to myself, but it also seemed he had never been there, that I hadn't spent all my time with him these past weeks. I felt the way a person must feel who finds everything she has ever known and loved didn't really exist and the future of her own existence is better left to those who insist that we all turn to dust anyhow.

I called Cherise and when she answered I couldn't speak, I gripped the phone and stared at the black mouthpiece but didn't know how.

"Is it *you*," Cherise finally said, "or is this the breather?"

I caught at the straw and began breathing.

"Hi, mom," she said.

God, that my own daughter can speak to me as if I'm a normal person, after knowing me all these years.

"Are you coming?" I asked.

She said sure. "Jake isn't here," she said, "did you want to talk to him?"

I said no. I couldn't bear to hang up and face my apartment alone, so I told her about Lydia's troubles with Simon and asked if I had done the right thing in telling him where she was hiding.

She didn't pause to think about it. She said in her opinion a person ought to be loyal to her friends, but that I knew the people involved better than she did so she wasn't prepared to say.

I told her she was being cloyingly diplomatic, why didn't she say straight out that I was a devious and conniving bitch who couldn't be trusted any farther than I could be seen.

"Well, you've had problems," she said. "We'll talk about it tomorrow."

"What would you like to do tomorrow?" I asked.

"Oh, mom," she said, exasperated, "don't take me to another movie."

The last time she had visited I had taken her to see *Grease* and she had thought it stupid except for the Sandra Dee number.

She said a few sweet things to me and then hung up.

Jack's note said he adored me.

I got exhausted walking around the apartment and wringing my hands and when I climbed in bed there was another Walter Pidgeon movie on the tube. This time he had Greer Garson with him and all their nine children were so cute in their raccoon coats I turned it off and tried to sleep.

Jack's letter said his star was attached to mine and that he loved me to the moon and back, what about a June wedding in Stanley Park. *Yours forever*, he signed it, and this made me weep, I got it out from under my pillow and put it in the shoebox along with the others so it wouldn't wrinkle and so that when I was an old woman scuffing about in my slippers at Gulf's Rest and Nursing Home I could get it out again and use it to prove to the world that I had been used and misled and humiliated and deceived at every turn by men who know only one line and that one the biggest lie on God's green earth.

Cherise came early on Saturday morning. I had got up early myself to unlock the door and tape a note to it saying, *Cherise, I had to step out a minute, be right back, you come right in.*

But she marched straight into the bedroom where I was hiding and told me that Jake who had brought her was not going to leave until I came out and at least said hello to him.

I wept, said I couldn't bear to, I said if she loved me she could do this much for me, she could go out there and tell him to quit my premises immediately, that I was in no shape to see him and that if I did anything might happen.

She went out and told him.

She came back and said he was sticking put.

I was seated on the edge of the bed, quivering, and she sat down beside me and took my hands.

"You've got to figure this out for yourselves," she said, "and stop putting me in the middle. I'm only an adolescent and the strain is too hard on my nerves."

She said a lot more, we both did, and inside a few seconds each of us was weeping.

"Go out and speak to him," she said, "he won't bite."

I told her I knew what he wanted, that he wanted to tell me that the divorce was final, maybe even that he had the papers to serve on me.

"Husbands don't serve the papers," she said, "a representative from the court does that."

"Then what does he want?"

"He only wants to see you. He wants to see for himself how you're doing."

I told her I was in misery, any idiot could see that.

She couldn't do anything with me and went out to tell him, I guess, that I was very upset.

He came in and sat down by me in her very spot.

He didn't say anything and I couldn't. I was crying and couldn't catch my breath and after a while he put one arm around me and patted my back.

He always used to do that, it drove me crazy.

Then he began crying too.

Cherise stood in the doorway watching us. She had on a red coat and looked like Little Red Riding Hood. She said we were both sensible people and ought to have our heads examined.

I begged her to come over and sit with us and Jake asked her too, but she refused to come.

"This happens every time you see each other," she said. "I'm fed up with nursemaiding you two."

I said I'd get up and get her some ice cream.

Jake didn't leave, he spent the afternoon and the evening and then it was too late for him to bother returning to his place so he spent the night, and that was exquisite.

Jack came in on Sunday. He came in smiling and shouting my name and then he saw it was Old Home Week and sat down in a chair to hang his head and to moan over and over, "So this is it, I've had it, you're giving me the kiss-off."

The three of us tried cheering him up, we told him there were lots more fish in the pond, I could give him Lydia's number for instance, he'd like Lydia. But nothing we could say worked and he shouted that he would like to murder us, all three of us, but in the end he went away quietly, although he told us it would never work, that we were too pig-headed and self-indulgent, too opinionated and stupid and ridiculous ever to find true happiness with each other.

"I hope I never get the brush-off," Cherise afterwards said. "I think I'd die."

The Only Daughter

T HE LANE upon which the child walked was long and straight, with high red-dirt walls to either side, which sometimes she could see above and other times could not. It was more trench than road, wide enough perhaps for three people to walk abreast, perhaps wide enough for a wagon. Yes, for a wagon, for she could see in the slippery mud where one had come and gone, though not when. The walls were eroded by rain and where boulders were packed into the dirt scraggly bushes, leafless now, made vain attempts at renewal. She walked mostly in the lane's middle, trying to avoid the collected puddles, since her shoes were new, or newish, and she yet took some pride in them. Suitcases half her own height hung from each arm. She had started the day with a ribbon through her hair, tied at the top in a bow, but at some point several miles back the ribbon had come loose and now lay unmissed in the mud. She wore, in addition to the shoes and a thin cotton dress, a black coat that flopped unevenly around her heels. A circle of mud, steadily expanding, caked the hem and seemed to pull the coat farther from her shoulders. From time to time, fretfully, she yanked it back. A single large button secured the coat; the button was ever travelling up to her throat; her heels were ever stepping onto the hem. The coat draped loosely on her, an adult's coat, inherited with something of that other person's shape still intact. The sleeves were twice folded at each wrist that her hands might be clear. It had had a belt once; she wished she had it now.

From time to time she paused and placed the suitcases on dry earth or on stumps, on weedy patches in the lane, and shook her arms until feeling returned to them.

She had been walking this lane since first light; she had traversed it for a portion of yesterday. Now the sun, although it brought no warmth, was directly overhead. It moved when she moved, and at what pace she moved, and stopped when she stopped. But she did not look often at the sun or sky; she kept her sight on the road, on her feet, for the lane was strewn with rock and brush, with brown puddles of varying size, with massive boulders that cropped up from floor and wall. Occasionally, where the land was flat, the woods encroached until the land all but disappeared. She went, at such times, the way the wheel tracks went, passing under pine and cedar, under hemlock and droopy locust, under willow and numerous other dusty, unswaying trees. Where red dirt receded, clumps of wild grass took over, competing with moss and clover, and here she took longer rests. With leaves and sticks she wiped new layers of mud from her shoes. Her feet were wet and cold, but she was accustomed to this and gave thought to it only when pebbles worked inside her shoes. She wore a grown woman's nylon stockings, which bunched at her ankles. Originally these had been retained by rubber bands just above her knees, but the bands, rotted already, had broken countless times and no longer held. One she sometimes chewed in her mouth, trudging along now at a diminishing pace.

Rests were more frequent now. Her shoulders ached. Her legs ached, and her arms and hands worst of all, though her feet ached too. Her shoes were too tight. The man at the store had told her they would loosen, but they hadn't. This morning they'd been stiff and hard, though still wet, and she'd opened a heel blister, getting them on. She'd bitten her lip and tears had come, but she'd kept them on. She was too cold to feel much anyhow. Her hands were blistered too. They were swollen some. The suitcase handles were sharp, like little razors. She'd tried wrapping leaves about the handles but they'd shredded in a minute. They'd been slippery too. Green stuff had got into her cuts and stung. Maybe it was her hands that hurt the most. She'd thought it was her hands, but she'd carried the cases a few feet and the ache had hit her shoulders again. She was hungry, but she wasn't going to think about that. The shoulder ache was worse. Pins and needles stabbed down from her neck; her neck was stiff. A stiff neck was nothing though. She could put up with a stiff neck. The shoulder ache made her groan; it made her grit her teeth. But after a while she'd decided it was her arms that hurt more, the bones stretched near to bursting. Nothing could hurt more than that. But she'd halt and put down the cases and dangle her arms and shake that pain away. She couldn't shake out the shoulder ache; shoulder was worse. She was hungry, but she wasn't going to think about that. Heck with that. What was bad was the button, which kept crawling up, gnawing a hole at her throat, always in the same spot. Maybe that was the worst. Like somebody digging at it with an ice pick or pinching that same spot over and over. This was the most maddening somehow, because such a little thing. You wouldn't believe a smooth button could be so sharp. The same place over and over, her skin raw. Like her heels. Her heels were bloody. These stockings were ruined. Well, she didn't mind that; she had plenty

more. Maybe a dozen pair. She had a hat too, but you didn't need
a hat out here. A hat would be silly out here. Mud was on her coat,
but she couldn't help that. Mud was nothing, you could wash out
that. She hoped you could. This dress she had on, you could sure
wash that. She'd done so herself, and ironed it too, not three days
ago. Not that a person would know it now. It was her shoes she
most cared about. They were pretty shoes. If she ruined them that
would be her bad luck because she had no other pair. But how
could you ruin cowhide? Cows got wet, they didn't ruin; no reason these would either. She was hungry, but she wasn't going to
think about that. Thinking about it only made matters worse.
Last night she'd thought about it anyway, but only for a little
while. Then she'd slept and thought about her aches. About
which was worst. It was awful, whichever way you thought, but
she wasn't going to cry about it any more than she was going to sit
down in this lane and quit. She didn't mean to walk this road forever; aches would mend, cuts and blisters heal. She'd been tired
before, tired a thousand times. Hungry too. But she'd got over it.
She would this time too. So she bit her lip and let her eyes stay wet
as they wanted to; she laboured on. She'd be there pretty soon.
This lane wasn't no endless highway going nowhere. She knew
where it was going. Her instructions had been clear on that score.
Git out fast. Go to him. This is where he lives.

Whenever she stopped now she would lie back, if that were
possible, and draw the big coat tight about herself, and close her
eyes. She would doze. But always, after a minute or two she would
start up as if from fright, and dig both hands into her coat pockets. The left pocket contained an unopened package of Luden's
Wild Cherry cough drops, and five or six black hairpins when
these did not happen to be in her hair. In the right pocket was a
small leather change purse, much scarred. She would open it and

empty it in her lap and count her money. Her fear was that she would lose this or that it somehow might be stolen. She feared pickpockets even here on this solitary lane, for long ago, in another place, her mother had screamed and yelled and cried because a pickpocket had got her money. She remembered that. She remembered her mother's alarm as she cried, "How can we live? Tell me how we can manage now!" She remembered her mother's alarm, and her own, but not how they had managed. She had noticed no difference in how they got along. They had moved, she remembered that. Her mother had been absent much of the time. This was because of the pickpocket. She knew that.

She had in her possession two quarters, three dimes, a nickel, and four pennies. Yesterday she had had more but the man on the bus had taken the dollar bill. He had taken the half-dollar too, and had seemed to want to take more, but she had bitten her lip, watching his every move, and thirty-nine cents had been miraculously returned to her palm. "How I know you're not cheatin' me?" she said. "How I know how much this bus trip is?" "You don't," he said. He'd had a cigarette dangling from his lips the whole time, and scabs on his hand. He'd had black hairs in his nose. "You don't. No, you don't. You don't know nothin', I expect." She'd not risen to this taunt. She'd kept her palm open, stretched out to him. "You want me to kiss it?" he said. "Maybe you want a glob of my spit?" She'd yanked her hand back, since it seemed no more change was forthcoming. She'd put the coins in her purse and the purse in her coat pocket, and staggered down the aisle with her two suitcases. She'd put the cases on a seat at the back where there was a big round hump in the floor. For resting your feet, she supposed. She climbed over them and sat at the window, which wouldn't open. "You see them racks?" he said. "Them racks is for the suitcases. Ain't you never travelled before?" He stood over her, his cigarette dangling, squinting at her. She'd thrown her body over the suitcases. "I ain't putting them nowhere," she said. "I ain't having my property stole."

He'd gone.

She talked to no one during the journey. The bus was nearly empty. A boy hardly out of diapers sat up front, making faces at her. She gave him her black look and kept her lips sewed tight. He came back once and said, "This ain't your bus. I never seen you on this bus before." When he went back to his seat his mother slapped him. She ought to have. She ought to have smacked him a dozen times. She curled up, making a careful, secret study of each inch of the interior. Cold wind came through the window. The tires whined. The seats were hard and squared off at the back where there was a rod you could lean your head against. The bus had a flat roof with rounded edges. The floor was nothing but loose planks. The seats weren't yellowy though, like the dinette she and her mother used to have. The terrain outside was mostly a blur, and she told herself it wasn't worth looking at. The window was smeary anyhow.

It wasn't worth a bit what she'd paid.

In the afternoon, and repeatedly after that, she moved up the aisle to remind the man with the cigarette where she wanted to get off and to wonder aloud if he hadn't passed it already.

"Nobody told me it was this far," she said.

"That's right," he said. "You're abducted. This here is John Dillinger at the wheel."

"I don't care who you are. You better stop at that crossroads I told you about."

"It ain't no crossroads," he said. "It ain't hardly nothing. Just a scratch in the woods, that's all it is."

"That's a big lie," she said.

"This here bus is heated," he told her. "Supposing you take off that there hot coat and try to relax yourself." She held her hand clenched over the purse in her pocket while she talked to him. She had no faith in him. He was one of them smart talkers, those her mother said you had to look out for. He looked to her like an out-and-out damn fool, with his stubbly growth of beard, with his scabs and dangling cigarette and his eyes squinted up so tight it surprised her he could see the road.

"Who you visiting?" he asked, but she locked her lips and veered back to her seat.

If he didn't stop where he was supposed to she didn't know what she'd do. She wondered what a body was supposed to do when it had to go to the bathroom. The boy up front got smacked again.

"It's going to rain," somebody said.

Somebody was always saying that. They got their brains out of a marble jug.

The man nearest her was eating a white apple. She'd never seen no white apple before. It almost made her puke to watch him eat it. But she watched every bite he took, and when he had gnawed it down to seeds and core she saw him drop it on the floor. She wouldn't eat no white apple no matter how hungry she got. She wouldn't eat no turnips either, or spinach, or innards of any kind. She wouldn't eat no dog either.

She had her cough drops, but she was saving them.

She gnawed her nails and kept her vigil; she didn't know when it was she fell asleep.

Near dark, the bus driver pulled to the side of the road. It was the bumps, and gravel hitting the underside, that woke her. "Somebody meeting you, I hope," he said. "I don't take no responsibility. This here bus line don't take none. Strange things go on in them woods. Wild animals, too. Naw sir, you wouldn't find me getting off at no godforsaken place like this. Not at night-time no how."

This angered her. It angered her because his saying it scared her and because she knew he saw it.

"I don't see no crossroads," she said.

He offered to help with her suitcases, but she held tightly to them. The boy who'd made faces was asleep with his mouth open. He had a booger hanging from his nose and snot smeared across his cheek. The woman beside him was smoking, staring in a dull way at nothing. She didn't have no nice hose like her mother had worn. She didn't wear no rouge or lipstick either.

It was a real dumb load on that bus.

She followed the driver to the front of the bus. He put a foot on the bumper and leaned his elbow on his knee. His shirt was bunched up, and she could see his ugly naked skin. The air the bus lights shot through was smoky. It did little cartwheels in the beams. "There she is," he said, meaning the lane.

But she didn't see it.

"There ain't nothing," she said. "You've let me off at the wrong place." She wanted her money back, but didn't say it. He was still pointing. "It's there," he said. "You can call it a crossroads till gold comes out your behind, but your calling it so ain't going to change it none. It's that little lane you see yonder by the stump. It ain't hardly more than a red-dirt path and you can beat my rear end till doomsday and I'd still stay ignorant of where it goes. There was a house there once, or a store. I never seen no traffic come up out of that lane. I never had nobody go down it before. Far as I know there ain't a soul lives down that lane. Maybe a few squirrels and rabbits, maybe snakes, if they's got souls. I hope you come for a long visit 'cause you going to be in no shape to leave if ever you get where you're going. Be solid night soon. Looks to me like you took the wrong time to pay a call. But that's the road you ask for. That's Spider's Lane. You ask me, you're going to wish you'd stayed where you was."

He was a big blabbermouth. She would have told him so, but he was wrestling the suitcases from her. He tugged them from her hands and crossed the highway and plonked them down on the other side. She saw the lane now. Vines grew over it at the mouth. She still didn't see no stump.

"There you go," he said. "Service with a smile. I come by first thing in the morning, you want to go back, but you got to wave me down. Ticket cost the same, coming or going."

She picked up her cases and started off.

"You're uppity," he said, pitching his live cigarette into the ditch. "But I don't hold it against you. I reckon you never had no one to show you how to behave."

She called him a son of a bitch, with her teeth together and her eyes slitted, just the way her mother would have.

He sauntered back to his driver's seat. Two or three faces were at the greasy windows, mutely studying her. She heard the gears grind. Groaning, its twin beams slicing the dark, the bus moved on and after interminable seconds disappeared around the curve, its four blinkers still flashing.

She didn't believe this was the right place. Crossroads was what she'd been told to head down. But the sign, rotted where it entered the ground and thrust back into the bushes, had the right words on it, splashed on in a faded paint. *"Spider's Lane. You go down Spider's Lane till you're about to drop. When you've dropped I guess you'll be near enough."*

"But I don't want to go."

"'Want' ain't got britches no more she can wear. 'Want' is dropped dead. I can't look out for you no more. 'Looking out' has finally got the best of me. You go."

"Yes'm."

"Are you going?"

"Yes'm."

"Then pull the covers up and let me sleep. Tuck me in."

"Yes'm."

She'd spent the night on pine straw in a hollow about a hundred feet off the road, camouflaging herself under broken branches, the coat pulled up over her head, the money purse in a fist up under her chin. She chewed on bitter pine bark and once or twice swallowed some. Her stomach churned. It was like someone inside trying to talk to her, refusing to shut up.

"I can't let you sleep with me. You'd kick. Now wouldn't you?"

"Yes'm."

"Sit there a while. Hold my hand."

"I will, mama. You rest now."

In late afternoon this second day she came to a creek and crossed it, carrying her shoes in one hand, her coat pulled up and bunched at the waist. Then she came back and again forded the stream, one of the suitcases riding at perilous balance on her head. The muddy bottom sucked at her feet. Green slime covered the rocks; she tried to avoid them. The water turned a thick brown where she walked. It trickled politely over the stones; up there a ways a skinny tree was down and twigs and leaves snagged on the skinny tree in the making of a forlorn dam. The stream swept at a good pace around it. There wouldn't be no beavers here. Beavers had better sense than to be in a place miserable as this. The woods here were thick and scraggly. Vines swept up over everything and hung still as ragged curtains from the trees. The earth was shaded, with pock holes scattered all over, each filled with an inch or two of water, and the creek was dark too, of an amber colour. She got the second suitcase across, though she nearly lost it once when she slipped. Her grip gave way on the coat bunched at her waist and the coat got wet from the knees down; as she reached for it her sleeve unrolled and it too plopped into the water. At the bank she took off the coat and squeezed what she could from it. Then she put it on again. It was heavier now. The sleeve was cold and soggy against her wrist. She shivered, and stood a moment hugging herself.

Mud squished between her toes. She knelt at the water's edge and let the cool water flow over her feet. She put her hands under, marvelling at how the slow current wanted to carry her hands along. Her stomach rumbled. She felt a wave of dizziness and knew she'd have to eat something soon. She should have spent some of her money for beans or a can of potted meat, but she hadn't been able to part with it. The prices alone were enough to make your gorge rise.

She thought of the cough drops in her pocket. Although here was food of a kind, she refrained from reaching for them. She'd never have put out good money for these cough drops herself. They'd been in her mama's shoulder purse, along with the hair-pins and rumpled tissues, along with the comb and the teensy mirror in the fold-up case. The change purse had two dollars in it then, plus the change. It had her pills too, in a tiny brown bottle, only six left. Six gone to waste. She'd tried selling these back to the pharmacy man on the corner but he'd laughed at her. "How do I know you ain't spiked them pills?" he said. "How I know where in thunderation they been?" She'd insisted but he hadn't wilted an inch. The skinflint. Yes, you paid good money for a thing, it cost you an arm and a leg, but when you tried selling it back to these devils you found out how worthless it was. Those pills hadn't helped her mama. She'd said so herself a million times.

But you never knew. Those pills were now back in her mama's shiny black shoulder purse and the purse back in the suitcase.

If ever she got to feeling run down the way her mama did then maybe she'd take them herself. Maybe they'd pep her up.

She examined her feet in the running water and wondered if she shouldn't wash her stockings now. They were bunched up wet around her ankles. She pulled them high again. They were streaked with mud, and stiff, nothing but pudding where her heels had bled. They had a zillion snags and runs. But there was no use now in opening up a suitcase and getting out another pair. In ten minutes they'd be as bad off as these. Best to wait until she got where she was going.

She cupped her hands into the water and drank. It dribbled between her fingers and down her chin. The water was cool, but tasted smoky somehow. It tasted burned. It didn't have the sparkle of city water. No telling what animals had dropped their leavings in it. Oh, but it was cool. She wiped wet hands over her face and neck and throat, for she was sweaty from all this carrying. Oh my, that felt good. Be nice to just dunk her head underwater. But the water stung her blisters; it pitched a fit at her sores. She winced, thinking maybe this was the worst pain. But it wasn't. The worst pain was all over now, including in her stomach where the water she'd drunk weighed like an anvil.

She thought seriously about taking off her clothes and bathing herself all over; there might be some advantage in this. It didn't hurt you none, her mama said, to be clean. But the air had a nip in it. She didn't want to end up coughing and moaning the way her mama had. Her mama had smelled. She'd run the washcloth over her mama and pat on the pink powder but in a little while the smell came back again. A smell sort of like a hot ironing board. Her skin was dark too, like the cover you ironed on. Though her mama hadn't smelled it. She'd said, "No, no, don't open the window! Can't I at least rest in peace?"

Minnows swam at her feet. They'd shoot off a little way, then stop dead still, then dart off again. They hardly paid any attention now to her wriggling toes. She lifted her arms and sniffed under her armpits the way she'd at times seen her mama do. She couldn't smell anything. She didn't need no bath. To bathe here naked in the open would be next to foolishness. First thing you knew somebody'd be flying over in an airplane. Or some thief coming along. Anyway she'd never in her life bathed in full daylight. Bathing was for night-time so you could go to sleep clean and dream nice pictures and wake up in the morning spick-and-span.

She looked hard at the suitcases. They'd got so heavy. My lifely goods, she thought. They weigh more than me. She wondered if maybe she couldn't lighten her load, maybe hide some of it away up here. Maybe take out the best things from the one case and stuff them in the other and go on along with that. She strode out of the creek, searching about for a good place. Maybe over there by that rotted stump. She'd never seen a place with so many stumps, or with so much rot. Some of it was black, too, like there had been a fire through here at some time. Long long ago, probably before she was born. Probably before her mama was born too. Before anybody was. Before there was this poor excuse for a lane or even spiders you could name it after. Probably a zillion years ago.

She saw no wheel tracks here and for an instant felt alarm. Had she somehow got off the main path? The tracks had come to be like company to her. But no, there they were, there they had been all the time. One set going one way, one going another. You could tell by how the horse hooves, if horse it was—mule maybe —left their prints in the ground. The one going was deeper; it had been carrying something. She wondered who had rode that wagon. Wondered if maybe it wasn't him. *Him*, yes, but she wouldn't say his name. It scared her even to think of him. What would he say when he saw her? Would he chase her off with a stick? *"Don't let him,"* her mama had said. *"You stand right up to him. Call him a jackal to his face, if that's what's come of him."*

She knelt over the bag before opening it; she listened, breath held, for any sound. Far off she saw a bird going. There was another one up in the big tree. Funny she hadn't seen it before. But she hadn't and maybe that meant there was a lot else she hadn't seen. Peeping Toms. Maybe this minute somebody was off in the bushes spying. Maybe him. Aw, heck no. That was foolishness. It looked more to her like no one was within a million miles. No one knew whether she was living or dead.

Everything was so still. Still and near to dead. She was going to have a hard time getting used to a quiet place like this. Even the creek bed seemed to feel it; its trickles were like little whispers over the stones.

"It's going to try me to my very eyeballs," she said aloud, just to give a voice to the place. "I don't know I can." Her voice shook. She laughed at herself.

She dragged both cases to the bushes at the side of the lane. She worked carefully and quickly, sorting out the goods, exchanging articles contained in one for articles in the other. Her mama's high-heeled pumps delayed her a bit. She placed the soft leather up to her cheek, her eyes closed. Closed and wet. Her mama had loved these pumps. She'd hardly worn them at all, loving them that much. She had a dozen clear memories of her mama in these pumps. Her mama had such beautiful legs. Ankles thin as twigs and her hips lovely as a moving picture lady. Your heart went up to your throat when you thought of mama in these pumps. You'd think heads would snap off the way men turned theirs when mama went by. "Oh, mama, damn you," she said. "Oh, damn you." She wiped the coat sleeve against her eyes and took bitter

sight on these high heels. Her mama had bought these for dancing first: *"I needed new pumps to go with my dress. Do you like them?
You don't mind my leaving you alone? You go to sleep early and I
promise I'll tell you everything went on when I come in."* Her mama
danced in these shoes, but only that once. They were hardly worn;
not a scuff any place. She saw her mama at the long mirror, turning, looking down at one lifted leg. Then turning and lifting the
other. *"Are they straight, honey? My seams? Aren't they pretty with
these new pumps? Am I pretty enough, do you think, to be seen in this
world? You can come with us if you want to. Monty won't mind."*

She bit her lips, told herself to stop this. "Stop it," she said.
"Stop this snivelling like a backward child. You quit it right now."

She'd take these pumps with her. Best be on the safe side. She'd
take this silver mirror too, and the jewel box. She'd take these
framed pictures of herself and her mama. Take these fancy scarves.
These white gloves that went all the way up to her elbow. In these
gloves wasn't mama grand!

She crushed down the lid and after an effort got it snapped.
Both sides were stuffed out fat. She couldn't lift the bag. Oh heavy,
too heavy. She stood up straight, screeching silently at the weight.
She kicked the ground in fury and tried again. She strained, apply-
ing both hands, tongue between her teeth, crossing her eyes, and
got it an inch or two off the ground. Hopeless. How could a few
doodads weigh so much? It beat her. "It beats me," she said. "I'm
stumped." The attempt made her giddy. It made her pulse race.
She felt a flush of scarlet on her face and half sat, half tumbled
down. Her knees shook. She let her head fall between her legs;
she watched the ground undulate. The taste of bile charged up
her throat. She couldn't stop the quivering in her legs. Her eyes
refused to focus. Her face was hot and she slapped a hand up over
her eyes, thinking, I've got what mama had. I've got a fever to beat

the band. Her head swam. Was this how mama had felt? Her heartbeat was racing, she could hear it going clippity clop. Yesterday? Was it yesterday morning she'd eaten the last dregs of what was in the icebox and poured out a bottle of milk that had turned? Gurgle-gurgle. She'd had saltine crackers and a smear of peanut butter left in the jar. She could see that clearly, the empty jar, but not where that was. She could see the man with the cigarette dangling and the four bus lights blinking against the dark. She could see the white apple the man across from her had and in her hunger she almost reached for it. *Did* reach for it, or for something, because a second later the apple spun away and bus too and in its place, head lowered between her legs, there was just her own hand wildly scratching in the dirt. I've slipped off the deep end, she thought, like that sister my daddy had. My yo-yo's come loose. Was she so hungry she'd now eat dirt? She half remembered a time when she had. As a baby she had. So her mama said. "You and dirt! You'd have stuffed wiggling beetles in your jaws if I hadn't kept you from it!" "Where was *he*, then?" "Him? Your papa? He was long gone. Or I was. You'd have had to chain me up like a dog to keep me out there." "What's he like? Did you ever see him again?" "Oh, once or twice. He come around. But our feelings for each other were all dead and buried by that time. I didn't know him from Adam, and wanted him less." "Would he know me now?" "Know you? Well, maybe he would. When you cry, when you want something bad and can't have it, you both have that hungdog miserable look. I reckon he might recognize that."

She got the bags sorted to her satisfaction. That one she was leaving behind she carried up through the woods, over a marsh that slurped at her heels; she hid the case away behind bramble bushes at the edge of a wide, untended, gullied field. She threw dead brush up over the hiding place. The bag looked safe enough there. She circled the spot, eyeing it from every angle, and pronounced herself satisfied. "Take a hawk's eye to find it," she said. "Anyway, I don't mean it to stay for long."

Something pricked at her ankle. She looked down with a screech. A black tick had its nose buried in her flesh. She picked it off, then saw another between her toes and rubbed her toes over the earth to erase the itch. She felt something crawling lightly, ticklishly, over her neck and she whirled in a fury, clawing with her fingers there. In a moment she was scratching herself all over, scrambling back through the marsh, feeling ticks all over. They were black ugly things and came loose with little tufts of white skin clinging to them. A pair of startled quail shot up in a sudden flurry of wings, startling her. In an instant other groups burst out of nearby bush and weed and cut in a swift, curving line through the sky. They circled high and disappeared. A crow cawed somewhere. She heard the rattle of something else too, uneven and distant, an echo perhaps, and stood stock still, cupping hands to one ear. It came again, a rumble this time. She darted free of the marsh, zigzagging out, the long coat yanked up to her waist and flapping. She dropped quickly down into a spread of weeds. It sounded like a wagon. It sounded like someone coming, to her. "Goddamnit," she whimpered, "I ain't ready yet."

For a long time, flat in the weeds, her head raised, she didn't move but stayed alert to all sounds, her muscles taut, her breath shallow and quick. What if it's him? she thought. What if he sees my suitcase on that road? What if it's stole, or he's got a gun and shoots me dead? She considered leaping up, racing back to the lane, yanking her suitcase off into the bush. But she couldn't take the chance. She didn't want to meet him like this, not in no woods and looking like a rat. She would meet him, had to, but not like this, like some brainless waif hiding in the woods, not knowing doodly-squat.

No further sound came. There was only stillness over the place. "There ain't nothing," she whispered at last. "I imagined that noise." Finally she got up, dusted off her clothes, searched her legs and arms for ticks, and returned in a run to the lane.

Nothing had changed. There her suitcase was and the babbling creek, nothing coming either up or down the lane. I dreamt up that wagon, she thought. I surely did. To calm herself she stepped her bare feet into the creek's cold water. Her mama had told her how to go about it: "You walk right up to his door," she said. "You hold your head high, too; I don't want him thinking I didn't know how to raise you. You watch out for dogs; he'll have those. You knock and when he comes you tell him who you are. You tell him what's gone on here. What's come of me. You tell him it's his turn now." She'd made it sound so easy, her mama had. But she hadn't told her it would take days and days and a million miles to get her there. She hadn't said nothing about how soon a full belly could start rubbing backbone. She'd have to eat something soon; she couldn't go on like this.

She stared down at the tranquil water at her feet. There was white sand washed up in this spot. The water was clear, numbing to her legs. Her legs looked split, like she'd stepped out of her bones. She flexed her toes, grimacing at the icy waves. "What if he don't want me?" she said. "What if he says I can go rot in hell?" Her mama hadn't answered that. Her mama, poor thing, had moaned and coughed and slept.

Minnows swam lazily at her feet, looking silvery in the light. Her body threw a zigzag shadow as she bent her face to the surface. A minnow was a fish. A person could eat fish. The minnows veered away as she lowered her hands into the water. Then they reassembled to drift somnolently between her fingers and legs. Her stomach growled; her mouth moistened. She reckoned people had eaten worse. Babies gnawed at crib paint and didn't always die from it. In the picture show, seated beside her mama, she'd seen ritzy people eating frog legs. That would be a whole lot worse. Once her own mama had cooked what she called brains, and made her taste it. She didn't reckon minnows could kill her.

She cupped her hands together and brought them up ever so slowly. Mostly they drifted free. Those few trapped in her hands shook their tails as the water dribbled away; then they stretched flat and still against her skin, looking so much smaller than they had in the water.

Eyes closed, making a face, she licked her palms clean. She swallowed without chewing and imagined she felt them flopping about inside her empty stomach.

She was stooping to gather up more when she heard the sudden clop of hooves, the creak of wagon wheels. She caught her breath and with a low cry dashed out of the water. She swept up her suitcase, swung it, and went tumbling behind it into the dense thicket at the side of the road. She burrowed herself down.

A wagon came into sight, empty and rattling, pulled by a mule, which walked with its head low and bobbing, bobbing and swaying. The mule was old and tired, dust-coloured, its knees bald; yellow pus dripped from its eyes; as it neared she could see flies crawling over the pus. It was chewing at the bit in its mouth and swishing its tail.

At the stream the mule stopped and drank. It made big slurping noises and once or twice flung its head around. One of its ears didn't stand up.

When it was done drinking it clumped in its traces, edging off twisty from the wagon to munch on tall weeds.

"Well, Buddyroll?" the man said.

He had a whispery, gentle voice.

The man in the wagon was standing, the reins secured by a hand tucked by thumb into his waist. He was idly surveying the stream, content apparently to let the animal loiter and graze. Was this him? She did not think it could be. Her mama had said he'd be a good height and thin and pretty nice-looking. He'd have a certain glint in his eyes that would make a woman go goose bumpy. He'd have a way about him that let you know he meant to get what he wanted and that you wouldn't mind it. "*That man whispered things in my ear I'll carry to my grave,*" her mama had said. "*I think sometimes of what he said to me and my hair still stands up. He could make a mummy's eyes pop out.*" Mama must of been joshing, for this one was nothing. He was red-dirt nothing. He had a big fat gut and muscly arms, all stubby. He wore a rumpled greasy felt hat pushed back on his head. You could see where the brim had shaded his face so the sun burned his nose and left red swatches all across his face. It was an ugly face. He had a stick in his mouth, moving it from side to side. He had bulgy jaws and meaty ears and a thick, streaked neck. His little pig eyes gleamed. No, this wasn't him. It couldn't be. Mama didn't have memory to beat a bat.

She saw him unbutton his pants and lift out his thing. He peed in a long wide arch into the stream. He had big calloused sunburned hands and sunburned arms and a red nose, but his weasel was puny and white. It looked like hardly nothing a human would want. He'd be better off not peeing at all than showing that thing. He shook it, bent his knees, and loaded it back inside. Him? The idea was so funny she almost laughed out loud. He wouldn't have sense to beat a cockroach. Him? The likelihood was plain disgusting. Her mama would never have let herself curl up to nothing looking like that.

He said something in a low voice to the mule, which turned and looked at him coldly. He hopped down and removed the bit from the animal's mouth. The mule rippled its haunches and went back to its feeding. It ripped up a tall growth of grass by the roots and ate it down to the dirt. It scraped the dirt off against a bald knee, then ate the roots. The man knelt by the stream, lacing a hand through the water. He pulled a rag from his pocket and wet it. He wiped the rag behind and around his neck. He dipped the rag again into the water and crossed over to the mule. The mule had an open puckered sore high on a hind leg. The man cleansed it. The mule swished him in the face a time or two, and rippled his skin again, and again the man said something to him.

Buddyroll, quit, it sounded like.

He put the bit back into the animal's mouth and hopped up into the wagon. He gave a small shake to the reins and sluggishly the mule responded. The wagon rattling started again. The man took off his hat as they crossed the stream, and swatted it against his leg. Dust flew up. The hatband had cut a line in his forehead, leaving a strip of white skin there. White and freckly. He didn't have much hair. What there was was reddish. She felt her face heat up, noticing this. His red hair, if you could believe mama, was where she'd got hers. He was how come she'd got her freckles, too.

He seemed to be smiling at something as the wagon creaked by, the smile slack on his face, as if he didn't know it to be there.

Her stomach rumbled. She shifted in her hiding spot, ramming a fist up against her stomach to quieten the emptiness.

"Damn son of a bitch," she said. "If he's mine I don't claim him."

Ahead, the road dipped and curved; it rose on to higher ground. A bit yonder from that point, trailing at a distance, she saw the wagon turn into a rutted yard.

He went on down the path, through an open fence gate at the rear of the house, to a weathered, leaning barn.

The house was as her mama said it would be.

A wide porch extended over the full length of the two front rooms, with two worn cane-bottom chairs tilted to the wall, and a wooden swing on chains that, except in summer, lifted the swing up to the ceiling. Two windows faced the lane, divided in the middle by a sagging pinewood door, the screen part open. Behind the front rooms, he'd added a hallway and two other rooms. He'd lived here, so her mama said, with a sick sister who hadn't taken lightly another woman's presence on the place. But the sister had passed on, her mama said. She'd died of craziness, if not boredom. An old sycamore, with a maze of thick graceful limbs, shaded one half of the yard. A stump across from it showed where another had been. A stone chimney went up at the side, and a bent weather vane with a rooster at the top guarded the roof of the house. She saw how he'd patched the tin roof with flattened-out cans. He'd put in a new windowpane not long before.

The place had lights now; it hadn't had electricity in her mama's time.

She was about to step up on the porch and peek through the windows when she heard him coming. He was whistling. She ducked low over the grass, hit the lane, and took off running. For the balance of the day she searched out the place, avoiding open fields, steering wide of his house. In the afternoon she crawled up in a tangle of vines and slept, pulling the black coat up over her head. It seemed to her she slept a long time but when she rubbed her eyes awake the same bird was alight, alight but silent, preening its feathers, on the same high limb. It was so blessed still out here even the birds had caught it. You couldn't hardly breathe because the earth seemed to want to sop it up like gravy on a plate. Her body itched all over. Her flesh was covered with bites, with scratches and welts. Bruises, head to toe. She took off her shoes and picked briars off the bottoms of her feet. They were black and swollen up some. You couldn't even see any more where the blisters had been; it was all raw now. She rolled the stockings down, gritting her teeth, wincing, as she peeled them away from the dried blood on her heels. That was the worst pain, these heels. These feet. These scratches and cuts and being stuck out here. Standing, she felt dizzy, and had to sit down again. Her head swirled. I've got what mama had, she thought. I'm going to waste away in these ungodly woods and go to my grave out here. She picked a black tick out of her scalp and flattened it between her two thumbnails. When mama went down she'd wanted to go down with her. She'd wanted to be shut up with her and have the lid closed on them. They'd said no, no you can't, but it seemed to her this had happened anyway. It was happening now. The lid was closing, but mama wasn't raising her arms to welcome her. Mama was stretched out flat, not saying anything. Come along, child. Come along, child. Mama's back was turned or she wasn't there at all: black space, cold black air, that's all mama was. She hadn't cried then, with mama being lowered down. She could have and wanted to, but she hadn't because mama made her so mad. She hadn't wanted to be mad, not at mama, but she was so she just bit her lip and hung on, and if anybody spoke to her or touched her she moved away from them. She hated how they whispered, as if her mama could hear. She kept moving away and they kept coming with her until more of them were huddled with her up by the tree than were down there by the tent where her mama was. She didn't know why they'd come in the first place. Nobody had asked them to. They had no right to be there. She shook when they touched her. She threw off their hands and had to edge away. She had to go on up as far as the tree, but still they kept coming with her. Snivelling, fluttering up little hankies to the nose. What she wanted was for her and her mama to be alone. Not being alone with mama, that last time, that was the worst pain. It was worse than bloody heels and that man on the bus with a cigarette dangling between his lips. It was worse than spending good money to come out here to this dismal daddy in this dismal place. In the end it was her mama alone. You couldn't blame mama for turning her back on her, for changing into black space, into cold black air that never answered a word you said. She felt dizzy now, and hot, and knew this was her mama's sweat on her brow. "I won't talk to you, child, but you can have that. I give my fever to you, along with everything else." Hunger wasn't doing this to her. Hunger wasn't worth talking about, because she had money in her pocket and could buy food, lots of it, any time she wanted to. She could eat weeds, like that mule. She could eat these cough drops in her coat pocket, but she wouldn't. Her mama had said, "Go to the store and buy me these cough drops to ease my throat, and get some little treat for yourself," and she'd done so, but her mama hadn't touched them. Her mama's eyes had rolled in her head. You could take her hand in your own hand and squeeze but her mama couldn't squeeze your own hand back. She'd sleep and you'd sit by the bed thinking how beautiful she was. You'd hold her hand and your own hand would burn. You'd watch her eyes move under the lids sunken and dark. You'd watch the tremor in her lips and dab a wet cloth over them for they were always dry. Sweat broke out on her brow and you could fold a cold wet cloth over her but the cloth got hot as fire in a minute and in the meantime the fever just went on elsewhere. She'd wake and cough and say, "I didn't doze off, did I?" "Can you eat, mama?" you'd say. "Can I bring you anything? Are you feeling better?" She'd pat your hand and try to smile. It broke your heart how she tried to smile and that was the worst pain. It was worse than blisters or having your belly gnaw or coming this far for nothing. Worse was what was back there, though it wasn't back there but with you every minute, which was what made it worse. Worse was mama not squeezing your hand after you'd squeezed hers first and then that hand not being there to squeeze although you could still feel her hand in yours. Worse was waiting for the squeeze to come and knowing now it wouldn't. "Mama, can I fetch you something? Can I rub your back or freshen them sheets?"

"Not now, child."

"All right, mama."

"Don't you be weary on my account, baby."

"All right, mama."

You could put your hand behind mama's head and lift her up; you could put a spoon between her lips and feed her like a baby. I loved bathing mama's feet. You could run a damp, cool cloth between her toes and sometimes that would make her smile. "You can turn the light off now," she'd say, and you'd go over and pretend to do it, not letting her know it was plain daylight and no lamp burning. She'd lean on you those days when she could cross the room, and she'd lean on you, coming back. "My right arm," she'd say, "is a pretty little girl. She's my left arm, too." Her lips would tremble when the real pains came and she'd turn her face against the pillow so you couldn't see it. You couldn't get a doctor to come. You'd call up on the store phone and they'd say do this, do that, and you tore home and did it but it didn't help none. You fed her pills by the pail but that didn't help none. "Does it help, mama? Does it relax you? Can you sleep now?"

"Oh, child. Oh oh oh. Oh, I feel like I've gone in the oven head first. Pull me out now. Grab my legs and pull. Putting a body head first into the fiery furnace is the one sure way they've found of making sure no ghosts lag behind. I feel my ghost has burned and the rest has yet to follow. You take my coat. You take my purse and my nice scarves and my new shoes. You take all the fine stockings the navy sees fit to give me."

The navy. You had to smile, thinking about that. You had to laugh out loud. Even her mama in her worst sickness could. One of her mama's old boyfriends, Monty his name was, sent these stockings to her. He got them from Ship's Store or foreign ports or off the black market and in they came, regular as rainwater. "I'm being swept off my feet by nylons," her mama would say. "It beats me what men will do. Why I only went out with that sailor-man once! I let him hold me tight on the dance floor, but dancing was all. I liked his arms around me. I let him kiss and hold me when his leave was up and I dashed down to see him when he left on the train. I pulled him back against the red-brick wall and I was the one held him that time. That time I was the one raining the kisses down. 'You come back,' I said. He said he'd write, but what I said was, 'Well, you know how sailors are.' I should have given myself to him. God knows, it's little enough. If his ship goes down and he doesn't return I'll cry and wish a thousand times I had. I think of that each time his nylons come. I think of it each time I pull one on."

Men loved her mama. Two had fought over her once, but she'd never spoken to either again.

"I won't be treated like I'm a lump of clay that they can mould and take and have. I didn't care a snake for either of them and they'd of saved themselves a heap of bruised knuckles had they asked me first.

"Your father wasn't that way," she said. "He never fought for me or raised a word to stop me when I said I was leaving that place. It wasn't him I was leaving, as I saw it. Only that place. He never so much as said 'Please' or 'Don't do it.' I know he was unhappy and cried, because his sister, crazy as she was, came one day and told me. She said, 'Come back and this time I'll try to be good.' But your father didn't try to sway me. You can't lock up wind, he said. He said he wouldn't try to tame it either."

Several times in her wanderings the girl caught sight of her father as he moved from barn to shed or shed to house. Once, she spotted him on the rear doorstep, calmly surveying the horizon. In late afternoon he came out and scattered feed from a bucket to a half-dozen chickens that flew down from trees. He appeared later with a pail and followed a footpath down to where two sows wallowed in muddy puddles inside a pen. Afterward, she saw him carrying in wood. Another time he was out by the fence gate, whittling on something.

She didn't see any dogs. She saw something streak across his yard once, but couldn't tell what it was.

For long intervals, when he disappeared inside the house, she lay flat in this or that field watching his back door.

Down beyond the fenced-off area was an orchard; she trampled about there, but what little fruit remained on the ground was wormy and rotten. A space of ground nearer the house had served as his garden in seasons past. She pulled a young carrot out of the soil and ate it quickly; she searched a long time for others but found nothing.

On toward nightfall, troubled by the rising cold, she followed what seemed to be an ancient path, trampled down in parts, in parts wild again, and eventually found herself regarding an abandoned, burned-out site inside a ring of scorched trees. Someone had lived here. Wrinkled sheets of tin roofing, blackened boards and black jackknife timbers covered the area. Bushes sprouted amid the rubble. In one corner, climbing up over a wall that remained partially intact, honeysuckle was taking over. She eyed that wall. She eyed the tin. She could fashion a roof of some kind where that wall was, and spend the night here.

She set to work clearing out that space. She worked on into dark, scarcely noticing she had.

The little room she erected was well hidden; you'd have to stand right up on it to know it was there. She had room for her suitcases and room to stretch out, though not stand up. She put in an opening at the front big enough so that she might crawl through.

She could hide here, she thought, for a million years.

Afterward, she lugged her suitcases up from the woods. She rested then in the cramped shelter, peering up at the streaks and pinpoints of night sky. For a few minutes she slept, although she did not intend to.

Later in the night she worked her way down to the creek and there, trembling with cold, washed herself. Like ice, the water was. It made her teeth chatter and her bones crunch up tight. But it felt good to be clean. It was like heaven, getting the soot and filth off her. She slipped naked into her coat, rolling up the dirty clothes under her arm. She hastened back to her shelter among the ruins and for long minutes sat shivering, waiting for warmth to return. She didn't think about hunger now. Being cold is the worse ache, she told herself. I've never known nothing worse than cold. Being alone in the world was a glory ride compared to being cold. If I stop shivering it will just go away. But she couldn't stop shivering. Her skin was so white and shaky she could see it even in this black hole. Her scalp itched; her hair was grimy, too; tomorrow in fresh daylight she'd go and wash that.

She felt about inside the suitcase for a pair of stockings—a new pair—and pulled them on. "Bless the navy," she said, for this was what her mama liked to say. "Him with his nylons, going to sweep me off my feet." She drew the hose up over her hips and tucked the extra length inside her panties. Her mama had kept hers up with garter belts or she'd rolled and twisted them somehow and they'd stayed up. Beautiful legs, old mama had. She felt about for a sweater and skirt and slipped these on. She got out a comb and raked that through her tangly hair, making low cries as the comb pulled. She wondered where her bow had got to. She rubbed a finger over her teeth and moistened that finger and set a shape to her eyebrows. She painted her lips with the tube her mama had said she could have. She rouged her cheeks the way her mama had showed her how.

She took out her money and hid it away inside a suitcase.

She hooked the purse over her arm and crawled out of her hole.

In the beginning the house was but a faint speck of yellow light low on the horizon, obscured now and then by the land's undulations. She crossed the fields with short bursts of speed, swinging her shoes in her hands, using his lighted window as her guide. Soon the house was outlined in full, with the sagging roof and the bent weathervane and the big sycamore at the front.

She crouched down where his last field stopped, from there inching her way forward. Smoke wafted up from the chimney; the light was flickering. He passed by the window once and she ducked down, holding her breath. She could hear faint sounds from inside and wondered whether he had visitors, maybe a woman. She wondered what her mama would say about that. Or maybe her mama was wrong about the sister being dead the way she was about him having dogs. But it sounded to her like music; it sounded like a radio.

She raised her eyes above the sill. He was seated on a log stool before the fire, whittling on a piece of wood, a carving of some kind. He was seated on a log although the room held plenty of nice easy chairs and an old settee that looked comfortable. It surprised her how clean and orderly everything was. The floor was of polished wood, a nice deep colour, with numerous old clocks on the wall and nice pictures, and lacy antimacassars on the arms of the settee and chairs. It was a whole lot better-looking place than she would have thought, and lots better and more roomy than the place she and her mama had. Her mama hadn't been one for keeping things straight, and she hadn't either.

She didn't see no sister. She didn't see no tramp layabout girl-friend either.

His shirt was unbuttoned. He had a curly ring of hair on his chest and clean hands and what looked to her like greenish eyes.

He had a drink in a glass down on the floor beside him and now he drank from that. He took three or four deep swallows.

An alcoholic, she thought. If he ain't alcoholic then my name is Clementine.

He was patting his foot to music. The music didn't come from a radio, but from an old Victrola over in the corner. The lid was up and she could see a fat silvery arm spinning over the phonograph record. She'd seen Victrolas like that in town with a big white spotted dog beside them.

She knew that song. It was an old one. Her mama had hummed it sometimes.

"You're his only daughter," her mama had said. "You go to him. I mean it, now."

She moved around the house and clumped noisily up onto the porch. She stretched up her stockings and brushed at her coat. She took a deep breath and knocked on his door.

"I'll try it," she said. "I'll give him twenty-four hours to prove himself."

Pretty Pictures

T HERE ARE PRETTY PICTURES and not-so-pretty pictures. You know that. We would probably agree which is which. There is the not-so-pretty picture of my wife kissing another man. But that's looking at it from my side. From her side it is no doubt a very pretty picture. We know how it feels, don't we, to kiss someone we are attracted to, illicit or otherwise. The picture isn't the same, illicit, but the feeling is. You go up on your toes with a feeling like that. You kiss, and you go up on your toes, illicit or otherwise; you go off into orbit. That's what the kissing does, and maybe the prettiness or the not-so-prettiness of the moment is somehow beside the point, and ought to be, somehow, not a thing that we dwell upon.

We've all been deprived of too many kisses and that is one reason we do it. Let's say that is one reason. There are other reasons, of course, but let's not dwell upon it.

I did not set out to tell you about my wife kissing another man. It was not a picture, at the start, I even had in mind telling you. It was an ugly picture, to my mind, which just jumped in. It got in front and momentarily dislodged the pretty picture I was contemplating telling you about.

Here it is, that pretty picture. My father and I are passing along the street and the sights I see seem very strange and unfamiliar to me. All the angles are screwy; they are screwy and cock-eyed. People look short, very short, and dogs and cats are practically foreign creatures, so small are they in their appearance. Children, other children, they are the smallest beings yet. You can look over fences you've never looked over before. You can see into certain windows, into houses, you've never looked into before.

It comes to me, in this picture, that I am riding my father's shoulders. That is where I am, up there on his shoulders, my legs around his neck, his hands gripping my ankles, my head above his head. My chin, at times, rests in his hair. I am laughing, I am at times waving my arms, so fond I am of being up there. I am delighted with this view of the world.

That is the pretty part. Here is the not-so-pretty part. We go through a doorway, and we both crouch. I do not know which doorway it is. Maybe we have circled the block and returned home and that is the doorway we are entering. The picture dissolves at this point. I know we are passing through a door, but what awaits us inside is not a picture I can see. It is not even out of focus, that picture. It is blank; it does not exist.

Here is an even prettier picture, a picture prettier than the first part of that picture was. I am again riding my father's shoulders. We are out on the street once again, but here is why this picture is prettier. I am eating an ice-cream cone. I am smiling, eating that cone. My father is also eating an ice-cream cone and he too is smiling. I have two scoops on mine, one chocolate and one vanilla, with the chocolate on top, and have just begun my licks. I have an entire double-scoop cone to look forward to. My father has a single cone, vanilla, I think, and he has not yet touched his. One of his hands grips my ankle. I have my free hand across his brow, to hold on, and sometimes I jiggle and that hand slides down to cover his eyes. He walks with one foot in the gutter, the other on the sidewalk, and up on his shoulders I weave from side to side. He says, How do you like your ice cream? and I say, How do you like yours? And we laugh, as though we have said the funniest thing in the world.

The ice cream melts and oozes over my fingers and it drops into his hair. It's a hot day, he says. Where do you want to go now?

Here that picture becomes not so pretty, what little there is of it, because I don't know where I want to go now. I want the ride to start back over; I want him to lift me to his shoulders, to hold my ankle, to walk again to wherever it was we bought that ice cream. I want him to walk on and off the curb as he has done, I want to slip and slide up there, and for my ice cream to drip into his hair. When he asks, Where do you want to go next? already that picture is closing down, the picture is dissolving, and a second later I will no longer be riding on his shoulders. The picture will vanish and I will not know where I have gone next.

This is what I felt when I saw my wife kissing another man. It is what I felt when I saw her coming out of his bedroom. I did not know where my world had gone or if I had a place within it. The door to that bedroom rattled as it closed, which was precisely what I felt inside, that rattling, and I could not say what was beyond that door or any other door. I think what I felt was that she had left her love behind that closed door and the only picture I had left was of that closed door.

So that is the picture I have now, of that door, and it is the only picture. It is the picture which keeps jumping in; it dislodges all other pictures. It is not a pretty picture, from my point of view, and I do not know what to do with it. I do not know where I can go next. It will not dissolve, that picture won't, and it will go with me wherever it is I choose, or don't choose, to go.

The door is not a part of her picture. Her picture is composed only of whatever it was that went on while she was inside. She has that picture, of what went on inside, and the next picture, as she closed the door, of my stunned face. The man inside the room, the man she kissed, he has his pictures too. I expect my father, for that matter, has his own pictures and that these do not include his riding his son upon his shoulders or of their eating ice cream and the ice cream dripping into his hair. It is a fact that I never in real life rode his shoulders, or even saw him once I had reached the age of two. Possibly he rode another kid on his shoulders; more likely, he didn't. I have never imagined that children were a part of this earth that my father cared for.

So the picture I have of myself riding my father's shoulders is one born of the rides I have given my own child, together with those sights I have witnessed of other men and women riding their sons and daughters. It is the picture I had in mind to tell you when I began telling you this, before I saw her kissing him and that door closing, because this, her kissing him and emerging from his bedroom and that door rattling shut with its full awful power, is not a picture I would, in the normal course of events, have mentioned. It is the one true picture, the one picture drawn from real life, but it is not a picture that will do any of us any good.